SCORPION

JACK CURTIS MYSTERIES
BOOK 3

TRISHA HUGHES

PREVIOUSLY BY THE AUTHOR

Autobiography

Daughters of Nazareth

Historical Fiction

Book 1

Vikings to Virgin – *The Story of England's Monarchs from The Vikings to The Virgin Queen*

Book 2

Virgin to Victoria – *The Story of England's Monarchs from The Virgin Queen to Queen Victoria*

Book 3

Victoria to Vikings - The Circle of Blood

The Story of England's Monarchs from

Queen Victoria to The Vikings

The Tartan Kings - *A Powerful & Rich Story of Scotland*

Crime/Mystery

Beware of Beautiful Days

Dragonfly

Chameleon

1

———

SATURDAY 20TH MAY

The thick double door beneath the sign, Neil's Bar and Grocery, was shut and a *For Sale* sign jutted from a side wall with an 'Under Contract' banner plastered across it. The blinds were down, as if the house too had closed it eyes and died.

That's all I had time to notice as my taxi whipped past. I couldn't tell the driver to slow down since I'd already given him instructions to hurry. I looked back as we passed and felt a tug at my heart. It looked like nothing had changed. And yet, it somehow looked different. Smaller perhaps.

We flew past Murphy's farm then took a sharp right-hand turn and it was gone, disappearing from my sight around a bend.

A left turn brought us to the two-roomed schoolhouse where I'd learned to read. It had grown immensely and a large sign stood proudly before the scattered wooden buildings stating I was looking at Richmond Primary School.

"That's it!" I called out before we almost passed it. "That's the church!"

The taxi screeched to a stop, gravel crunching under the tyres, bidding goodbye to my hopes of a discreet arrival. Heads turned to look as I quickly gathered my handbag and scarf from the seat next to me. I should have known the crowds would be spilling out of the church. My mother was well-known as the proprietor of Neil's Bar and Grocery, the town's shop and pub. The hub of Richmond. It was always going to be a big funeral. The years peeled away as memories flooded in and suddenly, instantly, I was laid bare and fragile again.

There was no escape. The driver was out of the car, taking my suitcase from the trunk, opening my door saying, "Here we are now love," in his strong, chirpy Irish accent.

I can do this. I can do this. I chanted to myself. *I can do this.* The vow that seemed so potent yesterday in my small house in Southport felt puny now. *Doing it* doesn't necessarily mean going into the church, does it? I was so late. Wouldn't it be more discreet to shrink back into the seat and wait it out, catch Kathleen later, on her way home? Or even better, go back to Hobart and lie low until all the fuss was over?

Harden up, I admonished myself. *You're a grown woman now not a sensitive child. You're a police detective. You have a career and a mortgage on a house. You have a life away from here. Get in there now!*

As I psyched myself up, I put my sunglasses on top of my nose to protect myself from the staring eyes, not so much the watery sun straining to appear through dark threatening clouds. Then I took the clip from my hair to let it fall forward over my eyes, a veil of sorts. The breath I took was so deep it hurt.

And then, I was stepping out of the car onto Richmond soil for the first time in twenty years. The air felt moist and cool, hardly like air at all, and the nausea that had been plaguing me growled again. I walked through the open gates of the little church yard. *Here I am folks, the entertainment of the day, the news that you'll pass on to each other whenever Mrs Neil's funeral is recalled.*

I fixed my stare beyond their curious eyes and it collided with the door of the black hearse, open like a yawning mouth. It drew me to it, inexorably. As I drew nearer, people began to turn and recognise me. One voice whispered, "Hello Samantha. Welcome home." Another murmured, "Sorry for your loss and trouble." Then there was a general murmur of greeting and sympathy. I acknowledged every one of them with a nod from side to side.

I remembered the names and faces of every one of them. I could draw lines between them on a whiteboard showing the relationships between them all. I remembered it like yesterday.

A man turned to greet me with a snigger.

"Oh yes, here she is. Samantha Neil. It's a welcome you're after, is it then?"

I knew *his* face too. He was one of the Kennedys, who always used to mock me from his high stool at our bar. Subtle alliances and old hatreds are never far from the surface.

At the door, they parted like I was Moses and they were the flooding waters to let me through. I walked head up, my back ramrod straight, towards the words I haven't heard for a long time: "Let us give thanks to you, Almighty Father…"

The priest was as bald as a Buddhist monk, a big man wallowing in emphases and pauses. "…gave to His disciples and said…."

Two other priests in purple robes stood behind him and the congregation was on its knees, heads bowed. It was the Consecration, the holiest part of the Mass. The quietest part of the Mass. In the silence, my heels sounded like horse's hooves as they clicked loudly down the aisle louder than they should have been. The sound echoed in the stillness.

People turned and nudged each other in the holy silence, their eyes travelling up and down my body. As whispers began to swirl in my wake, Father Doyle sensed the loss of his audience and looked up. Seeing me, recognising me, his eyes narrowed, two black specks of stone. Again I was gripped by the urge to flee, but the pull of my mother's coffin sitting there on the trolley before me, all polished wood and burnished trimmings, was stronger. It was covered in glossy funeral flowers already dying.

I clomped on.

The priest stopped the ceremony, his hands together in the prayer position, a pillar of forbearance, silently watching me. The two priests behind him imitated the pose, censuring me with that loaded, condescending silence they must get taught at the seminary.

I was almost at the top pew where my family was sitting. I could see Kathleen now, looking thin, far too thin, almost gaunt. She followed the eyes of Father Doyle, turned to see what was causing the disruption and when her eyes found me, pure exasperation broke across her face.

Now Sam? it said before she turned her head on its long, elegant neck away from me, back towards the altar. *Now?*

I couldn't blame her. It must look so careless, so uncaring, to crash in like this, turning our mother's funeral into the latest act in the long-running Neil drama. My sister would be grieving my mother's death sorely. I didn't want to add to that.

At the same time, I did blame her. I blamed them all – Kathleen, my mother, Daddy, even Nana Peg. These scenes I brought upon the family were never just my doing, though I got the starring role. They all played their part, though they live and die pretending the stage is not even there.

I realised the girl kneeling between Kathleen and her husband Donald must be Rianne, my 8-year-old niece. She stared at me with Kathleen's eyes from behind a veil of red hair not unlike her father's. Her expression told me she had heard all about her Auntie Samantha.

She and Donald pushed down to make room for me but Kathleen, in one of her childish gestures, stayed firm and solid. She would not move. Ignoring her, I squeezed and wriggled into the pew beside her.

Once I was on my knees, Father Doyle began again, "Heavenly Father, you gave your only son...."

The wood was hard against my kneecaps. The smell of incense sent another wave of nausea undulating but I knelt and stood and sat and knelt through the half-forgotten rites waiting, as I had waited out so many days in Richmond, for it to be over.

Why was I here? All the way through the early morning flight from Brisbane to Hobart, through every bump of the cab ride from Hobart airport to this church in Richmond. For twenty-three minutes and thirty-seven seconds, I'd been nursing the same question: Why? Why, when I'd spent twenty years not making this journey, when I had left it so late that I was unlikely to arrive on time anyway, had I nonetheless organised a last-minute ticket? Why did I feel I had to come?

And it wasn't just me. Why had Kathleen, who so long ago gave up trying to get me back to Richmond while our mother lived, made such frantic efforts to contact me once it was clear Mum was dying?

But in time for what, I asked myself? To visit the hospital and be confronted with a totally different mother, twenty years older, one who was weak and dying? To snatch a few words from her, say something in return, then watch her go? What difference could that possibly have made?

I knew how my eldest sister imagined the scene: our mother looking up to see one of her girls ushering in the other, meaningful looks passing between us all, a clasping of hands and forgiveness all round. Then the two daughters together at last, watching her die, smiles and tears, hands clasped or arms around each other, ushering her out of the world.

No Kathleen, too much has been left to curdle for too long for that to happen. No words, not even deathbed words, would have been strong enough to hold it all together. No, it was better the way it happened. Believe me.

The organ sprang into sound for the last time and an elderly voice began a quavering 'Ave Maria'. I looked up to the balcony and saw Mrs Mead, my mother's friend, chins a-wobble. While she struggled with the top notes, an undertaker stepped up to release the brake and glided the coffin down the aisle. Kathleen was crying, curling her sobs into her husband.

Outside, the chill covered us. Kathleen was immediately engulfed by sympathisers, a wall of backs around her. Seeing me alone, Donald stepped across and bent down to bestow a grudging kiss on my cheek.

"So," he said in the sardonic tone he affects, "the prodigal returns."

I have met Donald only a handful of times in the many years he has been married to my sister. When they were first engaged, Kathleen brought him to meet me in Surfers Paradise and that first encounter has always stayed with me. He enfolded her as the two of them sat opposite me in a restaurant, her holding out her hand to display the tiny diamond perched in the ring on her third finger.

"How is Kathleen doing?" I asked, ignoring the jibe.

"Wearing herself to a frazzle. Your mother had very definite ideas about this funeral and Kathleen, being Kathleen, is carrying them out to the nth degree."

This time the scorn was unmistakeable. Kathleen had always claimed that Donald and our mother were fond of each other, but when it comes to family relationships, my sister is prone to whitewash things.

"Is she still annoyed with me?" I asked, knowing full well she was.

"Your mother wanted to see you before she died and Kathleen promised she'd track you down. When she wasn't able to, well,...", he shrugged.

I couldn't give him the response that leapt to my mind and found I couldn't think of anything at all to say. Kathleen was the single thing we had in common. Communication between us was always strained when she was not with us. Just as the silence was stretching towards awkwardness, we were rescued by a loud shriek.

"Ahh," smiled Donald, turning. "Our keening friends again."

At the church door were four young women in costume, made to look old, with black wrinkles painted across their foreheads and around their eyes and shawls drawn up over grey wigs. I resisted the impulse to cover my ears.

"Keeners? What the...?"

"Professional mourners, one of your mother's many special requests," he shook his head, a look of disgust on his face. "She left pages of instructions, practically a guidebook. How to Have a Good Irish Send-Off." He smirked. "We had a wake last night, complete with those four weeping and wailing and flinging themselves on the floor."

I looked across at my sister, explaining to everybody what the sideshow was about and wondering how she could bear it. While planning all this, my mother would have been imagining her celestial proceedings from above, watching and weighing who did what so she'd know how to treat them accordingly when they eventually caught up with her, hopefully in heaven. She wouldn't have been thinking about Kathleen at all.

I felt a hand on my back and turned to see Eileen standing there with her husband Seamus.

"Samantha," she said sincerely, "I'm so sorry."

Eileen worked in our shop while we were growing up and lived with us until she married. I let her hold me. Her hug seemed to give the others permission to approach and now, people I hadn't seen for years, were coming across to grab my hand. Faces I remembered, names I'd forgotten. Names I remembered, faces I'd forgotten.

My mother was a great character, they told me. She has gone to a better place, they said. God would give me comfort. Only one old woman told me anything that sounded liked the truth and she got herself dragged away by the arm for it.

"Who are you?" she yelled, glancing over her shoulder. "I never heard Maeve mention you at all."

Then, out of the mass of well-wishes, came a particular hand and a particular voice, one I *did* know.

"Sam," he said, and my heart skipped in recognition as I took the proffered hand. A second one came to encircle mine in warmth and then he was there in front of me. Rory. Rory O'Donovan. All of him, looking down on me, our hands joined.

I had thought about Rory on the journey back. I won't say home because I haven't considered it home for many years. I've built a new life for myself and a new home in a little suburb near Surfers Paradise. I had planned my opening lines and the airy way I would deliver them, but in my imaginings, we'd meet again on a beach. Or per chance on the street. Not here, not at my mother's funeral, the last place I would expect to find him, or any O'Donovan. Not here, in front of everybody. Certainly not here.

"How are you, Sam?"

Extra weight had loosened his jawline. He was still the picture I have held in my head and heart but blurred at the edges, like a photograph out of focus. His hair was gone, his long, black, lustrous, beautiful hair. It used to flow down his back, soft, wavy and shiny as night-water. I used to sink my face in it, hook it through my fingers, knot it around my naked neck. All gone. Shorn and thinning and greying now. And he was wearing a suit. Any man's clothes.

I had to look closely for the Rory I used to know.

"I'm sorry for your loss, Sam," he said, the conventional phrase again but in his voice, low and concerned, it sounded different. Personal. "But oh, it's so good to see you."

The keeners choose that moment to raise their wailing to a higher pitch and he rolled his eyes at them. It was a look to share, confident of my amusement. Just like the old days, the two of us against our families.

Kathleen appeared out of thin air, violent and furious.

"How dare you!"

She was barely holding the anger in as she glared at Rory. I saw her jaw tighten and the well-remembered fire flared in her eyes. Her face, with a network of lines, registered fury as she fisted her hands on her hips.

"How bloody dare you! The cheek of you and your family. Coming here today."

I dropped my eyes to the ground, not ready for the backlash I knew would hit me soon enough.

Kathleen turned to me. "And you! Talking to him after everything he and his family have done to us!"

Keeping his voice soft, Rory said, "I haven't done anything, Kathleen."

"You're all alike, you O'Donovans!" She spat the words at him. "Don't think I don't know what your family is capable of! Don't you *dare* think I don't know that."

I lifted my eyes and saw the shuddering of her chest as she took great gulps of breath. The anger had brought the blood to her face and she was positively glowing.

"Leave. Now!" she said through gritted teeth. She would have pointed dramatically if not for the crowd now turning to watch, so she kept her hands clenched in tight fists at her side. It was as if she was trying desperately not to hit him.

"Your kin will be waiting a long time if they expect to be allowed through the gates of heaven. They have done so much to hurt our family. For one thing, they murdered our sister Merrell and you have no right to be here now!"

2

Merrell had been the beauty in the family. Three years younger than Kathleen and four years older than me, she was the one everyone turned to look at when we walked down the street. She was fun, carefree and endlessly amusing and fit without having to try. When I was thirteen and she was seventeen, she gave me her Easter dress she'd made herself three years before. She curled my hair and shortened the hem another inch just before church. 'Doesn't she look lovely?' I heard her ask my mother upstairs. 'Nice as she can be,' our mother answered, 'but she'll never be much to write home about.'

At the time of Merrell's death, she and Sean O'Donovan had been meeting secretly while I was totally besotted with his younger brother Rory and doing the same thing. But furtive looks and secret meetings were all we managed because the Neils and the O'Donovans hadn't seen eye to eye for as long as any of us could remember. If my mother knew what was happening behind her back, I knew all hell would break loose.

My mother's fiery temper was legendary and many said it the reason my father escaped this life when I was barely eight years old. No one spoke of him and I have precious few memories of him except for a thin man with very little to say to any of us.

Merrell's 21st birthday party had been the most anticipated party I had ever seen in my short life and everyone was invited to our small bar to celebrate. Later that night, when we were all exhausted and asleep, someone broke into her bedroom and ended her life.

My mother grieved so hard and fierce for Merrell who was about to make a fresh life for herself across the Bass Straight in Melbourne in a few weeks' time to start a new job as a receptionist with an advertising company. That's what Merrell told everyone but we all knew her real motive for leaving was to get away from serving behind the bar at the pub and find herself an agent and become a star. All her friends knew her plans and most were happy for her, even jealous. Not so Sean O'Donovan. He'd read something else in Merrell's beautiful green eyes that she flashed at him. He'd imagined a future and a family and Merrell leaving Richmond for a new life in Melbourne, before he even had a chance to try out for that part, was not what he wanted or expected. But she knew what she wanted and life in a small town five minutes from another small town wasn't it.

The investigation wasn't any more organised than a barroom brawl. Nobody took control of the crime scene. Mum must have run screaming in and out of Merrell's bedroom twenty times before the first of the police arrived. She even cleaned up a bit. Not that there was any real point in worrying about forensics. Out in Richmond, they hadn't had a murder for eighteen years and probably hadn't known what to do then. Which didn't keep them from messing around for a day or two. They were all just small-town nincompoops.

Everyone was watching everyone else but in mum's mind, Sean was the only one with a motive. Merrell was leaving and he hadn't liked it. Not the most convincing of motives but in Mum's eyes, there was no doubt about it.

The only problem was he had an alibi and that was Rory. Sean and Rory had turned up late in the afternoon to the party and stayed for barely an hour, obviously unwelcome. During the festivities, Sean was quiet and sullen while Merrell danced with every available man in the pub. It was Rory who took it upon himself to whisk Sean away before anything untoward happened. I still remember Rory leaning in close to me, the familiar smell of him filling my nostrils until I could barely breath, whispering an apology to me for leaving so soon, saying he had to get Sean away. He twirled my hair around his fingers as his beautiful blue eyes held mine and winked, saying he'd make it up to me soon.

So Sean's alibi was Rory. They'd both gone fishing long into the night and then they'd both gone home to their own beds at around midnight. Rory swore Sean never left the house that night but of course Mum never believed him. In her heart, she said, she knew it was Sean.

Merrell's death turned out to be the death of our family as well and my world changed overnight. For days, I was in denial, certain she would walk through the door, flinging her hair over her shoulders as she always had, a brilliant smile on her face, lighting up the room. I wasn't allowed to see her body so the denial went on for more than a week until I found myself at her graveside. Then I knew she was truly gone. I felt hollowed out and angry and somewhere inside me, a voice told me my life would never be the same. Her death burned a hole in my heart that was never going to heal.

Anger and grief filled our home from the moment we rose at six in the morning until we put our heads down on our pillows at night. Kathleen supported Mum, of course, while I kept quiet. Merrell was the only person in the whole family who had ever given me the time of day and she had been wrenched away from me. I was alone and desolate. In the weeks that followed, while policemen scratched their heads, I was reminded endlessly that I was forbidden from ever talking to Rory or his family and my heart broke.

Then one week later, Sean walked into the police station and confessed. He killed Merrell, he said, and he would never forgive himself for losing his temper. He went to trial but it was over before we knew it. He pleaded guilty, was sent to prison for life and as far as I knew, he's still there.

Two months after Merrell's death, at the end of my senior year at school and still forbidden to speak to Rory or even glance his way, I packed my own bags and moved out as well when Rory refused to see me or even talk to me, seemingly giving in to our families' unreasonable demands. I had only just turned eighteen, no big party for me by the way, and with an acceptance into the Queensland police force tucked away in my suitcase, I was determined that I would never set foot in Richmond again.

That was to be the last time I ever saw my mother again. Or Rory.

I was brought back to the present with the keeners warming up again and became aware of Rory's eyes on me. A deep flush began at the base of my neck and tracked slowly up my face. I panicked, pointed across at the undertaker slamming the hearse door shut.

"I have to go!" I muttered.

Kathleen had already stormed away from us towards Donald and that's what I did, almost running from Rory, decamping back to Donald who stood shuffling from one foot to the other with Rianne near the hearse. It was the shock, I told myself as I fled. It was this new Rory springing upon me when my mind was on my mother and Kathleen's intense anger that was making me revert back to the Sam of old.

But I know that's not the truth. I know it's Richmond. Not even back an hour and already I was regressing, the work of twenty years coming undone.

Donald explained that we were to stand behind the hearse and lead the cortege down to the old cemetery. His eyes glanced over to Rory who had obediently stepped away to a corner of the church where he could be away from the proceedings but still able to observe.

"Let me guess," I asked grimly. "Another special request?"

"Yep. She's to be buried with the rest of her own family. And according to the grand plan, we all have to walk there."

"To the old cemetery?" I gaped. "That's almost as far as the next village."

I was beginning to doubt I'd make it when Kathleen bustled up, her aggravated-big-sister expression still in place.

"Am I supposed to say, better late than never?" she grilled me, her kiss failing to connect with my skin.

"I'm sorry, Kathleen," I muttered apologetically. "Really I am. I didn't get your messages until a day ago and ..."

"Honestly, Sam, you're impossible," she interrupted. "Why do you have an answering machine if you don't bother taking your messages?"

I said nothing. I usually do pick up my messages as soon as I walk in the door but the past few days had not been usual at work.

"And couldn't you have let us know you were coming? Where were you when I rang, anyway?"

"At work."

"Work?"

She had rung at all hours of the day and night and had left five messages on my machine.

Her puffy, red-rimmed eyes were ringed with black circles gouged deep by distress, so I let her scold me. I didn't have to tell her my job as a police detective meant working all hours of the night and day. She knew that. What she didn't know was I had been working a murder case when I got the first message. I'd been so busy with the case, I forgot about the message until there were five of them waiting for me, every message sounding more and more angry and desperate.

Scolding me was one of Kathleen's favourite occupations, without argument or interruption. It was a relief when the undertaker slid across and whispered in her ear and she moved away again to line us up in the order our mother had dictated. Father Doyle and two of the keeners were to go in front of the hearse, the other two priests and the other two keeners immediately behind, then us. Was I expected when Mum made her plans, I wondered?

The black car slipped into gear and rolled out the gates as the keeners, no doubt professional actors, lifted the pitch of their noise another notch and started to hold their notes for longer. My mother must have been planning this event for months. Years maybe.

We trudged down the village main street, making slow progress past the two-roomed school, past the Lamberts' little farm, still with the same stench of dung mingled with sea salt wafting out, then past the post office with an assortment of stickers and flyers pasted over the windows. Rounding the curve in the road, I saw our house. Mum's house. The bar and grocery in the front, living room and kitchen behind, bedrooms above. When we reached it, the undertaker stopped the hearse outside the front door, turning off the engine for two minutes of silence. The keeners became quiet, thankfully, and now we could hear the sea.

Mum's house. Just a front-room bar and grocery shop but in her own world it made her someone. A home that was bigger than most others around and a business that was central to the life of the village that held barely 1,500 people. So central, in her mind, that when she talked about the shop, she gave it the name of the village.

"Mum's thinking of selling Richmond," Kathleen had said on the phone a year back. "This time I think she means it."

And this time, she really did. The 'For Sale' sign went up on the building that had defined her for fifty-six years and quickly attracted an offer. But before she had time to finalise the deal, she died.

Dead, Mum. That's what you are. But how can that be? How can it be over?

After one hundred and twenty blessed seconds of silence, the keeners recommenced their lament and we moved off again, up the gently rising hill. It was fresher up here, with a small breeze blowing off the sea and we could see right across to the mud flats of Samphire Island.

As a child, I used to look across to the island and imagine a shark. The jutting bit to the west was its nose, while the small inlet beneath it was the mouth and fin. Around it, on the three sides visible, are treacherous, waterlogged sands that have inspired a lot of folklore and legend. It gleamed at me now, flat and innocent in the almost midday sun.

We passed the old police station, once a burnt-out husk but now a holiday apartment complex with landscaped gardens and balconies facing the sea. We walked on past the higgledy-piggledy line of bungalows, each built without awareness of its neighbour, like a row of crooked teeth. Then the buildings stopped, the road narrowed, and we were in a country lane that hugged the coast.

My nausea had become a squirming mass, thick and threatening. I could no longer respond to Kathleen's whispers. I had to concentrate on my breathing and focus on the way ahead. Slowly, slowly, we tramped on until at last, we could see the cemetery, a patchwork of crosses and slabs of stone staring over a low wall at the sea, closed now to anybody who did not already have a plot inside.

We kept to the trees at first as long fingers of lawn stretched between the graves. I walked cautiously, not wanting to tread on any flowers or knock my shins on one of the smaller headstones. The sounds of Richmond Road had disappeared, replaced by snatches of birdsong.

Mum's open grave was there waiting for us and beside it a pile of earth, the surface cracking as it dried in the sun. To the back, tucked away where no one ever stepped, was Daddy's grave. A plain, grey slab simply stating Patrick Neil 1948 to 1988. No frills. No 'loving husband, loving father'. Just his name and details. Gone when I was barely 8 years old.

Catching the tail-end of whispered stories in the dark recesses of the pub, I remembered hearing that Daddy's widowed mother had held down two jobs to give her boy an education, planning for him to go to university. Except Daddy didn't cooperate. First he said he didn't want to go, then he failed the scholarship and that put paid to any future thoughts of advanced schooling. From there Daddy went to a hardware store selling nails and the like to tradesmen in town until his mother and Nana Peg, a Rooney by birth, sat down to a cup of coffee in a local café. Mum was still single and nearing thirty by then and beggars couldn't be choosers, both mothers agreed.

Apparently, it wasn't just the big age difference Mum objected to. It was the young man's lazy attitude that bothered her. Nonetheless, the two mothers pooled whatever spare money they had and put a down-payment on a lease for a pub that was meant to supply them with an income after the marriage. Within a month, Mum and Daddy were betrothed and within another month they were married. They had raised three daughters on the profits of that pub but it was a heart attack at forty that finally took him.

Four Celtic crosses stood sentry over the hole in the ground that was Mum's.

The smallest, newest one belonged to Auntie Norah. 'Norah Anne Teresa O'Donovan. 1920 to 1999. Ar Dheis De Go Raibh A Anam. May Her Soul be with God.

Nana Peg would have chosen this inscription for the woman who was not really our aunt at all but her closest friend. And Norah must have chosen to be buried here with the Neils and Rooneys instead of with her own people, the O'Donovans.

The second Celtic cross was for Nana Peg and I remember Kathleen telling me she had a full Irish Republican burial when she died, complete with tricolour flag draped over the coffin. I sent my condolences but I couldn't bring myself to go. I still hadn't forgiven them.

The third cross was a memorial cross for Uncle Barney, Nana Peg's brother, Barney Rooney, her hero who died during the Uprising in Ireland.

The last one was for Mum, and it waited, cold and still, as we all approached the grave. My chest tightened and I could barely catch my breath.

I turned to Kathleen. "Mum didn't ask for an IRA burial, did she?"

"Oh no. Nobody does that anymore," she whispered back, eyes sweeping over the crowd.

Father Doyle and the keeners joined us by the grave and the keening stared up again as we waited for the long string of people to trudge in and gather round. His face made his feelings very clear: he had no choice but to indulge mum's eccentric requests but he does not have to approve.

Finally, at the height of the keener's lamentation, they stopped abruptly and stepped back into the crowd. Silence reverberated.

As Father Doyle began to pray, I spotted Rory at the back of the crowd and behind him were the entire O'Donovan clan. All of them. Paddy and Brendan and Martin and Margaret and Benny and their assorted spouses and children along with his parents and an ancient man I knew would be Rory's grandfather, John O'Donovan. I was so surprised to see them all here that it took me a moment to register the woman who must have been Rory's wife, tall and elegant, holding two little hands that belonged to the boy and the girl who must have been his son and daughter.

I felt sick. It was physical, nothing to do with seeing the perfect family portrait. I've had twenty years to accept that while Rory O'Donovan may have been the love of my life, the one who spoiled me for everyone else, I did not mean the same to him. He had long ago moved on to marriage, fatherhood and children as Kathleen was more than happy to inform me. Not that I could talk. After hearing the news, I moved on too. I married and divorced three unhappy years later and since then, I've engrossed myself in my work, moving up the ladder from policewoman to detective. Work helped soothe my ruffled feathers but I never quite found my way back from mourning that lost possibility.

Good for him, I thought. Whatever I wanted to do with my personal life – and I will admit that at 38-years-old, I'm a little tardy with the answer to that question – I do know, I've always known, what I *don't* want. It's a list that seems to include things that are desirable to others: flashy cars, big houses, weekly trips to the shopping centres for expensive clothes, big televisions and face-lifts. And the top, first and foremost, outright number one on the list of 'Things That Samantha Neil Does NOT Want' is marriage and two children in Richmond, Tasmania. With Rory O'Donovan or anyone else.

Nausea swirled again. And again. I tried to beat it down, but pressure was swelling up into my nose and ears and I knew it was going to come. My throat constricted, my scalp felt clammy and hot. Death was a finality I could only comprehend in the dark of my bedroom when I was on the cusp of sleep. Like an electric shock, it hit me with a force of a thousand volts. It's the *end*. There's no blackness, no tunnel, no sinking into oblivion. It's literally nothing. And it was the nothingness, the utter finality, the horrific reality of ceasing, that scared me to the point of gasping for air.

My middle constricted and my head filled with the sound of somebody wailing. Father Doyle looked up from his missal, annoyance written all over his face because this was supposed to be *his* time. He should have recognised that this sound was different, rawer than the ritual cries of the professional keeners.

This time it was me.

I stumbled away, floundering in the only direction where there were no people. I could see the questioning faces of the crowd as I lurched away but it was as if they were behind gauze.

My feet were not working properly and when I almost fell, two strong arms grabbed me. My body recognised them as Rory's and I swayed towards him. But as I held him, vomit rushed up and I threw up over his shoes where it pooled on the grass around our feet. I tried to apologise but the next wave was surging up just as Father Doyle decided to continue with his prayers.

"You're all right, Sam," he whispered. "You're all right."

But I wasn't. What his wife must be making of this! When the heaving stopped, he placed a handkerchief in my shaking hands and watched as I wiped my mouth. I stepped away from him in an effort to stand on my own but the world came rushing in through my ears, spinning me into a vortex of blackness.

As I sagged, Rory took hold of me and let unconsciousness carry me off.

3

It felt like days later when I woke in a bed of weighty blankets pressing down on me. It's been a long time since I slept under anything so heavy. Gradually, objects in the room become familiar – the pictures and curtains. Above me, on the ceiling, strips of wood made a design of squares and the old smell of sea air and lavender came swimming into my nostrils, seeped with memories. I listened and there it was: pound, swoosh, pound, swoosh. The backing track to my childhood.

Mum didn't like the sea or beach. It was the sand, she said, the feeling of it between her toes, but also she blamed it for how it clung to the carpets, to our shoes, to the end of the bath after we let out the water. She didn't like the salty wind either because it spattered the windows with stains and scoured paint off doors and window frames.

The sea didn't care what she thought. On it went, raising the volume whenever we opened the windows or doors. Smashing itself against the shore and sending glitter-blue invitations to us to come and play.

A door opened downstairs releasing a buzz of talk. The funeral. No doubt the drink was flowing by now, the craic flying, the sentiment oozing. I was grateful for the queasiness that allowed me to lie here and avoid it. Twenty years on and nothing was different. Everything that drove me away is still here, in this village, in this house and I could feel it watching me and waiting. I rolled myself into a tight coil under the blanket and let the rhythm of the waves carry me away back to sleep.

"Sam. Sam! Can you hear me? Sam. Are you awake?"

It was Kathleen, standing at the end of the bed holding a tray with tea and toast.

"I am now," I grizzled.

"You haven't eaten a thing. That's why you're poorly."

I tried to sit up but my head felt like it was packed with gravel and it pinned me to the pillow. She set the tray down on the bedside table.

"Should I have let you sleep?" The softness in her voice caught me out. It was rare to hear it. "But I didn't like to leave without checking on you first."

"You're leaving?"

"I'm just shattered," she replied. "I'm going as soon as I can."

"I can imagine," I said trying to sit up again. The dizziness was easing now and the teapot began to look inviting. "You should go now."

"I wish," she muttered.

She launched into a long spiel about everything that had gone wrong as she tried to serve drinks and lunch and snacks and now teas to the ones who were hanging around. All with only Eileen to help her. It was a muffled complaint against me, useless as ever. I said nothing as the domestic litany of the day droned on until eventually she sighed to a stop and sat down on the bed beside me.

"Seriously, Sam. How are you feeling now?"

"A bit woozy," I replied feeling annoyed with myself.

"I rang Doctor Woods and asked him to drop by later."

"No need for that."

Her head was bent low and her neck bones protruded like knuckles.

"You don't look too hot yourself," I commented.

"Thanks," she grinned.

"You know what I mean. It's been a tough few days for you."

"Awful. The worst." Her eyes welled up. "Jesus, I can't stop crying. I thought I was all cried out but the bloody tears are gathering for the next flow."

Which is worse? I wondered. To cry too much when your mother dies or not to cry at all?

After Kathleen blew her nose and dried her eyes, I said, "You were very good to her."

And she was. Our mother was 76 years old when she died, apparently severely arthritic and chronically cranky, but Kathleen let it all flow over her. Not like me.

"Right," she sniffled. "But I have a favour to ask you."

She wanted me (needed me actually) to stay on in Richmond to sort our mother's affairs. Mum had auctioned the house and business a few month ago but it failed to meet the reserve price. She'd since agreed a sale with a German couple who had given up their jobs in Frankfurt to move across to Richmond, (why I'll never understand), but the contracts weren't finalised yet. The handover was this coming weekend. All this on top of the usual issues that arise after a death.

"I can't stay," she said. "I just can't. Rianne needs to get back to school and Donald is up to his eyes in work."

"Whereas the spinster sister has no life worth speaking of?"

"Oh, come on Sam!"

Come on: this was the first family duty I've asked you to do in twenty years. Come on: it was the least you could do for Mum and the family and might in some small way make up for all that trouble you inflicted on us all the years with your unforgiving attitude. Come on. Quite a load for two little words to carry, but such is the verbal shorthand of families.

"If you can't do it, I don't know how I'll manage," she begged. "But before you decide, there's something you should know. I just found out that Mum's affairs are being handled by Rory O'Donovan."

I guffawed.

"Really." She insisted, looking just as shocked as I felt. "He says he's been acting as her solicitor for twelve months now, ever since she started to seriously consider selling. Can you believe that?"

She was shaking her head, looking out the window, not at me.

"Apparently he has the will," she went on. "She arranged for him to come here and read it to us both tomorrow."

"Rory O'Donovan, Kathleen? Are you bloody serious?"

Mum? Taking her business to an O'Donovan? Talking to an O'Donovan, for God's sake. Especially to Rory O'Donovan. To Rory!

"I know. I was as surprised as you," she snorted. "I only heard myself a few hours ago. She may have forgiven his family for Merrell's death but I surely haven't."

"I don't believe it," I muttered incredulously. "I just don't believe it."

"He's downstairs now," she continued. "He's been there since he… since you…waiting all afternoon. He wants to know if he can come up and see you before he goes?"

"No!" I almost shouted as I pulled the blanket over my queasy stomach and shook my head. "No way. Tell him I'm not well enough to see anybody."

"Have some tea, Sam. At least have *something*."

She poured me a cup of tea and I wrapped my fingers around the warmth of the cup and found it tasted unexpectedly comforting. I nibbled some toast, again surprisingly good, as Kathleen sat on the bed again, closer this time. So close I could feel the tension humming in her and like everything else today, it brought me right back to my childhood. I remembered her circling around Mum's moods, senses on full alert, seeking a gap through which she might enter to say the right thing. Something I never accomplished. Usually she picked her moment with uncanny tact but not always. Not always. And we gave up talking about it years ago because we saw it too differently.

She poured me another cup of tea and said, "There will be money, you know, once the sale has been settled."

The sound of toast being crunched was loud in my ears.

"You should think about what you'll do with a lump sum like that Sam. Maybe pay off the house you have in Queensland."

"Thanks for your concern, Kathleen." My voice sounded brittle and I made a mental note not to sound like the bitter spinster I was. "It's a big 'if' that mum would leave me some money, and we both know that."

"Of course it isn't!"

"It doesn't matter to me, Kathleen. Things like that. I've moved on. I have a well-paying job that I love and I am self-sufficient. I know what Mum thought of me and I'm older now and not so easily hurt," I lied.

"Mum wouldn't do that. Surely you know that much about her? Surely you can admit that, today of all days."

My silence filled the room.

"It was Merrell's death that caused all this unhappiness, Sam. She never held a grudge against you."

I went back to chewing my toast as she sat staring at me. My silence was getting to her. It always did although this time I was not trying to upset her.

She sighed. "Rory told me just now that Sean gets out of jail in a couple of years, maybe sooner. Good behaviour they said after twenty years served." She snorted. "He's been the model prisoner. And he'll probably come back to Richmond to rub it in our noses." She swallowed noisily. "So I could use the support."

I stopped chewing my toast and let that piece of information settle in my mind. Sean out but my sister, the only one who ever truly loved me, was still dead. I felt my stomach lurch again.

"Jesus, Sam, will you please answer me?" she blurted out. "Is an answer too much to ask?"

I made my face blank, a sheet of glass that bounced her gaze right back. If I fired off the answer that was searing my tongue, in seconds we'd be quivering into a fight, our faces wrenched into hateful shapes, our memories leaping back across the years to snatch up the old insults and injuries that lay in waiting in this house. I couldn't let that happen, not today.

After a long time, my sister said, "You've something missing in you, Sam. Do you know that?"

The words were spoken in a hard, cool voice of someone who thinks she's being tactful. Then her eyes flickered and she blushed before picking up the tray to leave. As she reached the door, I called her gently. There was one more thing I needed to say.

"Kathleen?"

She turned eagerly, two hands on the tray, one foot in the door keeping it open.

"This business of reading Mum's will tomorrow."

"Yes?"

"I won't be there." Even I could hear the petulance in my voice.

I wanted to oblige her, and where I could, I would. But even the thought of this sick little scheme of Mum's made my blood boil. Kathleen and I sitting at her dining room table while Rory O'Donovan sat across from us, reading us her requests and bequests.

No. Sorry. No can do.

"But you have to be there." She looked at me as if I'd said I was about to dance naked down the street. "If you're not..."

"You can tell me all about it afterwards."

"I really think..."

"I'm not going Kathleen."

We were looking at each other across an impasse when the tentative sound of steps came down the corridor, followed by a male voice.

"Hello? Anybody there?"

And then, knowing it was the very last thing I wanted, Kathleen threw open the door, leaving Rory to enter the room.

"So Sam," he started after my sister had made her excuses and left us alone. "What's going on? Why are you receiving me in bed, like a courtesan? You don't look sick to me."

As he talked, he pulled out the chair from the corner and brought it over, close to the bed.

"Don't think I don't know what you're up to. Lying low and avoiding the mob downstairs. Avoiding me too, no doubt."

His voice took on the same Irish brogue I remembered so well. He was born here in Australia but his grandfather had taught him everything he knew about Ireland and his accent was pure Wexford, just like his grandfather's. The nasal vowels, the singing rise and fall to his sentences. But of course, it's *my* speech that's changed, not his. I was struck again by the newness of this man that I had once loved, the short hair that made him look so different.

"It's all a bit Richmond to me," I replied softly.

"I knew it."

"I hear you're a full-fledged lawyer and resident with a wife and family now." I said it as if I had only heard the last part of my speech today. Like Kathleen hadn't crowed about it nine years ago. "Was it the progressive liberalism that brought you back here or the cultural stimulation?"

"No need to sneer, city girl. It's a good place to live."

I raised my eyebrows in question. The Rory I knew could not have been happy here.

"I like that it takes me only fifteen minutes of traffic-free driving to get to work. That my nice house cost half of nothing compared to a similar place in Hobart, or any other big city. That after work, I can go walking in clean air or swimming in a clean sea. That I drink in a pub where everybody knows me."

"Stop it. You're scaring me."

He laughed, then waved towards the window. "Look at it. Look at how lovely it is."

The window framed Richmond in full seduction. Over to our right, the setting sun threw streaks of orange and pink and red along the sky and the Coral River borrowed the colours and flaunted them like they were its own. Waves shimmered around the curve of Halfmoon Inlet and on the mud flats of Samphire Island, foam glistened. Above it, seabirds circled and swooped, silver and gold wings flashing in the dazzling, dying light.

"When did you ever care about scenery?" I asked.

"I think I always did, Sam. I took that sight away with me everywhere I travelled and never saw anywhere that looked better. And when the time came, after I'd passed the bar," he hesitated, "to figure out where home was," he said that instead of what he meant to say: when the time came to get married, "Well, here I am."

Here he was, turning the chair around to sit into it, backwards, his thighs straining against his trousers, his bulk too close.

"And you? You've wound up in a big city. Surfers Paradise in Queensland, I hear."

"That I have." The lilt in my voice shocked me, returning suddenly. I made a mental note not to let *that* happen again. "I like that I'm surrounded by millions of people. I like that my four-bedroomed house is worth a ludicrous amount of money compared to here and that the price of it keeps rising. And I like that I can choose from a hundred bars where nobody knows me."

He tossed his head back and laughed, the way he always did. It was all the same: the crinkles round the eyes, the missing back tooth that showed only when his lips were stretched into his widest smile. I felt my heart turn over and I swallowed hard to calm myself.

"God, Sam," he laughed. "You haven't changed a bit."

"Of course I have."

He stopped smiling and said, "You look so much the same. I was surprised by that."

"I'm twenty years different. Just like you."

When I was that girl, I had one person who was all mine. A secret person, into whom I poured everything. Rory.

He lived up the road from me and was my own age, but while I was boarded at a good Catholic girls' school in Hobart, each morning his sister would drive him to school on her way to work. He never came into the shop after Merrell died just like I never walked up the side road that led to his family's farm. And if he, or any of his family, saw me or any of mine, our eyes automatically moved towards the ground or the sky.

But I saw him often. Obedient as always, we never gave each other even a hello. But we did look. Whenever I would sneak a veiled glance towards him, across the road or the church or the beach, I often found him looking back. We would get lost in those stares, but never for long. We were afraid of being noticed. Those few seconds could be so intense they hurt, almost enough for my heart to burst.

At night in bed, I would summon up in my mind our most recent encounter and run it through my head like a movie, milking it for detail. I had no time for the other boys with their bruised legs and dirty hands and slow minds. Boys who were always yelling and waving their arms, pretending to shoot each other with sticks from behind trees. For all their shouting, those boys could never do what he did: walk down a road alone. He was different.

Like me.

Years before, he had been an altar boy and every Sunday he was on show at Mass, performing holy chores. Holy communion became the high point of my week, those few seconds at the altar when I let out my tongue for the host and his hand was beneath my chin holding the paten, close enough to touch me. I watched him as he bowed low or rang the little bell, so much that even now as he sat before me, I could see 11-year-old Rory, good shoes and grey socks jutting from beneath his surplice, a sliver of shin revealed as he reclined on the altar steps. I remembered how the thoughts of approaching the altar could make my hands shake so badly I had to sit on them.

I thought I was keeping my secret safe in my heart. I thought Nana Peg or Mum, not even Kathleen, noticed. I was wrong.

Now his adult eyes were bouncing all over me, like they can't get enough of what they are seeing.

"How on earth did you end up with my mother as a client?"

"You were surprised?" he grinned.

"Stupefied."

"I knew you would be."

"It began nine years ago when I moved back here. If I was going to be living here, I decided I couldn't carry on avoiding Neil's pub. Most of the lads I hung around with drank there." His eyes dropped to his hands, twisting his wedding ring around and around his finger. "One evening after work, I gathered my courage and took myself in, when I thought the place wouldn't be too busy."

"Wow."

He nodded. "After taking the big step, she wasn't even there herself. It was Eileen Powell behind the counter. I asked her for a pint and Eileen stared at me goggle-eyed. 'Excuse me a sec,' she said and scuttled off, leaving me standing there like a right eejit. Three or four others began to gather behind me, delighted with the goings-on, others on the edge of their stools to see what was going to happen next."

I threw my eyes to the ceiling.

"I know. If they hadn't all been watching, I think I would have made a run for it. I was no nervous. After what seemed like a day, out she came, with Eileen running behind her. 'Can I help you?' she asked in her best frosty voice, her chest puffed out, and I knew straight away it was going to be alright because I could see that underneath the frost she was flustered herself. 'A pint of Guinness, please, Mrs Neil,' I said. She stood there for a full half a minute, just breathing, her chest rising and falling, with every-body watching. When she picked up a glass and pulled the tap, it was like the whole place let out its breath."

"And that was it?"

"That was it. I've been a regular ever since. I even," his face wrinkled with apology, "became fond of her."

I groaned.

"Her bark was worse than her bite."

A familiar feeling coiled inside me, deep and cold.

"So, a happy ending all round," I said. "How moving." I have never tried to make anyone else see Mum as I saw her, as she treated me.

He leant forward in the chair. "I want to tell you what I told her days, maybe weeks later." His eyes were magnetic as they held mine. "Sean didn't murder Merrell, Sam."

The words were like a bomb in the silence. I blinked a few times as the words sank in.

"Of course he did, Rory. He confessed. He was found guilty."

He was nodding as I talked. "That being so, but he didn't do it. He was with me the whole night."

I snorted. "So why did he confess to something he knew would send him away for life?"

"I don't know, Sam, and he never confided in me. And believe me I asked, begged, for him to tell me. I couldn't get it out of him. He was determined to go through with it."

"That's ridiculous!" I almost spat the words. "Are you saying this now to me because he's due for release soon and will be on his way back here. Is that your ploy? To make it easier for him? He may be free to live a care-free life but my sister will still be dead in her grave."

My voice had risen and I could feel emotion making my face hot and red.

"You know that's not me, Sam. I told the same story to your mother, explained everything I knew, and thank God, she believed me. Sean didn't do it."

While he spoke, I was shaking my head in disbelief. "Then who murdered her?"

"Again Sam. I don't know." He looked towards the closed door. "And she never said a word to Kathleen about it."

As I seethed, he searched my face again and despite my anger, I could see his eyes soften. He leant forward in the chair.

"I've often wondered how things turned out for you, Sam, but I never got the nerve to ask your mother. Our association, hers and mine, was very much on her terms and fragile to say the least."

"That sounds like Mum, all right," I conceded.

"So I never asked, but I often wondered," he repeated.

He leant closer still and picked up a strand of my hair.

"You never changed it," he said. "When you made your grand entrance into the church yesterday, that was the first thing I thought: *she never changed her hair.*"

He tugged the curl straight, then wound it around his finger. I let him, but only for a second, before jerking my head away and tossing my hair over the opposite shoulder.

"I see you're married?" I knew what the answer was but I wanted him to know that I knew.

He nodded. "I married nine years ago."

I had a follow-up line prepared for this inevitable moment but having invited it, my brain had now decided to evacuate. Silence lengthened and it was he who broke it.

"I have two children."

"Two? How lovely." *How lovely? Is that the best I could come up with?*

"And your wife, is she from around here? Would I know her?"

"No. I met her in Hobart when I was studying law."

"So you've done it all," I smiled my most charming smile. "Wife, kids, law practice, a big house in the country."

"I've been lucky," he nodded again.

Did he not remember that we never wanted all that? Certainly he was coming over as all grown up whereas I, since arriving back in Richmond, was reliving the most gauche horrors of my adolescence.

I am not normally like this, I wanted to scream. *I'm a police detective. I am respected, even admired. Reporters run after me.*

"What about you?" he asked. "Are you married?"

"Oh no. Not anymore. Been there, done that, you could say. Not my style. I'm a career woman."

"Never say never," he smiled, which made me want to slap him.

He saw the look on my face and said, "Hey. I didn't mean it the way you're taking it. I just meant..."

"I'm single because that's how I like it."

I wanted to add that after being kicked around by the people who were supposed to love me, I had come to distrust everyone. And it's true. I have learnt how to create myself, by myself and for myself, and I am happy with who I was.

"Look, I won't stay long, Sam. I dropped up here because I need to talk to you about your mother's will."

"Rory, I've already told Kathleen. I don't give a fig about..."

He held up his hand. "I know that Sam. We all know that. But can you just listen for a minute? Last January, your mother said to me, *'I'm not long for this world. I won't last another year.'* I laughed it off, the way you do, but she started making plans and she hired me to carry them out. So this is business. And this," he said reaching across to place the white envelope he had been holding onto the top of my bedspread, "is for you."

An A4 envelope with my name written on the outside in blue ink: Samantha Maire Neil. Mum's writing, still neat and small. At the centre, between the folds of paper there was something hard.

"Don't open it yet," he said, getting up. "There's something else you have to be given first."

He left the room and returned with a battered blue suitcase. I recognised it immediately. Six times a year, I used to fill it with uniforms and be driven to and from my convent boarding school with it resting on the seat beside me.

He heaved it onto the bed where it landed at my feet with a bounce.

"Jesus, it's heavy. I'm always surprised by the weight of paper."

"Paper?"

"It's full of documents, family photos and papers and newspaper cuttings. That sort of thing. The key is in that sealed envelope you've got there. You are the only one who is to have access to it."

I was astounded. "Me? Why me?"

"I don't know. I'm just following instructions. I was to make sure to give this to you myself and I was to tell you that the contents are for your eyes only, nobody else's. Trust me, she was very clear about that."

I felt my eyes harden. "I stopped believing the words 'trust me' when I was seventeen."

The words were out before I had time to think about the impact they would make. When did I become so hard?

I watched his eyes widen and watched as he took a quick breath, but he said nothing.

To hide my embarrassment, I took out the key and pulled the case towards me. The locks must have been oiled recently because one twist of the key and they snapped open.

It was crammed with all kinds of documents. Packets of letters tied with faded ribbon, a well-worn diary, newspaper clippings and manilla folders along with sheaves of photos and a smell of yesterday as strong as bottled perfume.

Half of me wanted to recoil, but the other half won and I found myself picking through the photographs: stiff sepias from the early part of the century, black and whites from the 40s and 50s and some from around the time when I was born, colourful prints of Merrell's 21st birthday party, prints that brought me back all the way to now taken presumably by Donald of Mum looking smaller and more wrinkled than I remembered her, clasped in Kathleen's arms while together they watched Rianne blow out the candles on a birthday cake.

Damn you, Mum, I thought as I rummaged through, reluctantly at first, then greedily, until I became aware that Rory was looking down at me, which was all too much for me. I replaced the photos in the suitcase and snapped the clasps on tight.

"What was she up to?" I asked.

"I honestly don't know. Apart from the fact that it meant meeting up with you," there was that grin again, "I've treated it as if she was just another client."

I ignored his comment. "How was she so certain I'd come back?"

"If you didn't, I was to get your address and bring the suitcase and the letter to you. I was to make sure to put it into your hands myself."

I tried to imagine myself in my house in Surfers Paradise, answering the doorbell one ordinary day and seeing Rory O'Donovan standing on the other side of the door, holding the battered suitcase. What the hell was she up to? And him too, with his hair-touching and his 'never say never', and 'you haven't changed a bit.' I was crazy to come back and now I have been delivered this.

"You can take it back." I pushed the suitcase towards him. "I don't want it."

"Oh Sam..."

"You, more than anyone else, knows why I can't forget what she did. You know!"

His eyes roamed my face. "I'll never forget," he whispered.

"So take it back!"

"I can't. I was employed to deliver it and now you have it." He nodded to the A4 envelope. There's a letter inside. Read it," he demanded as he turned towards the door. "And I'll see you tomorrow." Then he was gone, the sound of his footsteps loud on the wooden stairs as he descended.

My hands trembled as I took the sheet of paper from the envelope. I almost came undone when I read the first line but forced myself to read on.

My Dearest Samantha,

A letter from the grave, what do you think of that? I got one as well from your Nana Peg when she passed on so I can imagine some of your feelings as you read this. By now you'll have the suitcase and seen what's in it. Most of those letters, photos and records were kept by your Nana Peg, I don't think that woman threw away a piece of paper.

It was always in my mind that we should sort out these papers someday, destroy the rubbish and the private stuff, and give the rest to somebody who could put together what truly happened to Merrell. When your Nana died, she suggested, among other things, that the right person should be you.

After days of shuffling bits of paper in and out of different piles, I came around to agreeing with your Nana. You were the one for the job.

There is a danger in me doing this, Samantha, I won't pretend I don't know it. I'm afraid of the anger in your heart and what you may do because of it. But I think you should know all the secrets that I have uncovered, and others I have been told. I'm also hoping that when you read these papers and see these photos, you'll understand why it was so terrible for me when I found out you had gotten yourself mixed up with an O'Donovan. I've played that last evening in our kitchen so many times in my mind and I greatly regret how we both overreacted. At the beginning, I was afraid that if we did make up and you came back home, you'd take up with him again. Your grandmother feared that too, I know. You see, the Neils, and before them the Rooneys, and O'Donovans have always feuded. And there were other things to consider. Things you have no concept of. Auntie Norah was caught up in it as well. It might be hard for you to understand now but, at the time, the feud was real.

Yet I was always expecting something to happen that would bring you back to us. Always. Until Nana Peg died and you didn't come back for her funeral. I knew then that I'd go to my own grave without ever seeing you again. That's a hard thing to do to a parent, Samantha, but I forgive you as I hope my will makes it clear. Everything I have, I leave equally to you and Kathleen. I'm sure you agree it's a tidy sum. Invested wisely, you'll be free from money worries and able to do whatever you want. You could afford to take time off your detecting. But not until you do two last things for me. I want you to read the diary enclosed and I want you to find out who really killed Merrell.

So there you are. Think of it as me trying to make amends, of trying to put things right between us. I regret I won't be there to watch you but I'll be looking down from Heaven. (Keep that in mind as you work and you won't go far wrong.) I'll be praying for you as I always have.

Always, Samantha. I want you to know that.

That through it all I was always

Your loving

Mammy

My heart broke as I read the letter and by the end of it, tears were running freely down my cheeks and great gulping sobs were filling the silence. For days, thinking about returning to the place I thought I'd conquered consumed me in my spare time. It was a place where self-pity had me spinning scenarios about what would happen if I refused to come. Now this evening, with her letter burning in my hand, I felt wretched. If there weren't fifty people downstairs, I'd go to the sitting room fire and toss it in, then watch it burn.

Death is supposed to be the final act but so much is left unfinished when someone dies. It's as if they have walked offstage in the middle of the performance expecting to come back later and tie off loose ends.

My body felt like a sack full of sand. Outside through the window, the daylight stretched itself into a long dusk and with a final sob, I got up from the bed and opened my own suitcase that Kathleen must have brought up here for me while I slept.

I pulled out jeans and walking shoes, got dressed, and sneaked down the back stairs. From the front room, the sound of the party continued, only muted now. Only the stragglers, those who cared most for Mum and the ones who remained for the free drinks, were left. I made it to the back door without being seen just as a shadow appeared through the frosted glass.

I muttered a curse and stepped back quickly, hoping I hadn't made myself obvious, while the familiar band of the nearby ocean belted away its usual tune. Then the figure knocked on the door.

There wasn't much I could do. They'd seen me. I could run like a frightened rabbit back to my room or I could harden up and open the damn door. I opened the damn door.

Standing outside in the cold grey courtyard, with a small suitcase at his feet and looking bedraggled, was my ex-partner Jack Curtis. Parked behind him, in the family's private spaces, sat a mud-splattered red Mazda.

Jack had been my partner at Surfers Paradise station for almost five years before he left to start a Private Investigation practice of his own. After twelve years of seeing the worst things that people could do to each other, it was the skeletons of five small children found in the hinterland of Surfers Paradise that finally broke him.

What he should have done was take some leave and see a psychologist, like everyone suggested. But Jack never listens to anybody. He was just tired of seeing a broken justice system routinely fail children who've already been treated like disposable playthings. He did everything he could to balance the creaking scales of justice, the same scales many people want to believe are designed to protect the vulnerable in society. But those scales don't shield anyone, even our most innocent victims. Their function is to balance the lines of bureaucracy. And Jack simply broke under the weight.

Everything in life hinges on a split-second decision or submitting to a whim. Then, like tumbling dominoes, events follow. In a perfect world, you make the right decision and the best of results come. But sometimes good people make the wrong decisions, and that was Jack. He resigned from the police force and I'm sure he regrets it every day of his life.

Since then, our paths have crossed twice with cases he has helped me solve. Over the five years when we were partners, he was the best mentor anyone could have asked for and our relationship became one of friendship as well. Looking at him now, as if he'd walked all the way from Hobart, I realised how much I missed him.

I stared at him. I was suddenly conscious of my puffy eyes and my tear-streaked face as his eyes widened in surprise when he saw me. I knew I must look a fright.

"Remember me?" he asked with a smile. "I'm an ex-policeman and a Gemini. I love Indian food. Italian, too. And Mexican. Well, pretty much all food. I have a major sweet tooth too. No living family, but you know that sob story. I also love walks in the moonlight and Margueritas. Anything else that might jog your memory?"

He winked then laughed, throaty and packed with self-assurance while the lines around his eyes crinkled in a ruggedly attractive way that probably made plenty of women act foolish.

I stared at him in shock and it took me a few stunned seconds to respond.

"What are you doing here?"

He grinned. "Hello to you too."

"How did you find me?"

He looked coyly down at his fingernails. "As you know, I'm a detective. And a pretty good one, at that."

His eyes raised, travelling over my face, and the smile drooped as a small frown creased his forehead.

"I remembered you telling me your mother had died," he hesitated for a second. "Plus, you told Inspector Grayson where you were going," he added. "Getting to Hobart was the hard part. Once I got there, it was easier. Everyone knew about the funeral and everyone sends their condolences, by the way." He smiled. "Even the rental car attendant."

My boss, Inspector Grayson. I should have known he'd tell Jack. Not that it was a secret but Jack was the last person on earth I expected to see outside the back door.

He didn't mention my dishevelled appearance or my tear-stained face because that wasn't Jack. But he missed nothing.

"Why are you here, Jack?"

Unwillingly, my voice cracked.

He stepped forward to within a few feet of me before speaking softly.

"Because life is too cruel to go through it alone."

The remark pierced me like an arrow. Unwanted tears sprang to my eyes yet again. As I wiped them away angrily, he spread his arms wide and I fell forward, now sobbing, into them.

4

A splash of cool water on my face was all I needed, I told him. I disappeared inside, leaving him to wander around the yard behind the pub.

Five minutes later, I found him standing beside the row of giant gums that stood majestically at our gate, blocking the horizon. Long shards of bark were peeling off their trunks and lay in circles on the roots below them like skins. These trees were gluttons for the heat. They dot parks and fill forests and some years, they burn to almost nothing. But they are unbothered. This is their home and they always recover.

As I crunched my way over the gravel driveway from the house, Jack turned and looked back at me, squinting a little. Without saying a word, I waved him on to follow me across the long lawn, down a path overgrown with melaleuca scrub and far enough away from the noise in the bar. We pressed on, down to the edge of a sandy cliffside, down to the beach and on to the water's edge. We stood in silence for a few seconds, he with his hands in his pockets and me with my arms folded defensively across my chest, taking in the sky brushed with wispy clouds as a brisk westerly blew. The cool breeze was sending ripples over the water as the tide was coming in. It was approaching its highest point and from where we were standing, it was impossible to tell the moment when its seemingly unstoppable advance was about to go into retreat.

"I'd forgotten whatever it was that used to soothe me here," I murmured, my eyes riveted on the stretch of water before us.

He turned to face me, concern written all over his face. "By the looks of you, you've had one hell of a day. I'm sorry I was late and missed it. I'm thinking you could have used the support."

I took a deep breath and nodded, getting a nose full of Brut or Polo from his direction, as I tried to push my emotions deep down inside. Then I told him the story from the beginning of the day. I began with the clomping down the church aisle, interrupting the mass at the worst possible time, to the thunderous looks Father Doyle sent my way. I told him about the keeners and I had him doubled over in laughter. It made me realise there was a funny side to all this horror. Suddenly, I was giggling along with him. Then I told him the full story. There was so much I'd buried for the past twenty years and I wasn't sure where to start. He knew I'd left home to join the police force and that my childhood had been difficult. But anything deeper had hurt too much to tell anyone. I went on and told him about my history with Rory and finally Mum's letter and her request that I find out who killed my sister.

"It's like Mum has jumped up out of her coffin, waving a letter at me like a traffic warden with a ticket."

That was when his smile disappeared.

Jack looked at me for a few seconds in silence then turned back to let his eyes roam over the sea. Gulls skirted the sky and with a sudden shriek, one dived and disappeared then broke from the water, soaring with its fish. He watched silently and I knew he was gathering thoughts ready to deliver a speech.

I have always liked Jack. Men who take too much care of themselves and their clothes can appear vain and over ambitious. But Jack has stopped caring about what other people think of him long ago. Another thing that has always struck me is how he can stare into the distance as though he can see beyond walls, to a place where everything is clearer.

He sighed before turning back to me.

Here it comes, I thought.

"Sorrow is a thing with teeth, Sam. And although it sometimes seems to fade away, it returns from time to time to bare those teeth."

He ran his hand through his hair as he spoke.

"Can I give you a bit of advice? From a friend?" he continued. There was a calm, understanding expression on his face as he asked the question.

I nodded and shrugged. "Sure."

"You can never go back."

I nodded understandingly. I knew what he meant and he was right. Even if I wanted to, there were obstacles in the way now between Rory and me. His wife and children. My job. The fairy tale where we went back to the way we once were and walk happily into the sunset wasn't about to happen. It wasn't even the whole issue. It was going back to a time when I was loved, truly loved, and loving that person back with all my heart. That was the core of the issue and I had always thought that part was over and done with. But seeing Rory again, I was surprised because I thought the romantic in me had been burned at the stake twenty years ago.

Jack's gaze was intent, watching thoughts flit across my face. He always said he could read my mind just by watching my eyes.

I sighed. "I think I need your help, Jack."

The words were out before I could stop them. I'd spent my whole career proud of the fact I didn't need anyone's help and here I was doing exactly that.

He whistled softly through his teeth. "You're asking for my help?" A hand clutched his chest, feigning shock. "Now I'm freaked."

I grinned. "You don't get freaked."

"Trust me," he said. "I'm Richard Dreyfuss on the back of the boat and the shark has just jumped in my face."

"Ha ha, funny man. But I really think I could use your help."

Jack has the sort of brain that can unravel anything and make sense out of it. Somehow he can join random unconnected details and make them look like dot-to-dot drawings that even a child could do. He can collect details like a spider, weaving a web one strand at a time. He has the ability to reach back and pluck details out of the air when most people would have overlooked them.

It was that skill I needed now, if Mum and Rory were correct, and if I was to follow this through to the end.

I sighed. "I want to dig a little into Merrill's death, to do what Mum wanted me to do, but there are obstacles everywhere. For one, my job is waiting for me so time is limited. Then there's the animosity that simply radiates between our families. And as for Sean, he confessed, for goodness sake."

"Well," Jack began hesitantly. "As you know, every criminal investigation has loose ends. Most of them don't matter if you get a confession or a conviction. But if there's this doubt about the final result, we have to go back to the original investigation and look for something that was missed."

"And of course, there's Rory in the mix as well."

An expression I couldn't understand pleated Jack's forehead. "Do you want to talk about it? I'm all ears."

I took a deep breath and released it in a little puff of air. "Where do I start? I was this gangly teenager," I began, "with sharp pointy bits instead of female curves. I was plain and awkward and he could have had anyone he wanted. But he chose me. And I felt beautiful, just by association."

My voice cracked and I raised my fist to cover my mouth so he wouldn't see the quiver.

"I've never felt like that since, Jack," I managed, wiping the wetness from my eyes. "God. Look at me. Who is this person?"

I could see my reflection – desolate and hollow – mirrored in his eyes.

He stood listening, letting me finish without saying a word. That's what Jack does best. He listens. But inside I knew a jumble of words and emotions were jostling around fighting to get out.

I cleared my throat and continued as he watched me silently. So I wouldn't have to see the expression on his face, I watched a flock of birds rise over the water and fly towards the horizon as I spoke.

"He had this aura about him, a sense of confidence and knowledge, like a guy who knows he's two moves ahead of everyone else."

I swallowed and blinked rapidly, trying to keep the tears buried inside. "There he was, someone so perfect in every way. His hair, his eyes and he was so different from everyone else. And he loved ME."

Jack shook his head. "How stupid can a woman be?"

My eyes popped open as I turned to face him, anger flushing my face. I swallowed noisily, to cover my hurt.

"Gee, thanks Jack. Thanks for being so supportive."

"You're stupid because you are the most beautiful woman I know. You're stupid because you look in a mirror and you see something totally different from what everyone else sees. You see a lop-sided grin, that is, by the way, sexy as hell."

Colour rose in his face for a second and I could see he was a little embarrassed by his admission. "And you see...God knows what you see."

He threw his hands in the air. "But you're beautiful. You're smart. You're confident. And you leave other women for dead."

He hesitated for a second, searching for words, while I gaped at him.

"If there was one thing I could give you, I would give you the ability to see yourself through other people's eyes because only then would you realise how very special you really are."

He looked down at his feet, then back up again. A muscle in his jaw worked, tightening and flexing as he struggled with what he wanted to say.

His eyes studied my eyes before speaking. "The point is you don't see the whole picture. You don't see who you truly are. You may have lost your faith in the world but you haven't lost your values. Your personality shines through your eyes and you are..." he hesitated and sighed, "simply stunning."

Even in my confusion and sorrow, I found a laugh. "Wow! That was quite a speech," I said to hide my embarrassment. I could feel the heat rising in my face. "I've never heard you talk for so long before."

He smiled almost sadly. "Then listen to me now."

His voice was so soft, I could feel my chest contract at the softness in his eyes.

"He was the lucky one."

5

———

SUNDAY 21ST MAY

"Can I do it?" Rory asked. "I've always fancied pulling my own pint."

I handed him a glass. "Let the first one run off. What's in the pipes will be stale."

"I can't get used to this place being closed," he said tilting the glass as the creamy black liquid poured in, then letting it settle.

He and I were together, alone in the pub, the business that sustained our family for generations, now closed. Kathleen, Donald and Rianne had already left for Hobart that morning, after the reading of the will, and it had been a long morning alone with the ghosts and memories. Later this evening, I planned to meet Jack to catch up and have dinner with him in a little restaurant incorporated in The Richmond Arms Hotel, where he was staying, overlooking the Coal River. If he stayed for a few days, and he promised he would, I had in mind an evening cruise one night around Hobart.

A plan had formed in my head as I lay in bed staring at the ceiling the night before with the words from Mum's letter running through my mind. *Find out who killed Merrell,* she wrote. Her final words down on paper.

Jack's face jumped into my mind, standing at the back door, concern written all over his face. Jack, my mentor, who had forgotten more about solving crimes than I would ever know. Under the bed, the suitcase lay inert but ready to unveil all the secrets I would need and if anyone could help me, it was Jack.

I was pleasantly surprised, I admit it, when I answered the pub's doorbell at 3.30 this afternoon and found Rory once again standing on the step, tie loosened, an excuse on his lips to call in and tell me about the German buyers. I brought him into the kitchen but it felt too awkward to sit him there and the sitting room would have been worse. I felt trapped.

"Would you like a drink?" I asked nervously, and without waiting for an answer, I turned and walked through to the pub instead.

There we were, with the shutters closed so no one would try to peek in, and all the lights on. He sat himself on the high stool behind the bar and watched as I uncapped a fizzy orange drink for myself and walked around to the customer side to pour it, putting the counter between us. The place smelt of smoke and alcohol and it felt abandoned.

"Everybody misses it," he said looking around. "And it looks like it'll be closed for quite a while."

"Is that what the Germans said?"

"They don't intend to open again until they've done major renovations. Probably closer to the warmer months when the tourists return."

That meant waiting until November or December. Richmond is one of those sleepy towns that burst into life for a few months of the summer months and hibernate for the rest of the year. Quaint. Historic. Clean. The locals cling to their traditions and complain about the tourists who sweep in from the mainland, although they don't complain about the money they bring with them. These tourists arrive on weekends bringing children, dogs, quinoa, kale and bottles of Tanqueray and spend money on anything and everything.

The favourite hotel of tourists has creaking stairs and gloomy hallways and baths with clawed feet and overlooks the historic peer that juts out into the bay. I remember Daddy carrying me on his shoulders and buying ice cream cones at the kiosk near the Old Town Hall.

"When are they arriving?" I asked, raising my glass to my lips.

"Next Sunday."

"Oh. So soon? In seven days?"

I hadn't been here for twenty years, vowed never to return, and here I was, shocked that it would all be gone in just a few days. It was hard to imagine.

"Is that too soon for you?"

"Oh no. The sooner the better," I said as I spun my glass on the wooden bar.

"I thought you might hang around for a bit." His eyes held mine. "It's been so long since you've been home. And then there's your mother's request to clear Sean."

I shrugged. "This isn't my home anymore, Rory. But yes, I may stay on for a few days and see if I can come up with anything. But clear Sean? Don't expect too much after twenty years. And let's not forget, Sean confessed."

I lifted my drink again and our eyes met. The air between us became charged as I swallowed and put the glass down with an unnatural awareness.

"I was telling Margie about your mother and her bequest...the suit-case, I mean...and she dug out this for you."

Margie. His sister Margaret and the most vigilant member of his family who never spoke to our family.

He reached over to his briefcase and pulled a yellowing newspaper cutting on the counter between us. "It seems our two great uncles, Barney and Dan, were friends. Did you know that?"

I shook my head. "Nope."

"Friends and comrades. They ended up in an English prison together, for drilling IRA soldiers and for playing the Sinn Fein trick of the time, carrying on as if the British courts had no jurisdiction over them"

I smoothed the paper out on the counter, careful not to tear the brittle paper, and started to read.

Unprecedented scenes of excitement accompanied the trial of two Mucknamore men, Ibar Rooney and Dan O'Donovan, at the Wexford Assizes on Tuesday last. The two prisoners were brought out and put in the dock and immediately began to speak amongst themselves, ignoring the order for Hats Off. They were forced to remove the hats from the prisoners, leading to shouts and jeers from some among the assembled crowd and it took some time for the magistrate to bring the court to order.

The magistrate said he would bind them over in sum of £50. He asked, 'Do you intend to go to jail?' to which O'Donovan said, 'We do not recognise this court!'

There were cries of 'Good on you Dan!' and 'Up the Rebels!' and 'See you in six months, Barney!' Some members of the public even began to sing. The magistrate ordered the court to be cleared and an ugly conflict broke out as the police set to do with baton freely used.

I looked up at Rory. "What year was this?"

"Spring of 1921, just before the British Empire agreed to a truce. The Brits were scathing but plenty of the Irish too thought the whole thing a joke. Their laughter stopped when the IRA got going."

"Which I guess is where the great-uncles came in? Soldiers of the Irish Republican Army? Comrades together in jail?"

"In and out of jail. Comrades and best friends, Margie said. But they took opposite sides after the treaty with England was signed."

"I vaguely remember Nana Peg tell us that our family voted for Fine Gael and the O'Donovans for Fianna Fail. Is that why they had a falling out?"

He shook his head and shrugged. "I don't know. It still doesn't account for why they were so much at loggerheads in our generation," he went on. "Other families were Fianna Failers and we weren't expected to shun them like we did with you and yours. I've asked gramps but he's shuts up and refuses to talk about it."

"My thought is it had to be something to do with Auntie Norah."

"Possibly," he nodded. "Anyway, I thought you might want this, if you're going to dive into that suitcase your mother left you."

I nodded, thoughts on meeting up with Jack pushed to the front of my mind.

He sipped his beer in the silence.

"Do you enjoy your work?"

"Enjoy?" I put my elbow on the bar and rested my chin in my hand. "I don't know if enjoy is the right word for what I do. Fulfilling is a good word. Rewarding is another. Riveting at times. Sad as well." He had no idea the misery and pain that people inflict on each other. Although he was a lawyer, so maybe he did.

"What sort of law do you practice?" I asked.

"Nothing exciting. Corporate law with the government. Mostly land titles."

I nodded. "My job makes me feel like a seer sometimes," I said. "Someone who looks through the smoke and mirrors and come up with the culprit."

"Quite flattering, I'd have thought."

I let my hand drop to my glass and began twisting it in circles again.

"And what about you? Are you still taking pictures?" I asked.

"Not so much anymore. Pictures of the kids and Leanne but it's been more than four years since I've picked up a camera." He held up his mobile phone sitting on the bar. "Mobile phones these days do a good enough job." He smiled. "And finding the time is a problem."

He reached into his briefcase again. "I brought these along for you to see. You can add them to the other pictures in the suitcase."

He lay a large brown envelope on the bar counter between us, the flap was unsealed. He pushed it towards me.

I brought out a sheaf of black-and-white photographs, all of the same woman, doing all kinds of things. In the park, at the beach and one where she is lying naked on a tousled bed. It took me a minute to recognise her, then my hand flew up over my mouth.

"Jesus, Rory."

He was laughing. "Don't you like them?"

"Look at her! My God, just look at her."

"I know. Gorgeous, isn't she?"

So young. So unguarded. So trusting. Me, but not me.

Jack's words from last night jumped into my head and for the first time, I had an idea of what he meant.

"How can you say I haven't changed?" I muttered, staggered by her naivety, as I flicked back through the pictures, faster than I wanted because I was aware of his eyes on me and my young image. Each black-

and-white showed me in different positions: lying, sitting, on the side of the bed, sheet folded strategically across my thigh in one shot, thrown emphatically aside in another, my head back and laughing. I felt so embarrassed, I couldn't look up.

I put the photos back in the envelope quickly, feeling shaken. Once I knew and loved every inch of this man's skin, and the time we had together was between us as heavy as a shroud. But everything that had happened since was also there, crowding the goodness out.

"Sam." His voice was as gentle as a summer's breeze when he leant across the counter towards me. "Why don't you stay in Richmond for a while."

A flash of wrecking-ball anger whipped through me.

"Don't look at me like that, Sam." He stared down at his drink.

I snorted. "I don't think I'll be able to last until the German couple come."

"Why not stay at Prospect House? Or one of the B&Bs?"

"That would be worse," I muttered.

I felt annoyed at myself because I'd sent Jack to the Richmond Arms Hotel last night because it had a pub and a restaurant attached. Prospect House would have been a much better option but I hadn't been thinking clearly at the time. On the other hand, knowing Jack, he would have been uncomfortable in a boutique hotel. The Richmond Arms was more Jack.

Suddenly, I glanced at my watch. 4.15. I'd organised to meet him at 5pm and I had to shower and change yet.

I stood up and reached for his glass.

"Are you finished? I'm meeting someone at 5 o'clock."

His eyebrows rose. "Someone?"

"A friend from Surfers Paradise. He arrived after the funeral and is staying for a while to help me."

He raised his eyebrows higher and nodded slowly but didn't comment. Then he took a deep breath before plunging in.

"I want to tell you something. I lied to you yesterday. I don't love living here in Richmond. My family does, but it's killing me."

My heart shuddered. My stupid, treacherous heart.

"Sam. I'm so sorry." He leaned across the table, closing the space between us and making my heart thump. I wanted to lean back but I couldn't.

"Can't you feel it? This unfinished business between us?" he pleaded. His eyes looked like a beaten puppy's eyes.

His hands, folded across the bar counter, lifted and reached over to touch my hair.

"Stop it!" I almost yelled, pulling away.

He let his hand drop but his eyes stayed on mine.

"People fire the words off like a joke, *'my wife doesn't understand me'* but it's no joke when a marriage is awry," he explained. "I'm not saying I'm blameless in it, I know I'm not, and I know she feels every bit as bad as I do. But we haven't been good for a long time. There. That's the first time I've said it out loud to anyone. But we haven't."

He leaned back. "When your mother approached me last year about looking after her will, it meant I was going to see you again and I felt like a small light had switched on for me. I didn't think you'd come back here, so I used to imagine going to Surfers Paradise to find you, what I'd say, how you'd feel and I dreamt that seeing you would take me out of this terrible paralysis that is squeezing..."

I'd heard enough. The anger was resurfacing.

"You talk about unfinished business," I interrupted, speaking slow and low, trying to control the anger that was building. "You talk as if we mislaid something and now we can reclaim it. YOU deserted ME remember? Without so much as a good-bye. I can no more go back to where I left off than I could go back to being a toddler."

I swallowed loudly. "Please leave."

He stood quickly, scraping the chair on the rough tiles in the process.

"I know I let you down, Sam. But there were extenuating circumstances. I should have followed through with them and talk to you about them but I didn't. I was wrong. But now you're here again..."

He stopped when he saw the anger in my eyes. "I'm not saying our feeling are the same as then," he added, "or there aren't complications. But the feelings are there still. I know they are."

He gathered his briefcase and stood still for a second. "Will you stay long enough to do your mother's wish then? Find Merrell's killer?"

I straightened my back and flexed my shoulders, as if I'd run ten kilometres. He was staring at me.

"I may. I'm not sure yet."

And with one last look, he nodded, then turned and left.

I took the glasses into the kitchen along with the brown envelope and made my way upstairs. I sat on the bed and slid the pictures out of their envelope to look again at the face and body that seemed so foreign to me. As I looked my sight blurred and I squeezed my eyes shut trying to clear the mist. I found I couldn't and the tears that have lived in my chest for twenty years, forever waiting for their chance to erupt, overflowed yet again.

I let them come this time, finally becoming loud and harsh and ugly, the sort of sobs that nobody wants to hear.

Eventually they subsided. I pulled the suitcase out from under the bed, hid the envelope under the folders and photos, then made my way to the shower. Jack was waiting for me and that was all I wanted to think about right now.

6

Autumn leaves were swirling across the entrance of The Richmond Arms, collecting against the walls. It hadn't changed in all the years I'd been away: a block building with log and rock cladding designed to make it resemble a German Schloss in an imagined copse of the Black Forest. It made me wonder if the German couple who'd bought Mum's pub had seen it and let the idea grow in their heads to imitate it on a much grander scale.

A dozen cars were parked in the car park and music was faintly audible. Jack was sitting at a covered outside table exhaling puffs of frost into the cold air while buried in a black leather jacket that was more a fashion item meant for winters in Surfers Paradise than a coat for the bitter winters of Tasmania. Perched on his head was a beige woollen cap with the words RICHMOND written in bright red print inside a heart and under his jacket, I glimpsed a sky-blue Hawaiian shirt with yellow hibiscus flowers patterned on it. If that was all he had on under the jacket, leather or not, it was no wonder his cheeks were red from the cold.

He saw me coming and stood up stiff kneed and grimaced. His hands were buried in the pockets of his jacket but he took them out so he could take the cap off, leaving little tufts of hair standing straight up from his head. Behind him the sun was dipping low over the horizon, making the colours of the trees shimmer in reds and golds, like some beautifully mixed rainbow.

"It's freezing here," he grizzled as I approached him, a cloud of vapour billowing from his mouth. "I've forgotten how cold it gets in Tasmania at this time of year. Even the trees look bloody cold."

I reached over and straightened his hair, grinning. "Let's go inside the pub, old man. It'll be warm inside."

"Hey! Not so much of the old man, thanks very much." He pulled his coat together across his chest as we crunched our way towards the entrance and mumbled, "I'm barely five years older than you."

I grinned wider. "A grumpy old man at that."

He snorted but held the door open for me to enter first.

Inside, the pub was beautifully warm and goose bumps popped up on my arms. The glow from the roaring fire in the dining room gave the small seating area a deliciously cosy feel and in the soft light, half a dozen diners of various ages sat at linen-draped tables centred with flower arrangements showing not the slightest hint of droop. The upholstered stools at the bar were done in soft beiges and tans, the wooden ones stained and distressed to look old. The designer, striving for calm and serene, had achieved that with a sense of limitless cash.

Half a dozen teenagers, a couple looking underage, had taken over a corner of the lounge beneath a string of fairy lights. The girls were wearing skin tight jeans and short tops and over the back of their chairs, bulky jumpers and coats were tossed carelessly.

Ten minutes later, we were seated, each with a glass of Heineken in front of us, the sweet scent of pine filling the room. Spread out beside us were old newspapers Jack had produced.

"I thought you'd be having a good day being a tourist," I said, looking at the newspapers as I watched him wipe the beer froth from his top lip.

His eyes folded into wrinkles. "I didn't come here for a holiday," he stated. "I came to support you. And if this Sean O'Donovan has spent twenty years of his life in jail for confessing to a murder he didn't commit, he must be protecting someone else. I want to know who that someone is." He smirked. "The sooner I do that, the sooner you'll be back home in the warmth of Surfers Paradis, giving me a hard time again."

He hesitated, his head cocked to the side. "Right?"

"Of course," I replied.

The words were out fast, too fast, and the heat rose in my face.

An eyebrow rose as Jack's eyes roamed my face but he said nothing.

Framed behind him on the darkening waters of the Coal River was a tourist boat, bedecked with strings of dainty white lights. People bundled in coats were leaning on the railings, all peering into the distance. Even from this distance, behind the windows at their backs, enormous floral displays of white and yellow blooms were clearly visible. The contrived elegance cruised past the tavern moving smoothly towards the historic Richmond Bridge, while waves, glimmering like thousands of tiny diamonds from the golden light of the sunset, softly lapped the sides.

My eyes returned to Jack to find his chin resting on his hand and his gaze on me. If anyone was watching us, it would look like we were on a first date and still stuck on the awkward getting-to-know-you stage.

He moved his head sideways to block my view of the boat, his eyes questioning me. For the first time, I noticed shadows beneath his eyes and creases in the contours of his face. The lines around his eyes had deepened as well since the last time I'd seen him and it made me wonder what was causing the disturbance in his life. As friendly as we were, I knew there were still things he held back from me.

"Of course," I repeated, more firmly this time. "But what about your own work?"

"*Surfers Paradise Investigations* is officially on hold for a while," he said, picking up his glass and taking another sip. "Maybe permanently," he added.

I sat back surprised. "What? But you love that business, Jack."

He gave me a *you've got to be kidding* look.

"That soulless box of an office? A room only big enough for me, a desk, a filing cabinet with a cupboard they call a kitchen overlooking a busy main road? Are you joking?" he snorted and shook his head. "No. I'm temporarily retired."

"Besides," he added, his eyebrows wiggling, "who needs to maintain an office and employ a secretary who secretly carries a torch for me?"

Jack humour.

"Then why aren't you off playing golf?"

"I have actually hired a hitman to knock me off if I ever leave the house in tartan trousers."

"Not a golfer then?"

"No."

"Well what about your dog and cat?" I asked, as an afterthought.

"The animals are with Frank and being well looked after. The three of them get along like a house on fire."

I pulled a face at the name 'Frank'. He had a reputation as being untrustworthy sleazy weasel and thankfully I have very little to do with him. But he and Jack seemed to have a vague working relationship going, so who was I to argue? We only solved the last case with help from Frank.

"Why is your business on hold?" I asked, sipping my own beer.

"After that last case, I've discovered I'm not very popular with a lot of unsavoury characters. Go figure," he grinned sheepishly. "Which is why I'm thinking of moving on to another sort of business. Still getting rid of trash like child molesters but without the hindrance of the police force. I've finally accepted our justice system isn't black and white and I'm striking out on my own."

He smiled disarmingly and I was vaguely alarmed at how serious he seemed.

"With Frank?" I tried to keep the scepticism from my voice and failed. "You can't find someone better?"

He waved away my comment and grinned. "Frank's alright when you get to know him. His help's been invaluable, especially when I left the force a couple of years ago. Everyone said I needed time to heal but in fact," he looked down at his drink, "I was scared. Frank helped." His eyes raised to mine. "If it happened again, I would be sitting with Nurse Ratchet instead of Frank."

"You're not talking vigilantism, I hope?" I asked, sounding alarmed.

"I'm not talking anything right now."

"Are you being deliberately evasive?" I asked, my voice full of scepticism. "Yet again."

"It's a character flaw," he admitted with a grin. "It may even be genetic." He shrugged. "On this occasion, though, I'm being straight with you.

I'm as much in the dark as anyone with my future. All I'm saying is I've finalised the contract on the office space and all the old paperwork is in a spare room at home. I own my home and I have money in the bank so this," he waved his hands over the papers, "came up at the right time. When I turned up yesterday, you looked as pale as a ghost and your eyes looked like they were swollen."

I absently twisted my beer glass on the table, watching the circles join.

"I didn't think I would react the way I did. It's been so long since I've seen my family, I thought I'd be immune to ... everything."

The words came out sounding raw, exposing the emotion I was trying to hold in.

"And then Rory gave me that letter Mum wrote to me and it opened the floodgates. I feel guilty that I've been so callous towards them for so long. It was really just hormones and youth that made it all seem worse. I was just an angry kid hitting out at the world. But instead of facing the anger head on, I ran away."

I could feel the betraying tingle behind my eyes as tears welled up and I quickly rubbed them before they fell.

Jack was watching me, his right eyebrow cocked. I focused on his concerned face and said, "Anyway, I don't want to talk about it. Not right now anyway. Can we please proceed?"

He cleared his throat. His normally relaxed expression had changed and was replaced with the faintest tightening around his eyes and mouth. He simply nodded but I could see a tighter set to his jaw.

"Okay." He pushed his beer glass to one side and brought the papers before us on the table. "Back to why we're here."

Jack has always been a workaholic. When we worked together, he grizzled and grumbled but his solve rate was near perfect. Which is why Inspector Grayson tolerated the ignored phone messages and memos tossed in the bin.

"I spent the day doing research." He glanced up at me without raising his head from the paperwork on the table. "The case is public information now and with it are dozens of photos of Sean O'Donovan online. I read up on what happened and the investigation that followed and as you said, it was like the Keystone Cops did the work."

He took a sip of his beer, instinctively glancing over his shoulder to check if anyone was nearby listening, giving me time to reflect on this man who had befriended me a few years ago.

Jack was known to most in the police force as a blue flamer, or someone who wanted to change the world before it self-destructed. He was carrying baggage from a horrific case at Mount Tamborine so he probably thought he had something to prove, not just to the world but to himself. His past left him too troubled to make many friends and the outcome left him a solitary man. As a result, he took too many chances leaving everyone sure in the fact that he would either burn out or get himself killed.

Eyes the colour of a hot summer's day silently regarded me. When he spoke, his voice was soft. "Despite the standard of the police work done, Sam, Sean O'Donovan confessed to the crime. As far as anyone is concerned, the case is closed. Solved."

He rotated his shoulders as if his neck muscles were tight.

"I get it. I really do. Your mother wanted you to look into it because she thinks he's innocent. Her dying wish if you like. But what gave her that idea? Why put this on you after all these years?"

I nodded slowly. "I know Jack. It's a guilt thing, I think. But what if she's right?"

"What evidence did she have to make her think he was innocent? Rory O'Donovan's insistence that he was? Is that enough for you?"

"Rory was his alibi, Jack. They were together when the crime was committed."

I shrugged and shook my head.

"I'm not defending him. I'm just trying to do what Mum asked me to do. At least for a few days. After that, I'll let it go and head back to Surfers. I can't stay much longer than that anyway. I have a job waiting for me."

"Okay," he nodded again. "One thing I did find," he continued, "was that the lead investigator was a man by the name of James Russell. He was fifty plus back then so my guess is he's retired now. He'll be over seventy. Another search told me he still lives here in Richmond." He shook his head and pulled a face full of mock surprise. "Why would anyone do that?"

I knew exactly what he meant. For much of the past two centuries, Richmond was the kind of town where people resided because they didn't have the resources to go anywhere else. Even if some citizens looked further afield, people like Rory, the majority elected to look no further than the boundaries of the state and eventually found themselves back where they started because they discovered little more than another town or city where strangers ignored them. At least in Richmond they were acknowledged and welcomed.

"Anyway, he's first on our list of people to talk to," Jack muttered as he took another sip of his beer. "Hopefully tomorrow."

I nodded. "I know James Russell. Or I did. He was this nice guy who was always scribbling in a notepad taking notes. Do you think they've been stored somewhere?"

"I've already checked," he said, shaking his head again. "I spent most of the morning in the police station." He smirked. "I'll call it that but basically it's just a six-room shed with a desk in the front room that serves as a reception area. They have the files of everything going back thirty years or so but they were not about to hand anything over to me. Not without talking to Captain Marshall in Hobart first. The only information I've discovered were from some old news articles I googled." He waved a hand over the papers spread out on the table between our drinks. "Reception here at The Richmond Arms printed them for me but there's an awful lot missing."

"I'm not surprised," I muttered. "There wasn't much of an investigation to start with. And no one seemed to know what they were doing. And then when Sean turned himself in, everyone seemed to breathe a sigh of relief because they had no idea of what to do."

"The murder was a sensation at the time," I continued. "People saw it as a tragedy that should only happen to people living in the big cities and not one of their own. The case topped the headlines in Tasmania for weeks, probably the country, and according to the papers there were no hard leads. But if Sean hadn't killed her, someone else crept into Merrell's bedroom and killed her while my family slept. And behind them, they left a trail of blood and glass."

My emotions bubbled up again and I gulped some beer before continuing, taking the time to settle myself.

"And then out of nowhere, two weeks later, Sean pleaded guilty of the crime despite Rory supplying him with an alibi at the exact time when Merrell was being murdered. At the time it didn't register with me. I was in hell myself, suffering from the loss of both Merrell and Rory at the same time. I was like everyone else and simply accepted Sean's statement without looking any closer."

I'd been talking quietly, almost as if I was talking to myself. Going over and over the painful events in my head.

"Small town stuff, Sam." Jack's voice brought me back from my reverie. "You hear this all the time. Our best bet is to find James Russell and see if we can jog his memory about the case. It would have been a big case back then so I'm guessing he'll remember most of what happened. If he's still got all his senses." He grimaced as he scratched his chin. "Fingers crossed."

I was silent for a few seconds, teeth biting my bottom lip.

"What?" he asked, his eyes staying with mine.

"Mum also gave me some documents and old photos in a battered suitcase I used when I was at school. Along with a diary." The words emerged quietly. Almost painfully.

"A diary?" He cocked his head to the side. "How old?"

"I don't know. I haven't even started reading it yet. But it looks ancient."

"Secrets from the grave." He grinned. "You may find a few skeletons rattling around in there."

"If it gives me some idea of why the Neils and the O'Donovans were feuding, I'll be ecstatic. This feud between our families has been going on for as long as I can remember. I don't even know if Kathleen knows what it's all about."

His face stretched into a grin. "Well if there's any secrets lurking around, I'm just the one to flush them out."

"I wonder if Richmond is ready for your charm and charisma," I smiled.

"And don't forget about my notable empathy and all-round sensitivity."

"Okay old man. First thing in the morning, we'll just see what you can extract from them with your sensitivity."

I glanced up at the menu board. "Can we head over to the bar and order now? I'm starving."

Jack clamped both hands on the edge of the table, pressing hard, and rose to his feet.

"I thought you'd never ask."

7

Sleep was impossible with so much running around in my head. I stared at the ceiling motionless, willing my brain to stop thinking. I was aware of the warm comfort of the bed and the weight of my head against the raised pillows and the small of the air – different from my home in Surfers – faintly pungent and more autumnal than wintry, a smell of earth borne on an erratic wind. Gazing fixedly at the window, I could see that the room was darker than the night outside and that high constellations were patterning the faintly luminous sky. I had the strongest feeling like I was travelling back in time.

Suddenly, I was shivering and the sheets felt cold. I held them and duvet over my head but it still wasn't enough. In the end, I gave up and I climbed out of bed. I shrugged on my chenille dressing gown and pulled the suitcase out from under the bed.

I dug around for a few seconds, avoiding the envelope Rory had given me, and pulled out what looked like a diary.

I flicked through the pages all written in a beautiful flowing script, although faded by age, until I came to an entry.

The one small lamp left most of the room dusted with shadows so I turned to point it more directly onto the words and started to read.

. . .

Diary 4th July 1922

Independence Day in America and now in Wexford too.

It's very late on Wednesday and I'm sitting in the ladies' room of the Portsmouth Arms, locked in one of the water closets with a candle. It's the only place around here that it's possible to be alone. I can't think straight after meeting Dan. He's thrown me in a heap and I need to set my thoughts down to steady them.

But before I get to Dan O'Donovan, let me just write the words: the Republic lives! The fight is over and the so-called National Army has been defeated! We won. The Republic was...is won. Watching the soldiers in their fancy-free Stater uniforms making their surrender was so gratifying, especially hearing them swear they would never again be disloyal to the Republic.

Our side doesn't have anywhere yet to house prisoners, so all we could do was march them out of town. Within a few hours they were back, green uniforms turning up everywhere on the streets and pubs.

And that's how we came to meet Dan. Norah and I were walking up through the town, talking about going back home to face our ordinary lives. I can't imagine how I'm going to do that. And if it's bad for me, what about poor Norah? How she'll face her family, she doesn't know. She is nothing short of petrified. The thoughts of a Republican victory will sicken her father and the thoughts that she was part of it, fighting against her own brother.

And now that everybody knows about herself and Barney, she's terrified they'll get wind of that too. And there are still things she finds hard to talk about, especially her family. And I need to respect her privacy. I admire her loyalty.

We sat for ages until lack of sleep caught up with us. As we were turning into Slaney Street, at the top of the hill, we saw two men arm-in-arm, one tall and dark wearing the green uniform of the Free State Army, the other shorter and fair, in the trench coat of the IRA Volunteer. We recognised our two brothers, their free hands holding a bottle of beer, leaning into each other and singing.

Dan looked down and saw us. 'There's the girls' he called and foolish, foolish, I felt my heart take an excited tumble as he began to drag Barney down the hill towards us, laughing and nearly knocking him over he was so fast.

'Look at the state of you,' I said to my brother, ignoring Dan O'Donovan.

'Ah Peg,' Barney said, 'don't be like that.'

'Barney, you're drunk!'

'A few drinks, is all. Just a few with my friend here...'

'Friend now is it?'

You'd think he'd never heard what Dan O'Donovan has been saying about us.

'It's a grand thing that happened today.' He turned to Norah. 'Don't you think so, Norah?'

Norah didn't answer because my brother was barely able to stay standing but he still had his feelings all over his soft, silly face.

While Norah blushed, Dan leaned across and whispered in my ear, 'It's grand to see you, Peg Rooney. You're looking fine tonight. Let's all go for a walk.'

My traitorous heart twisted inside me.

'No,' I cried so the three of them looked at me in surprise.

The road was full of shadows and trees along the way and although part of me was tempted, another part - thank God - made me resist.

'No,' I repeated, 'You're drunk.' And when I looked at Norah, I was pleased to see her nodding her head in agreement. I thought she might have been sorely tempted to step out with Barney but I should have had more faith in her decency. Only an eejit like myself would even consider it.

And before he – either of them – could answer, I turned back up the street. Norah followed but looked back with a smile at Barney and I heard my brother let out a laugh.

What a sad state we were in. Me with my heart pulling me to an O'Donovan and hers pulling her towards my brother Barney.

Diary 22nd July 1922

Norah came down to our place for a few minutes this evening, her first time out of the house since we came back from Wexford, a full four weeks ago now. Her mother sent her to the priest's house for a Mass card and she was under orders to go straight there and back. She said she's locked in her bedroom, let out only to help with cooking and washing. She sneaked up to our place, coming up the back way and tapping on the back door.

You could see she was frightening herself with disobedience, the way her eyes were darting about the place, ready to be off. But she looked better than the last time I saw her. That time she was sick with dread. The sight of her disappearing up the road to her house, head bowed to the wind, back bent over the handlebars, face pale as candle wax, it nearly made me ill to see her so.

Her disappointment tonight when she heard that Barney was still away with the boys was deep. She had been counting on him to give her comfort and I thought how nice it must be to have your own boy to lean on like that. Whatever their troubles at least they have each other.

'Has it been terrible?' I whispered to her. She said she hoped the worst was over and I'm afraid to think what that might mean. I asked her if she had regrets of what we had done for the Republic and she said 'No,' so vehemently I almost jumped. 'I'd do it again tomorrow,' she added.

Her job is gone, for definite. Everyone in Wexford knows what she has done and since the Staters have reclaimed the towns, Republicans are next to dirt in the eyes of the business community. So she is confined to the house with nothing to do but assist her mother. But she's too bright for that.

We said nothing about her brother Dan since he is firmly back in the enemy camp now and even Barney is sickened by his duplicity.

We have worked out a way to keep in touch. Going to the church to pray is the one thing her family won't disallow so we will leave notes for each other under a loose stone around the back of the chapel. I said I'd get a letter to Barney if she wants to write and leave it there. This should, I hope, prove some comfort.

Diary 3rd August

Wexford was honoured today with a visit from a military motor and who should be driving it but Mr Dan O'Donovan himself. When people saw it, they trooped out to the road to have a gawk and saw who it was who had managed to get himself a promotion. That afternoon, we heard the sound of an engine roaring down the road and as it passed our place, it let out a loud honk from the horn. The nerve of him! We ran to the window and I nearly fainted with surprise when I saw Norah sitting in the passenger seat beside him. She looked tiny in the big front seat, shrinking down into the leather with her hand on her hat to keep it from blowing off. The look on her face spoke her humiliation.

Off down the road he drove, then he must have turned at the cross because in less than a minute, he was back, parading past our place again, blaring on his motor-horn once more, rubbing our noses in it, as well as Norah's. Up and down he went, fifty times if he did it once, until he made sure everybody in the village saw and heard him.

Diary 8th August

In the paper today is a half-page picture of six State Military men, including 'Lieutenant' O'Donovan, the six of them sitting up on the same motor Dan drove out here the other day. He is leaning back and staring straight into the camera, his peaked military cap at an angle, but the face beneath as blank as the opening into a cave.

They have all the same look on them, the six army men in this photograph, with their strutting heads, their polished guns and self-appointed titles. They think they awe us with it all but it's the opposite. Their finery is English-bought and for all their swaggering, you can see the knowledge of that in their eyes. They know they have to live with it. Give me a battered trench coat any day with a loyal heart that beats beneath it.

My eyes were scratchy now from reading the faded print and even though I was intrigued, I knew that if I didn't get some sleep, my mind would not be fresh tomorrow. And I needed that more than anything at the moment. The diary could wait. Jack couldn't.

I glanced at the clock and was surprised I'd been reading for close on an hour. I closed the diary, marking the spot first with a scrap of paper before placing it back in the suitcase and climbing back into bed.

Except for a few sounds, the small house stood in absolute silence, as though the world outside its walls had ceased to exist, nothing now beyond its doors. The quiet in the room was so deep it could have been drifting outside of time.

Lying on my back, I stared at the light-fitting that had captured moths, now lying dead in the frosted glass bowl in the white painted tongue-in-groove ceiling. The regularity of the joinery, straight as lasered lines, seemed to mock me.

8

MONDAY, 22ND MAY

Monday dawned bright and cool with leaves shivering their way to the ground. I donned boots and a warm coat over my long-sleeved T-shirt and jeans and stood on the porch as I surveyed the trees, hugging myself to keep warm. No cars passed on the road and all seemed peaceful. I took comfort from the quiet. From a gum tree, a black cockatoo soared into the sky and was lost in the morning mist.

"I'm okay," I said aloud. "Better than okay."

In the future, I would speak less to the shadows when my healing was complete.

Breakfast consisted of black coffee and what was left over in the fridge from the wake. Scraps of cheese, some pickled onions and slices of celery and carrot. Grimacing, I made a mental note to pick up some groceries in the afternoon.

Jack pulled up right on time, just as I was pulling on my coat. In his hands were two takeaway coffee cups.

I held my hand out to one of the cups, fingers wiggling. "Oh my God. Give it to me. You must be psychic."

"I didn't think there'd be much in there to eat. I had a 'continental breakfast'," speaky fingers, "at the pub. I'll bet anything you weren't as lucky."

I shook my head. "Black coffee, no milk, no sugar. And rabbit food." I shuddered.

"Well, hopefully this will get you through until lunch. Let's see if this James Russell has a land line then we'll see if he's up to a visit from us this morning."

While I stirred sugar into the coffees, Jack pulled out his iPhone and googled to see if there was a listing for a land line. Surprisingly, there was. It was rare these days because most people had plans that only included mobiles. We tried calling but there was no answer so we decided to take the short drive and hope he was at home.

By the time we headed off, the sun was blazing and the last vestiges of the chillness had evaporated.

The little bungalow James lived in was the same house he'd lived in for the past fifty years, surrounded by huge trees and built in the 70s not long after he would have made detective. In the driveway was an early model forest green Commodore, splattered with mud on the fenders and lower doors. It was the sort of car they're going to outlaw when emission regulations come into force because entire Pacific Atolls disappear every time you fill the tank.

We crunched our way up the gravel driveway and rang the doorbell, happy to wait in the sunshine until he answered the door. The air smelled faintly of pine, wet rocks, smoke, and autumn leaves. Gnats bomb-dived my face, surprisingly, given the coolness of the morning.

The familiar-looking man in the plaid flannel shirt and baggy track pants who answered the door had obviously been asleep. His face was red on one side and his white hair, some of it starting to yellow, was sticking straight up in patches where it should have been pushed over his bare scalp. He had become one of those elderly men with a permanent wary expression, seemingly afraid that at any second somebody might take advantage of him.

He opened the door but not the screen and looked quizzically at Jack, then me, and said, "Can I help you?" His scraggy eyebrows raised in question.

"Mr Russell? I'm Samantha Neil. And this is a friend of mine. Jack Curtis."

Jack nodded but said nothing.

"May we have a word with you please?" I asked. "We need to talk to you about something."

"Really?" He stayed where he was and looked harder at me. "Samantha Neil you say?" He craned his neck forward as he squinted. Then a smile spread across his face.

"Well, I'll be damned." The smile spread further across his face. "It's been, what, fifteen years?"

I smiled back. "Twenty actually."

"No! Where do the years go?"

He opened the screen door and stood back, beckoning us both in.

"Come in. Come in," he said, self-consciously smoothing down his hair.

He offered us a seat on a three-seater sofa and asked, "Can I get either of you a coffee or tea?"

We both shook our heads and thanked him as he settled himself into an adjoining single recliner. A well-used hand-crocheted rug in brightly coloured squares was lying half on the chair and half on the ground.

"To what do I owe the pleasure?" he asked, not showing the least annoyance at being disturbed from his nap.

Age had turned his face lumpy and his scalp almost bare. Somewhere in the back of my mind I remembered James as a widower and looking around I thought I was right. The house probably looked just the same as when his wife had passed away, when I was still a teenager. The living room was crowded with relics of a lifetime. The walls were thick with photographs, both family shots and scenery, as well as children's drawings. Every tabletop was littered with ornaments. Limoges figurines, little lacquered boxes, glass paperweights, books and more framed photos. They could film an *Antiques Roadshow* here for a month. Soft music drifted through from another room.

"It's real nice to see you again Samantha. You've grown into a beautiful young lady."

I glanced over at Jack and saw his mouth twitch.

"Can't see how I could be of any use to you both though. Nobody needs a 78-year-old guy. People look right through you at my age."

The melancholy frankness of the observation silenced me for a second but James didn't seem to be seeking sympathy.

"I'm sorry to barge in like this Mr Russell but we need to ask you some questions regarding Merrell's murder." I hesitated. "Do you remember Merrell? Her murder was twenty years ago."

"My oh my." The softness in his voice reflected the sadness in his eyes. "Of course I remember that. I don't remember what I had for breakfast yesterday but I can remember things from forty years ago like they were yesterday." He looked at me sorrowfully. "And especially Merrell's case."

He shook his head. "I'd spent twenty-five years on the force and people were telling me that it's best to let the sadness go. But I never could. It was a terrible business."

Jack leaned forward. "I read some old news articles that said you were in charge of Merrell's investigation."

James snorted. "There wasn't anyone in charge of that investigation. I wasn't even on the job any more. I retired at fifty-five a year before the murder and went into my brother-in-law's security business. It was Captain Davis who asked me to come in and help out. And seeing that it was Merrell who was murdered, I was happy to lend a hand."

"So, you weren't on the case from the beginning?" Jack asked.

"No. I came two days in." As he shook his head, his jowls wobbled. "Everyone was chasing their tails. Nobody was in control of the crime scene, not even the Captain. They were all running around making a mess of everything like a bunch of idiots."

He leaned back and crossed his arms over his ample stomach.

"I was never content we'd gotten answers to every question. We had three different teams of evidence techs go through there, each with different samples. Some tests got performed three times, some didn't get done at all. Everybody thought somebody else was running leads. It was a mess. So Captain Davis called me as a special to lead the investigation and I said, okay. Not that anybody was actually listening to me anyway."

"Can you tell us what you remember, Mr Russell?" Jack asked as he pulled out a notebook from his jacket pocket.

James seemed to settle himself deeper in the chair, looking up towards the ceiling, deep in thought.

"The crime scene," he began, "didn't point in any particular direction. The first police to arrive found the French doors to the balcony open. It had rained for the past few days but harder that evening, right at the end of the party, Merrell's birthday party I seem to remember, and there was a mess of deep shoe prints in the flower bed under her window, which made it look like several people had walked around the area. There was no use looking for tyre tracks because there had been fifty or so cars there earlier in the day for the party. One of the panes of the door was broken out and the glass was scattered on the tiny balcony outside. There was quite a bit of blood on the jagged glass and on the inside of the door and carpet. The blood trail ran into Merrell's bedroom where, by simple count, there appeared to be a towel missing, suggesting that the killer had used it to bind a wound."

I glanced over at Jack jotting down notes in his notepad as James continued.

"I'm sorry to say this," James said, ignoring Jack and looking at me, "but your mother trampled on any evidence there would have been by running around and up and down the stairs, wringing her hands, touching everything and screaming."

I nodded but said nothing. I remembered hearing the screaming but I was told to stay in my room.

James was gazing out the window, his eyes focused on nothing in particular and I didn't want to break his trail of thought.

"Blood grouping classified the blood in the room as O and all the Neils were tested and were found to be B. That left no doubt in anyone's mind that the intruder was O. But that's the most common group of all and half of Richmond is O, so we couldn't tie it down at all. The techs lifted a couple of good prints from the door handle that had remained, despite the rain that pelted the side of the house that night. No way to date prints, but the best guess was that they belonged to the murderer. And of course, Sean's fingerprints were taken, and they matched some of the partials at the crime scene. But you know as well as I do that latents at a crime scene don't come in ten-finger sets. You get partials, lots of them, smears from a couple of fingers, whatever, and that's about all you can work with." He hesitated. "One thing you should know is the Tim Logan issue we had at the time."

"Tim Logan?" Jack asked.

James sighed. "Tim Logan was the head of the fingerprint lab here at the time. I don't like gossiping about a man, especially when he's not around anymore to defend himself. But Logan was barely sober in those days. Most of the time when he showed up for work, he didn't know one end of the microscope from another. And damn, when I started comparing his report and the lifts from the scene, they didn't all match. Close. Very close. But there were several minute differences in some prints."

"So Logan made a mistake?" Jack asked.

James hesitated before replying. "Possibly."

"Are you saying Sean could have been innocent after all?"

"I'm telling you what I'm telling you. And when Sean confessed to the murder, there didn't seem any reason to go back over the prints again."

"Didn't they print him again when he came in to surrender?" Jack asked.

"No, they didn't, because they already had the other ten-card from Logan and at that stage, I was the only one who had noticed any discrepancies."

Jack glanced at me quickly and I noticed an eyebrow twitch upwards. It was a gesture I remembered from when we worked together that meant, *'Remind me later about this'*.

"Can you describe the scene, Mr Russell?" Jack asked.

James turned to Jack with a small smile. "Please. Just call me Jim."

Jack nodded his thanks and waited.

"She was on the bed," James continued, "which was still made, and she was in her robe and undies. No vaginal trauma, no tearing," he looked over at me, "sorry Sam, but the rape kit was positive for semen. Then again, that could have been from any time in the past forty-eight hours. But someone smacked her first, damn hard too, then grabbed her face. You could see the bruising in both cheeks. The hit on the left side of her face made finger stripes, meaning we were looking for someone who was right-handed. Again, most of Richmond is right-handed."

He thought for a second, chewing the inside of his cheek. "Let me see if I can remember." His forehead creased as he thought, then cleared as a memory surfaced.

"That's right. The police pathologist thought the intruder whacked her on the face, then sort of covered her mouth with his left hand and rattled her skull against her headboard. She died of an epidural haematoma. Lividity and the bleeding from the scalp wound showed she was alive for several minutes after she was beaten but the pathologists can't say whether or not she lost consciousness. Probably though, since she didn't call for help."

James was reciting this like a prayer. Merrell's murder was twenty years ago but for most people I knew in law enforcement, the details of a big case were burned into their brains. And especially a murder is a small town like Richmond.

"And no one heard the noise of her head being banged against the bedhead?" Jack asked, his face showing his surprise. From working with Jack, I knew he had a head full of questions so I let him go interrupted.

James shook his head. "The storm was in full blast by then with loads of lightning and thunder." He looked over at me. "Your mother and Kathleen were downstairs doing some last-minute cleaning up that would have involved some noise but your mother came upstairs to check up on you kids before going to bed herself. She just happened to go into Merrell's room first."

I'd gone to bed before the end of the party. Rory wasn't there so I had no reason either. The party was beginning to slow down by then and most guests were making their exits. But I remembered hearing the storm and wondering where Rory and Sean had gone. After the excitement of the day, I fell asleep almost as soon as my head hit the pillow.

"Do you remember the time of death, Jim?"

"Well, you know, it was an Irish party. They were eating all afternoon, so it was hard to tell for sure from the stomach contents, but the pathologist said around 12.30, give or take. Right around midnight, according to the phone records, she gave Sean a call that lasted for about 10 seconds and soon after that she was dead."

"Is that when Sean came into the investigation?"

He nodded his head. "The police had already spoken to Sean as part of the initial canvas but he claimed to know nothing. But when the phone records came in from Merrell's phone, and her only leaving a short message on his voicemail, they brought him back in."

He hesitated before continuing. "To tell the truth, Sean was the last person I'd have thought of. He and my daughter were in the same class in high school and I knew him from church."

At the thought of church, I felt my face redden. It brought back memories of watching Rory in the sacristy and what had happened the day before in the pub.

"But you know," James continued, shaking his head sadly, "it's the ones you think you know that fool you."

"About a week later, we had this big meeting just to see what we'd missed, which was quite a bit, let me tell you. By then, three of Merrell's girlfriends had said she'd made up her mind to drop Sean and that she was sick of all the trouble there was between the two families. I got a subpoena for Sean's prints and sure enough, the prints matched with the doorknob and a lot of other partial lifts around the room. So now I was thinking, maybe the call at 12 pm was to whistle his butt over there so she could tell him in person."

James closed his eyes for a second before continuing.

"Anyway, the prosecutor from Hobart wanted to question Sean but the O'Donovans had already hired a lawyer who wouldn't let him talk. There was a lot of cat-and-mousing for more than a week with the lawyer saying, '*Those fingerprints mean nothing. Sean was climbing the drainpipe every second night to be with Merrell. Besides, a lot of them were only partials.*' And the girlfriends who said Merrell was planning on getting rid of Sean, well, they gave that part up too."

"Sean was fooling around with Merrell right down the hall from her mother?" Jack asked.

James pointed a finger at Jack. "I asked that same question. She used to put the television on, Sean's lawyer told us, to hide any noise." He snorted softly. "We were just about to get a search warrant for his clothes and shoes and to see if he had any cuts anywhere on his body when he walked into the police station, without his lawyer mind you, and admitted to everyone he'd done it."

Jack nodded, looking down at his notes before speaking again.

"You said there were questions that weren't answered. I have a couple as well. Can you tell us what your unanswered questions were first please?"

"Well for one, the broken windowpane. The glass was all *outside* on the little balcony, outside the door. Meaning the window was broken from the inside."

"That was my first thought," Jack smiled wryly. "But maybe he arrived hoping for romance, not knowing what was on her mind. Maybe that's when she says, 'I'm done with this' and he loses it and smacks her. When she passes out he panics and flees, not knowing how bad she actually is. But if you're already inside, why not just open the latch and leave?"

James chuckled and pointed his thick finger again at Jack with admiration. The knuckle was crooked and swollen with arthritis. "But breaking glass, well, that makes a noise. If you want to escape, why raise that kind of ruckus?"

"So you didn't like him for the crime?"

"No, I'm not saying that. I'm saying I had a few more questions. But we had his fingerprints in her bedroom and on the door and his shoes matched the shoe prints left in the mud outside her window. His blood was type O as well and there's motive because she was going to drop him and leave Richmond to live in Melbourne," James looked at me, "or so your mother said."

He held up three fingers. "Motive. Opportunity. Evidence. The trifecta."

He turned back to Jack and leant forward.

"And he gave us this weak alibi when first questioned that he was fishing and drinking with his brother Rory until after midnight. But nobody saw them and he couldn't say who sold him the six pack of beer they were supposed to be drinking."

"And Rory backed him up?" I asked.

James nodded his head and sat back. "Very adamantly, as a matter of fact."

Rory had already told me they were together but I didn't want to interrupt the flow of the questions. Still the question was a valid one. Why had Rory given him an alibi?

James scratched his head absently. "You know, it was all a part of the initial investigation, but I remember the report couldn't have been more than a page long. I probably still have it."

"Really? Here?" Jack's mouth gaped.

"Yep. In the back room. I didn't have anybody working with me and I was in a different office every day or two so I figured I'd rather keep all the reports here at home where I could get to them whenever I wanted instead of heading down to the station." He looked from Jack to me, both of us staring at him in shock. "I'll show you if you like."

He used a chair arm to hoist himself to his feet and wobbled a bit with the first step. He was somewhat stooped now behind the shoulders but he remained a big man, well over six feet. When he was young, he must have received a lot of attention on the street.

He motioned for us to follow and then opened a door two down from the kitchen. He turned and looked over his shoulder at us. "I haven't been in here for years."

The room was even more crowded than the rest of the house with all manner of things crammed in.

I laughed. "Did you ever hear of a rummage sale, James?"

"My daughters are even worse than me. Don't want to part with anything their mother owned. Let them figure it out when I'm gone," he laughed. He turned sideways to get past an old wardrobe and reached a metal filing cabinet with rust peeling off the hinges.

Despite not being in the room for quite some time, like most hoarders he seemed to know exactly where everything would be. He pulled out the bottom drawer and crouched over it for a few seconds before lifting out a file and making his way to an old cane chair in the corner.

As he turned the pages, licking the tip of his index finger from time to time, he ignored the chair that creaked threateningly below his large frame.

"Here we go," he finally said.

He skimmed quickly through the report for a second then handed it to me.

It was just as he recalled. A short interview, two days after Merrell's death. Rory stated that Sean was with him all night after the party, fishing and drinking before heading home.

It had to have been a lie. Sean couldn't have been with him because Sean had admitted killing Merrell at the exact time Rory said they were fishing.

"This is gold," I whispered, looking up at Jack who was holding his hand out for the report. I handed it to him and watched him skim through it.

"It is?" James asked.

"Absolutely."

Jack was still reading but lifted his head and said, "This report points to two options."

Somewhere inside, a snake uncurled in my stomach. I had a feeling I knew where Jack was going.

"Rory was lying about Sean's alibi, which opens up the question: Why? Did he do it to save his brother from prison or was Rory involved somehow as well?"

My eyes popped open and I was about to ask a question of my own when Jack held his hand up to stop me.

"I'm just throwing out scenarios, Sam. Bottom line is he covered up for his brother. So maybe there's more to it than everyone thought."

I was shaking my head. *No way. Why would Rory be involved?*

"Don't like thinking I missed the boat like that," James murmured.

"And then there's this. We have evidence here that a practicing lawyer lied his ass off to the cops twenty years ago to keep his brother out of jail. He won't want this bombshell to come out."

James was nodding his head. "Those two boys were joined at the hip in those days. You never saw one without the other. They even looked alike. Same build, same colouring and probably the same shoe size. Remember the footprints in the mud outside her balcony?"

I was incredulous. "You both seem to forget that Rory didn't have a motive. It was Sean with the motive."

Jack stared at me for a second. "So the bottom line is he flat out lied."

I couldn't argue with that but I wanted to see what other evidence James had. Even as the thought came to my mind, Jack was picking through the file and had lifted out a sheaf of photographs.

Jack glanced over at me. "You might like to pass up on these, Sam."

I knew Jack was protecting me from the grisly crime scene photos of Merrell but my face still reddened, perceiving a slight when none was intended.

"Pass them over when you've seen them, Jack," I said firmly. "It's not my first investigation and I've seen crime scene photos before."

"This is different, and you know it." His voice had softened and for a second, I almost did a rethink. This was Merrell, not some stranger who'd been murdered and I'd never developed a taste for grisly photos. It wasn't the blood that bothered me. When I was young and playing hockey, I'd seen more than my share of scalp wounds and teeth flying like popcorn kernels as a result of a misdirected stick. It was the fact that it always seemed undignified and voyeuristic to be looking at someone who'd come to a tragic end and you were looking at her as an exhibit, a collection of visible traumas with no sense of the life that had animated her.

Jack on the other hand seemed to confront the photos with sad determination. There was nothing about it he liked but it was part of the importance of the job.

He nodded before looking down at the first photo. His eyes moved sadly over the photo before passing it on to me.

Merrell's face stared back at me and I involuntarily inhaled sharply before I could stop. Once so beautiful, now broken and bruised. The shots of Merrell's face and neck were so revealing, I had to bite my lips to stop them from trembling. Blood had coagulated in a thick clump at her crown and rusted the mass of black hair for several inches below. The scalp wound at the back of her head, portrayed in a close-up, was a smile about an inch across, the laceration bloated by the walnut-size haematoma beneath it. It looked like Sean had placed one hand over her mouth, gripping damn tight, as he rattled her head back and forth against the headboard. On the right side of her jaw, just at the point where it met her skull, there was a faint oblong bruise. Sean had given her a solid whack across the left side of her face. Rich with blood, Merrell's rosy cheeks had bruised easily and the strafing of an open hand was clear, with three streaks left by the fingers. The lowest of them disappeared into a whorl of colour and in a close-up, you could see a tiny break in the skin from which a trickle of blood had browned.

I swallowed noisily and cleared my throat before talking but even so, my voice sounded shaky even to my own ears.

"The break in the skin on her cheek," I began. "Was that from a ring?"

"That's what we thought," James said, sounding a little preoccupied. He reached over to take the photo from my hand. "You know, seeing these, I recall I got into a little something with the police pathologist. He was not accustomed to homicides and a little prickly about it. Looking at all of this, I wanted to say that slap on Merrell's cheek came several minutes before she got the wounds on the back of her head. Look here. See the difference in the colour of the bruises. Bruising doesn't continue long after death." He reached over for another photo Jack was holding.

"Look at this, too." He pointed to the photo taken of Merrell's left hand. She had long, elegant fingers but that wasn't what had James' attention. There was a rusty smear on the left knuckle.

"The tech put a heamastick on that. It was her blood. And there were traces on the left side of her face. My thought was that Merrell wiped it off her cheek when that little cut started bleeding. But that's the only blood on her hands. She never reached back to touch her scalp wound. Must have passed out before she knew she was bleeding."

"What was the issue with the pathologist?" I asked.

"Seemed to me that Merrell was with Sean, or whoever, for a while. They talked, he smacked her on the cheek, she wiped that little faint trickle of blood from the cheek, and then he wallops her against the headboard, maybe ten, fifteen minutes later. Dr. Grice agreed that the slap came first but she wasn't with me about the colour of the bruises. Said that could have been related to the closeness of the vessels to the skin. And that tiny little cut would have been stanched when the assailant grabbed her. So we never agreed about the timing. She thought she got slapped and was just stunned by that when he grabbed her again and pounded her head."

"Why stunned?"

"Well, there was no sign of a struggle. She didn't even turn her head as he's bouncing it off the furniture. And look at her right hand. You'd have thought she might have fought back and he would have grabbed it. No bruising at the wrist. Same with the left hand. And there weren't any foreign skin cells under her fingernails which tends to show she didn't fight off her assailant, and presumably knew him. DNA these days might show something different but we all figured he caught hold of her pretty fast."

"And what was the significance of the timing?" Jack asked. "What did it mean to you if there was a lapse between the blows?"

"Well, if she's slapped and sits there with the assailant for ten minutes, instead of screaming for help, it's got to be somebody she knew."

"Maybe an intruder held a knife or a gun on her."

"And then beat her to death instead of using the weapon?"

"A gun makes noise."

"So does breaking a window. Again, it's more likely someone she knew."

"It all fits with Sean being the murderer," Jack commented thoughtfully.

"And Sean had a ring on his right hand as well so everyone was patting themselves on the back."

Jack held up the file. "Can we take this report with us, Jim?" he asked.

James shrugged. "Sure. It's public record now."

My hand strayed to the filing cabinet. "What else do you have in there, Jim? Any chance we can have a look through your files to see if there's any more information we need?"

"Be my guest," he answered as he stood back to let me kneel down in front of the cabinet. I pulled out a handful of files and handed them to Jack who put the bulk of them on the ground, keeping a fat one on his lap to go through while I kept searching.

"Do you know the names of the girls who spoke up and said Merrell was going to drop Sean?" Jack asked, his eyes scanning every sheet he turned.

"I think they're actually in that file you have there." James leaned over and pointed to the file Jack was holding. "I seem to remember one was Deanne and another one was Jessica. Can't remember the third one or which of them was the ex-girlfriend of Sean's."

I looked at James over my shoulder. "An ex-girlfriend? I didn't know there was one."

James chuckled. "Sean was one handsome young man, Samantha. Why wouldn't he have girlfriends?"

He was right. Sean had been almost 21 years old and had to have been seeing someone before Merrell.

"Here it is," Jack said, holding up another report. "Jessica Summers."

James clicked his fingers. "That's right. Jessica Summers. Jessica Danvers now. She married a local boy and moved away. Murdunna, rings a bell. Hell of a long way out of town if you ask me. But she may not be there anymore."

He chewed his lip for a second before continuing.

"She was a nice girl, so far as I remember. But that young man she married not long after Sean went to prison," he shook his head sadly. "He was into drugs and anything bad that was happening. She divorced him when he was in prison but when he got out, he begged her to take him back. Two months after that, Johnny sold some crack to an undercover cop and he went back inside. Still there, as far as I know. If Jessica's father had let her go to university, things may have turned out different for her. But he wouldn't let her go. Said she was just a woman and a woman's place was in the home. More specifically the kitchen."

He leaned over again toward the file on Jack's lap. "Do you see anything on the report there?"

"It's difficult," Jack said, peering at the report. "It's hard to make out much on this fax. There's a photo of her here though. A class photo by the look of it. She would have been what, seventeen at the time?"

James did a so-so thing with his head. "Maybe a little more. Eighteen? Nineteen? I seem to remember she'd just left school."

He turned to me. "She went to that same convent school you went to Samantha, but she was a couple of years ahead of you."

He turned back to Jack. "She talked her head off on the initial canvass," James said leaning over to look at the photo.

Jack turned the photo around so James could see it.

He nodded. "Yep that's her. She also said Merrell and Rory seemed to have words on the day she was killed. Before the party. That's the kind of stuff you're interested in, right?"

"Exactly," Jack replied.

I jumped in. "She and Rory had words? Don't you mean Sean and Merrell had words?"

"Nope. I remember because I was as surprised as you."

"Did she tell the cop that because it seemed odd at the time?" Jack asked.

"Not hardly. The cop said to tell him everything she remembered and she did, even how many pastries she ate at the party," he chuckled.

"Why were Sean and Rory at the party? I thought the families were on no speaking terms," Jack asked me.

"The whole town was invited. I suppose Sean and Rory felt they were included. Not that they stayed long."

Jack had pulled out his mobile phone and was busy googling while I made a pile of the files to take with us.

Jack looked down at me. "Looks like we're heading out to Murdunna after we leave here. There's a Danvers listed."

I glanced at my watch. 11.00 am. From memory, a trip to Murdunna would take around 40 minutes. We could grab a bite to eat afterwards on the way back to Richmond.

"Let's do it," I said resolutely, picking up the files just as Jack reached over and took them from me.

"Thank you for your time, Jim. If you think of anything else, please just let us know."

Jack reached into his coat and pulled out a business card. "This has my mobile phone number so don't hesitate to give us a call."

"I'll do that," James nodded. "I wish you luck."

9

———————

It felt good to be sitting next to Jack again. As the trees whipped past, we travelled in a comfortable silence, each caught up in our own thoughts. Ahead of us, the land was falling away and in the distance, the sea was pressed down under a dark sky. The early morning sunshine had slowly disappeared and with the heater warming the inside of the car, condensation was steadily running down the window creating rainbow patterns. The clouds were so low, they seemed to be kissing the sea. Dark and swollen they promised delivery soon.

Forty minutes later, we arrived at Murdunna. We passed a tea house, a post office but that was basically it. Richmond was not a big town but Murdunna was so small and isolated, I wondered what made Jessica and her husband choose to live here in the first place. Looking at the few cottages scattered throughout the area, the population would barely be four hundred people. When she moved here eighteen years ago, there would have been even less. Another five minutes' drive would have taken her to gorgeous Eaglehawk Neck and the rocky outcrops and cliffs of Pirates Bay where New Zealand lays 2000 kms to the east. Further on still and she'd have been close to a thriving community near the convict settlement of Port Arthur. But instead, she chose Murdunna.

Beside me Jack snorted and I knew he was thinking the same.

We slowed to a crawl, scanning the house numbers on the scattered letter boxes, the crunch of our tyres on grey gravel splitting the silence. Some houses had no numbers at all.

"You'd think they'd all have numbers on their boxes," Jack mumbled. "Even just to make it easier for the postman."

Not too far away, a vacant building loomed reminding me of Vlad's castle, it's turret-like stacks reaching high into the cloudy sky. Broken windows were less eerie than the empty ones but they still resembled great gaping eyes of a beast waiting to consume me.

No more gothic novels for me.

Jack came to a stop outside a forlorn-looking red brick house badly in need of repair. Paint was peeling off the windowsills and even the weeds were having a tough time surviving in the dry earth. Parked in the front of the house was a blue Datsun that had to be fifteen years old.

Jack turned the car off and the engine ticked loudly as it cooled down.

"No Venus de Milo statues or koi ponds here," Jack joked.

He paused and turned to me.

"Do you mind if I handle this one? I have a few questions I'd like to ask her after talking to James and it might be less of an inquisition if only one of us does the talking."

I shrugged. "Go for it."

The woman who greeted us at the door was barely recognisable as the girl in the photo James had given us. Age had been unkind to her. It had coarsened her skin and sucked the life from it and like many girls who get married and relax once they had a husband, she'd put on an awful lot of weight. She had once been pretty, looking at the photos, very pretty, and looking closely you could see the remnants of that cheerful appealing face within a pudding of flesh. All there was left was this person who looked much shorter now in a droopy shirt, leaving you to wonder what illusions made her put on stretch pants.

"Good morning. My name is Jack Curtis," Jack said, introducing himself. "And this is Samantha Neil." He nodded to me then looked back at the woman. "Would you be Jessica Danvers?"

Behind her, an elderly man yelled out, "Who is it girl?"

She turned around and shouted back, "It's for me, Dad. Go back and watch television."

She turned to face us, her eyes wide. "Samantha Neil? Really? From Richmond?"

I smiled, being friendly. "Hello Jessica."

"What on earth can you possibly want from me?" she asked, looking directly at me.

It wasn't just the question that surprised me. It was the hidden animosity behind it that took me by surprise. As far as I knew, she should barely remember me. Yet there it was, a tiny frown furrowed between her eyebrows.

Jack must have noticed the look as well and stepped in.

"We're sorry to barge in on you like this." He glanced over her shoulder to the shuffling figure. "You must be very busy. Your father?" he asked.

She lifted both hands up and patted her hair, hanging limply around her heart-shaped face, into place. Her nails had been ferociously chewed to jagged edges and her pink fingertips looks as fragile as a baby's. She looked like a beauty queen who had missed her pageant by twenty years.

"He wanders around here like he's on a treasure hunt. My biggest problem is to keep him from picking up the phone. He gets on to all sorts of youth centres and police clubs and promises them thousands of dollars. I finally had to just give him a book of cheques from a closed account." She shook her head and gave Jack a coy smile. "He loves to write cheques."

Jack chuckled along with her and I noticed a blush rising up her neck.

"If you're not too busy, may we come in?" he asked, managing to look sympathetic. "We won't take up much of your time."

Still standing guard at the door, she looked at me through narrowed eyes. "What is it you want?"

"We'd like to ask you some questions regarding Sean O'Donovan, if you can spare a few minutes," I smiled resolutely.

Her eyes narrowed some more. "Don't know what you could possibly want to know from me after all these years. Why don't you ask him? He's not due for a parole hearing for another three years so he has lots of time to spare."

She shot me a frightening smile that personified the Grimm Brothers *'better to eat you with'* line. I almost stepped back.

Jack's eyebrows rose slightly but he showed no other emotion. Having dazzled at warm-up, I let Jack take over.

"We won't take up much of your time," he repeated.

She took one quick glance at me then stood back and waved us into a dark living room with worn, neutral coloured carpet, joining up with the dining room. On a corner hutch was a shrine to all things Catholic. A large crucifix stood at centre stage, complete with thorns carved around the base and painted in vivid detail. A cast of supporting players was also present, some in sculpture, others framed and under glass. Our Lady of Something, palms spread, heart pumping red. Saint Francis of Assisi, feet hidden by bunnies and lambs. Saint Therese of Lisieux, head veiled, arms laden with roses. The rest, though vaguely familiar, I couldn't remember. Beside a tattered, stained blue sofa, a heavily printed armchair held the old man, his attention glued to a large flat screen television where a news reporter was explaining the outcome of the law case involving Britney Spears and her father.

Jessica led us through to the dining room and waved to us to have a seat at the small table, her eyes wandering towards the television along with her father's. It gave me a chance to take her in.

She radiated sadness. It didn't feel as though she belonged here because everything in sight belonged to an older person: her father. The house seemed to trap her in its web, the past sucking her dry. If she asked me, I'd have said pack up and leave and put him in a nursing home where he could be properly looked after. It would give her a chance to live her own life. My guess was she wouldn't be asking me my opinion.

She tutted and shook her head. "What a mess."

While she tutted, I glanced around at the dark room. There were a lot of prints of Greece on the walls – the royal blue water and rocky hillsides – and they somehow looked out of place amongst the dark wooden furniture. The various tables and shelves held not a single personal photo. No baby in a silly hat. No dog asleep in the sun. No sign of Jessica as a child anywhere.

When the show went to a commercial, she turned back and caught me looking around and her mouth soured. Once again, the intenseness of the look took me by surprise.

Jessica didn't bother with the standard beverage offer. If she'd offered, I would have accepted because I make a point of never refusing coffee or tea in unsettling situations. It helps to establish some small bond of informality. Declining often renders an interview subject less likely to open up. By the look on her face, the only beverage on offer would have been arsenic.

"This isn't an official interview, Jessica. May I call you Jessica?"

Jack's voice came out soothing and a touch personal.

Her hand lifted to her hair again as she nodded.

"We're just following up on a few unanswered questions regarding Merrell's murder following the death of Samantha's late mother. Did you know she passed?"

Jessica barely nodded. "Yes. I did." She glanced quickly at me, dragging her eyes away from Jack, and muttered, "Sorry for your loss," sounding anything but sorry, before turning back to Jack.

"Before her death, she requested that the police follow up on a few leads that weren't investigated at the time of the murder," he lied.

Her mouth soured again. "She never liked me." Her eyes swivelled to me quickly. "I'm sure she mentioned that I was just a bitter witch who was angry at being dumped by Sean who had moved on to Merrell and became one of her harem."

Bitterness crackled in the room but neither Jack nor I said anything in the stunned silence. In the next room, her father muttered, "Bloody ads," just as the news program appeared again.

"Be assured Jessica," Jack picked up quickly as if the bomb hadn't exploded in the room, "nothing of the sort has been insinuated. Mrs Neil felt rather sorry for you actually."

My shocked eyes spun towards Jack whose own eyes had caught mine. "Isn't that right, Samantha?"

"Nothing's been said against you, Jessica," I agreed.

Her thick brows drew together as she squinted at me, trying to figure out whether to believe me or not. Satisfied I wasn't trying to fool her, she shifted her weight in the chair and looked back to Jack.

"We just want to know what you remember. Nothing more, Jessica," he smiled.

"Well, I don't really remember much after all this time," she said. "The event stands out, of course. How often does a friend turn up dead a few hours after you've been at her birthday party, murdered no less? But who knows with the rest of it? What's it been? Twenty years?"

We both nodded like synchronised dolls.

"Of course," Jack continued. "But memory can be funny. Sometimes you can say to a girl, just for an example, do you remember what dress you were wearing that day? And they do?"

"I do!" she said instantly, smiling for the first time since we'd come through the door, showing uneven stained teeth. "It was a little blue sundress with white sunflowers flowing down one side. I looked good in it, too."

Her quick laughter drove her back into the chair, pleased with herself. "Whenever I want to impress, I always wear blue."

She wriggled a little in her seat. "Sean always loved that dress. He used to call me his little Blue Jay when I wore it because back then, I could sing too."

The smile slowly disappeared as she glanced towards her father. "I had something to sing about back then," she whispered sadly.

Sympathy filled Jack's eyes when she turned back to us.

Like a switch, the wounded voice turned into venom.

"I'll tell you something else," she continued, her eyes flashing quickly at me. "Sean told me he was going to dump Merrell."

Sitting opposite Jack, I had relegated myself to the role of taking notes while he buttered her up but at those words, I was jolted. As she talked, her hand moved to her stomach and smoothed her dress.

"Are you sure it wasn't the other way around?"

The words were out before I could stop them. I hadn't stopped to think before asking the question, and I saw Jack's eyes drop to his lap, a frown on his face.

Jessica's head spun towards me, her face three shades darker as her blood rose, plainly feeling challenged. "Why? Do you think no one could possibly do that to your oh so gorgeous sister?"

Her mouth twisted in an ugly smirk.

"Guys being the way they were, they were always being sucked in by her la-di-da ways," she sing-songed. She nodded decisively, like she'd put me in my place. "But your sister was a total bitch," she sneered. "And everyone but her family knew it."

Over her shoulder, I could see Jesus staring down from a picture on the wall between the hutch and the fireplace, His eyes fixated on me as if He was about to tell me he smelled trouble.

Jack leaned forward, his eyes drawing her away from me. I found I'd been holding my breath.

"Did Sean say he was going to do that on the night of the party?" he asked softly.

"I'm only guessing," she muttered. "He told me he was going to do it days before the party so maybe he did. I don't know. I *do* remember wondering how Sean could have killed her since he and Rory left the party early that night."

She glanced sideways at me and smirked again.

"Merrell didn't even notice. She was too busy tramping around with every other guy at the party."

I dropped my head and scribbled in the notepad, trying not to show the anger building up inside.

"I don't want you thinking I'm taking Sean's side," she added. "Because I'm not. He was a louse to me. You know, woman say, *'He took the best years of my life?'* Well, he really did. I was the girl from the neighbourhood he was too good for as soon as soon as *she* crooked her finger at him. Three years we were going out together and then with one look from her, he was gone. And I could have had a ton of boys in those days the way I looked." She shifted in her seat, looking offended. "It still aggravates me."

Jessica looked down at her plump hands for a second. "But I'll tell you the truth. I'd have had him back in a heartbeat." She swallowed noisily. "He just confessed to killing her before he could do it."

Putting her jibes aside, I felt sorry for her. People get stuck in love and sometimes they never recover. They never come back from mourning that lost opportunity. The best love of my love had done much the same thing to me. He'd turned his back on me just when I needed him most and it was the brother of Jessica's lost love who'd done that. It made me wonder if I'd never had the courage to leave home and move to Surfers Paradise, would I be like Jessica, mourning that lost love?

Jack caught her eye again. "Let's get back to the day of the party, Jessica. Do you recall anything about Rory and Merrell?" he asked. "One of the officers mentioned that you recalled Rory having words with her."

Her eyes widened in surprise. "Did I?" she asked.

Most policemen I knew would be waiting for the moment when they could say, 'don't pull that rubbish with me,' but Jack was being earnest and kind. It was like talking to somebody's grandfather who was in a rocking chair on his front porch.

He reached into his jacket and pulled out the report casually, as if it were just another piece of paper he would have in his pocket. Jessica spidered a hand on her forehead as she read the highlighted part. Eventually, she nodded.

"That's right. I *do* remember seeing them talking. Merrell went stalking off and I remember the look on his face. It was like he hated her. Did I tell the cop that?" she asked innocently.

Butter wouldn't melt in her mouth, I thought.

She leant over and put the report back in Jack's hand without reading any further. "I don't recall even telling them that."

It was like I was in the audience of a theatre, watching a play unfold before me. Except they were talking about Rory now, not Sean.

"But you said he looked like he hated her?" Jack persisted.

"There was a lot not to like. I don't want to speak ill of the dead," she glanced at me again, "but I have to tell the truth. Merrell was just a spoiled brat with a very sharp tongue. She was gorgeous, so there were always boys chasing after her, the whole damned cavalry, but she managed to stay aloof from the ones she didn't want. The ones she wanted had no chance." She gave a soft snort. "She thought she was better than everyone else and those morons believed her."

"Is that what Rory didn't like about her? Her attitude towards his brother?" Jack asked.

She shrugged. "She was wild, leading his brother astray. Who knows what they argued about? They were talking loudly so from a distance I could hear him saying that his father hated her and her family too. Merrell already knew that but she didn't care. She was just egging Sean on to be spiteful and Rory knew it."

I had to stop myself from gaping. This wasn't the Merrell I knew. Could I even believe anything this woman was saying? The statement fizzed in my brain like an aspirin fizzing in a glass of water.

Jessica took a deep breath. "But Rory never believed Sean did it."

"Didn't he?" continued Jack, allowing none of the surprise and shock I was feeling ripple through his expression. He maintained a purely conversational tone. "When was this?"

"That day. The day Sean was in court pleading guilty. I was there. Sean and I had broken up a couple of months before, but I wanted to support his family," she muttered. "I was just looking for an excuse to see Sean again."

Jessica was looking past me, gnawing on what was left of her thumbnail, her eyes half-glazed over like she was caught in a memory. She finally winced, pained by the memory and probably the futility. With her eyes closed, I could see her face was blotchy from lack of care.

"Anyway, Rory thanked me for coming. He was really sad and he just said to me, 'He's innocent, you know.'"

Adrenaline slashed through my veins and I forced myself to sit still. But I had to intervene.

"And did you ask how he knew that?" I tried to match Jack's mild tone, but again, Jessica's response was sharp.

"You want to talk or listen?" she barked at me.

My molars clamped tight.

"He was his brother, wasn't he, for God's sake!" she added.

She tsked as she shook her head in disgust, then paused, maybe daring me to interrupt. I clamped some more and stayed silent.

"And if you'd bothered to read that report," she nodded her head abruptly towards the report in Jack's hand, "you'd know he said they were together fishing."

Jessica and I glared at each other for a moment before Jack spoke up again.

"Thinking back, Jessica, do you remember Sean having any serious cuts around that time?"

She considered the question for a moment before saying, "No."

"Would you have been aware of the cuts?" he asked as if he was asking the time.

Jessica fixed him with a knowing eye.

"I'd have known," she nodded cautiously. "We dated for three years and I was sure I was going to marry him. I mean, the truth is I saw him less once Merrell came into the picture, of course, but I'd have known." She nodded again, glancing at me with a smirk plastered over her face. "I'd have known."

"How is that?" I asked, seeing Jack wince in my peripheral vision. But I couldn't help myself. Her antagonism was almost palpable in the stuffy room.

Jessica wheeled back, her eyes flashing at my audacity to question her.

"I'm saying I'd know!"

She glanced over her shoulder at her father, aware that her voice had risen almost to a shriek. When there was no reaction from him, she turned back to me and glowered before lowering her voice and speaking to Jack.

"I was seeing less of him but I still saw him. Right? I'd have noticed." Her chest rose and fell as she tried to control her temper. "Everybody knew there was blood all over that bedroom." She turned back to me. "I'm not that bloody dense."

I absorbed the answer without arguing further, but those kinds of retrospective 'would-haves' were always garbage. If the man she loved told her he'd cut himself mending a wire fence, she wouldn't have thought twice about it.

I looked down at my notes in silence, seething. I felt completely off kilter, bombarded with new information I didn't know how to process. That left me with a hopeless feeling I abhorred.

"Was Sean right-handed?" Jack asked softly.

"Mostly," she replied warily.

"Mostly?"

"Yeah. Mostly. He wrote lefty sometimes, always ate lefty, but did everything else with his right hand. When he played tennis at school, he'd shift his racket from one hand to the other, playing forehands from both sides. But mostly, he was right-handed."

Jack folded the sheet up and placed it in his pocket. "You were correct before. Sean is coming up for parole soon. If he was innocent, his lawyers may want to speak to you to see if they can speed that up."

"The hell they will!" she answered quickly. "This isn't going to become my new profession. James Russell called me. And I agreed to speak to you," she glanced at me and jerked her head, "and her, out of respect. But I'm not repeating everything forty times to a bunch of lawyers so they can pick what I say apart and start with the finger-pointing. And I'm certainly not talking to any reporters. They just write what they want anyway. This here, today, that's the end of this for me."

"Well, no one knows anything for sure," Jack said, trying to smooth her ragged nerves. "This could blow over in a week. I hardly think you'll be dragged into anything. It's just questions we had since you were Sean's girlfriend. There wasn't anybody else who knew more about him then. You have to know how important you are."

Jack was good. I had to give him that. He knew instinctively what would soothe her.

We were all silent for a second. "Still," she muttered mollified.

From the lounge room, an angry voice shouted, "Where's my lunch, girl?"

The old man stood up slowly and turned to face us, pointing his cane towards what I assumed was the kitchen, making it clear what he wanted. He was in track suit bottoms and an old t-shirt with a soup stain running down the front. His hair was wild and his full grey beard looked equally as untamed. The frames on his heavy glasses must have been thirty years old but behind them, the eyes were quick and mean.

Jack greeted him with the barest of nods as he stood up. The old man was on the verge of having a serious tantrum and his rage was filling the house.

We were putting our coats on and out the door before either he or Jessica said another word.

10

We reached the car before I muttered to Jack, "You two seemed to get along just fine."

As he opened the car door for me, he grinned, "Charm and charisma, Sam. I can't help it if women love me."

"Well, she sure didn't like me. And that's an understatement."

I was looping my seat belt over my shoulder as Jack sat down in the driver's seat.

"Why were you asking about Sean being left or right-handed?" I asked.

"Remember when we were talking to James? He said the coroner wrote that Merrell had marks on her face but finger stripes on her left cheek, which meant the killer was right-handed. I was just confirming what Sean was."

"He also said half of Richmond are right-handed."

Jack turned the engine on and said, "You knew this wasn't going to be easy. For all we know, Sean was telling the truth and he did kill Merrell. But it also leaves us with the question, if Rory knew his brother was innocent, why did Sean say he killed her?"

It was a rhetorical question I knew I didn't have to answer. But it was the basis of the whole investigation. Why did he say he'd killed

92

her? What possible reason could it have been? Was he protecting someone?

Jack was sitting still, tapping his fingers on the steering wheel, with his eyes closed. He once told me that the trick to solving violent crimes was to focus on the suspects not the victim. For me, it's always been the opposite.

In the silence, the only sound was the engine purring and the heater humming.

As the silence stretched on, I asked, "Are you still here?"

He opened his eyes and turned to me. "Don't take everything Jessica said as the truth. She's the angry ex-girlfriend, who has the fact that Sean ruined her life just about tattooed on her forehead. Hell hath no fury, I've heard."

I nodded. Something was bothering me too but I couldn't put my finger on it. Something dancing around in my brain that disappeared just as quickly as it appeared.

"Lunch?" he asked, interrupting my thoughts.

"Hell yes. And a drink." I jerked my head in the direction of the front window. I could see Jessica peering out through the lace curtains with her father behind her, his mouth opening and closing like a puppet, no doubt berating her for not having his lunch ready.

I looked back at Jack. "I need a big one after that episode."

"I'm yours to command. Where do we go?"

"From memory, there's a nice pub in Sorrell, about half an hour from here on the way back to Richmond. There're actually two pubs in the centre of town to choose from. You'll be surprised at how big Sorrell is. It's twice as big as Richmond."

Jack grinned again. "Wow! That big, eh?"

He put the car in gear and headed off in the direction we'd driven in, occasionally glancing over at me from time to time as we drove. Music played on the radio, something bluesy that rattled the speakers. Closing my eyes, I could picture fields of sugarcane in Queensland but when I opened them, I saw the wind bending trees and twisting them like an arthritic old man. I'd give this a couple of more days. Three at most. And then I wanted to get back home. There were too many ghosts here.

"Is all this becoming too painful for you?"

Jack's quiet voice brought me back from my thoughts.

"If you want me to do all the investigating, I'm happy to do it," he said. "It must be upsetting for you to hear all this about your sister."

He was right. It was unsettling. I'd had this idea of my sister as being nothing short of a saint. Growing up at home, she was this person who wouldn't hurt a fly. She helped out in the pub. She helped me with homework and even tried to make me as glamorous as she could when I was getting ready to go out. Hearing Jessica talk about her in such a derogatory manner, was nothing short of disturbing. How did I miss that?

I shook my head. "I'm fine, Jack. Really I am. I've had twenty years to come to terms with all this. But hearing that your sister wasn't the angel you thought she was is pretty unnerving."

"Well, let's not forget we're hearing this from a woman who had a grudge against her. She is seeing things differently from most people."

I nodded as I watched the scenery fly past.

He glanced over at me. "I've been thinking we should try and see if there is any traces of the blood from the crime scene still in the evidence room in Hobart. While I was at the police station yesterday, they told me all evidence was sent to the main police station in Hobart."

"Are you thinking DNA?"

He nodded, keeping his eyes on the winding road. "Yep. Twenty years ago, they didn't have the capabilities they do now. But if some blood remains in storage, I think we have a good shot at seeing if we can match it up. They had blood evidence from the house, right, from the French door. That's clearly the murderer's." He glanced over again. "Just don't get your hopes up."

"But we don't have blood samples from Sean. At least James doesn't think so."

"We have fingerprint lifts from the room. Lots of them were identified as Sean's. If I'm not mistaken, they can extract DNA from old fingerprints."

"They can?"

I was stunned. All of this was new to me and it made me realise how much I didn't know.

"I'm not sure, but we can try. I know it's been done before. It only takes a speck. With so many prints, we're bound to get something. You can get DNA off the bone from a chicken wing somebody ate. Or a cigarette they smoked. Who knows, maybe your friend Rory was right and Sean was innocent. But, in any case, if it is Sean's blood, then we can stop searching."

He glanced at me then turned back to the road. "If all else fails, we may have to consider a visit to Sean in prison. He'll have to be willing to give us a sample to extract his DNA though. And then there are hoops to jump through." He glanced over again. "And going down that path is going to take a lot more time than you're willing to allow, I'd say."

A road sign appeared directing us to The Pembroke Hotel. "This will do," Jack muttered, indicating as he made a right-hand turn.

"What I'm hoping for," he continued, "is a detective at the Hobart police station who will be able to direct us to someone who can help us." He glanced across at me again. "I can do that alone if you prefer to stay here in Richmond."

"You have no sway with the police anymore Jack. Especially not here," I reminded him. "You're not a policeman anymore. Leave it to me to call and arrange a time and we'll both go. I'll contact them this afternoon and see what they can tell me. Who knows, maybe we'll get lucky."

The Pembroke Hotel came into view with an almost full carpark.

"Okay. That'll leave me time to go through the files this afternoon. Dinner tonight again to go over things?"

"Is it your shout?"

He grinned. "I'm unemployed, remember." His eyes shifted sideways at me and the skin around them crinkled. "Oh ok. Sounds like a plan. But first, let's have lunch."

11

Twilight at 4 pm was something I was unused to in Surfers Paradise. Surfers was a city that never seemed to sleep and glowed brightly 24 hours a day. This twilight had leached the colour from the village as we drove through it, lying silent and still in the deepening shadows. Apart from the small brightly lit supermarket where I bought some meagre food supplies, the buildings were starting to disappear into their own darkness. The silence seemed total.

The afternoon's breeze had turned surly and cold with gusts whirling across the carpark after Jack dropped me off. It snapped at my collar and as I looked up at the darkening sky, ominous clouds were building on the horizon. All around me, except for the wind, was utter silence.

A note pushed under the back door greeted me when I walked in to the pub. Without looking, I knew who had left the note and with my treacherous heart tumbling around in my chest, I read it.

I miss you Sam. Call if you want to talk.
Rory.

. . .

I swallowed hard as I read the short note. *Did* I want to talk? Or perhaps I should be asking myself, *should* I want to talk?

Although the pain and the longing was less acute this time, a niggle of a thought wormed its way forward and whispered, *Is this a precious second chance?*

Unbidden, a memory of Rory's wife and two children, standing hand in hand at the back of the mourners at Mum's funeral, suddenly jumped into my mind and instantly the guilt followed.

Almost immediately, I remembered it was *his* weakness that had cost us all hope of happiness. *He* had been the one who had pushed *me* aside. After two weeks of frantic messages sent to him, *he* had chosen not to reply to me and to avoid me.

The memory fanned my anger again and I screwed the note up then tossed it angrily in to the sink.

Glaring at the sink, I breathed in shallow breaths and almost reached in to rescue it before spinning around and heading into the pub. I needed a drink to settle my frayed nerves before calling Hobart Police station.

Ten minutes later, a glass of cool white wine in my hand, I spoke to a detective and was surprised to find that the report on the blood samples were still available. Apparently they were kept indefinitely in a small storage unit together with all manner of evidence. Also, to my surprise, after explaining the reason for my call, they were more than happy to set a time at 11 am the next day for us to talk to the station captain who could discuss the reports with us.

I had a strange feeling of accomplishment, as if things were finally falling into place. The step was a small one but it was a step forward nonetheless. Feeling almost cheerful, I marched upstairs to retrieve the suitcase from under the bed before I could change my mind.

After lowering the shade over the back door window in the kitchen, I sat at the table sorting through the photographs with solemn tenderness, the past alive again and rising from every image.

As I sipped my wine from time to time, the ancient heating system rumbled into action, gurgling and hissing, and now the house sounded as though it was suffering from indigestion.

With the suitcase resting near my chair and a second glass of wine beside me, I opened the diary and thumbed through the entries to where I'd left off the night before. I swivelled my chair around to make sure the ceiling light was right above the diary before beginning.

Diary 12th August

Barney and the boys captured a barracks tonight. It was after midnight before we got word of how it went. Daddy and I were counting the day's takings when the knock came to the bar window. We looked at each other and, putting the cash away in the strong box, he gave me the nod to answer it. I slid open the big bolt on the door and there stood Tipsy, Barney's friend, all excited.

'What are you doing out there?' I said to him, sweeping him inside before he was seen. I knew by the look of him that things had gone well.

'Come in lad,' Daddy said urgently. He made the offer of a drink and needless to say Tipsy didn't refuse. It went like clockwork, he said, with over thirty men all firing from four points. Oh yes, Mr Michael Collins and his followers have learned their English lessons well tonight, he said. We'll all sleep well on it tonight.

Diary 13th August

The Army sent a massive contingent today led by none other than Lieutenant O'Donovan. We were appraised of their intentions in advance and our boys gave consideration to staying put and fighting it out but we knew we'd be outgunned and outnumbered so decided to get out in advance to spare bloodshed. But some of Barney's friend were taken prisoner and are in Wexford gaol.

The soldiers they have put in place are very jumpy, knowing they haven't seen the end of us. Several times a night a mobile patrol is sent out in case we decide to make a return call. The fools do it every two hours, you could set your clock by them. Can they really be that stupid?

Barney sent a message that Molly and I are to join him and Tipsy and go up there and help free them. Let's see how Lieutenant O'Donovan likes that!

Walking was far from comfortable with a canvas sling of ammunition around my waist and a bomb held in place by strips of an old torn sheet tight against my skin. The bomb was the bomb was the bulkiest item between the size of an orange and a small cabbage. The belt that held the pair of guns strapped down along my two sides also dung into my flesh. But the discomfort was like a crown to me and a joy to be doing such work for Ireland. Looking down at myself, I had a premonition of how my body might look twenty years from now.

'I'm like Ten-Ton-Tessie,' I laughed to Molly.

'Just walk easy, else you might blow up,' she replied with no smile on her face.

There were many miles of nobody and nothing and we walked in silence, Barney with steady deliberation and something weighing down his steps. Norah, most likely.

A spattering of rain began to fall when we heard a rumble of a lorry in the distance, sounding like it was coming our way. Tipsy looked back first. 'Oh Jesus God! It's them!'

'We're only walking, remember,' Barney reminded us. 'We're not breaking any law. Stay calm.'

The lorry pulled in close beside us, revving. Then it pulled ahead and drew itself crossways up ahead, blocking our way. The engine stopped and a soldier jumped down. Dan O'Donovan to be sure.

'These are mine,' I heard him say to the other soldiers in the car. He stood beside the car, waiting, his legs planted wide, his hand on his gun.

He looked fine, there's no denying it. Six foot two of manhood in its prime, all shiny boots and buttons. The very picture of a soldier. I felt ashamed of my dilapidated coat and if I was shabby, the others beside me were next door to tramps. One look at us told the story of this war's injustices.

'So,' said Dan approaching us, dragging the word out. 'We're a little far from home, aren't we?'

Silence.

'What brings you to this vicinity?'

Barney gave him the prepared line. 'We're visiting,' he said.

Dan snorted. 'Of course you are. And the person to be honoured by this visit?'

'An aunt of mine.'

'And looking forward to seeing the rest of these people, is she?" he said looking at Molly and Tipsy.

'She's a hospitable woman.'

The conversation was going nowhere so I spoke up. 'Going for a walk is not a crime, Dan,' I said.

He turned to me. 'You know full well I could take you all in for questioning.'

His eyes travelled down my body and I felt a blush rise to my cheeks. He was staring hard at where the bomb was pressed between flesh and fabric. I looked down and saw a streak of whitewash down one side of the coat from painting wall slogans the night before.

'We're whitewashing the sheds at home,' I said, then realised he hadn't asked me a question.

'Is that a fact?' he smirked. 'I could come and see them to admire your handiwork.'

His taunting was hateful and I was flooded with a longing to say so. If we were alone, I would have said, 'Okay Dan, we are enemies now. All right. So be it. But let us please have respect for one another. Not this smallness.'

He threw me a look like I was something stuck on his shoe, then turned his attention to the boys. 'Hands up,' he said. And four arms were raised. Tipsy started smiling like a drunkard because the attention had turned away from me. I thought if he wasn't able to control his face, he'd give us away.

Dan ran his hands down the torsos of the two men who used to be his friends in the most mechanical way, like he'd no expectation of finding anything. Then his eyes turned slowly, carefully, pointedly to me. His face was quizzical as he let his look travel down to the centre of my mother's coat, as if he could see right through it. How did she think I could fool anyone, especially him with any eye for the female form.

'New overcoat?' he asked.

I shook my head. 'It's Mammy's.'

'I was thinking it wasn't your style. And what might have you wearing your mother's coat, I wonder?'

'Do I need a reason?"

I was done for, I thought. He's going to search me. He was capable of it because conventions didn't matter to him. One touch of his hands and he would have known it wasn't flesh he was feeling but solid steel.

'Open it!', he said.

The realisation that whatever it was that we had for one another was now *gone suddenly came to me. He and I were enemies. This must be what people meant when they talked about hearts breaking, I thought. I understood the phrase but I hadn't understood the actual pain, not until now. Heart. Breaking.*

I was forbidden now from loving him and what felt like an irrevocable thought gripped me: I'll never love another. You were the only one for me, Dan O'Donovan. The tragedy of that, the knowledge of how deep it went, pulled my eyes up to his. 'Search me if you like.' I thought. 'Do your worst, do whatever you want, because it makes no difference to me now. I'm bereft anyway.'

He just stared at me. As the moment grew and grew between us, I saw him decide that he would. Then I saw him change his mind. Then change it back again. And again. Indecision danced forward and back in him until finally, he dropped his gaze.

He turned to the others and gave them all a peremptory shake of his head. 'Go!' he shouted. 'But ye'll stay out of trouble if you know what's good for ye.'

And of course, we almost ran. And as I ran, I felt his eyes boring into my back.

At Wexford, the sunset was dripping liquid orange and gold when the rain-filled potholes all along the bridge glowed full of its light. I went behind a copse of wet bush and divested myself of my load. My flesh was screaming and pink indentations turning red were made into my flesh. I barely felt relief when I untied the straps and belts placed the bomb carefully on the grass, the heat of my body still on it.

I handed the bomb to my brother just as a wet star came out along the horizon. Soon there were dozens, then too many to count. I thought, if the soldiers didn't come soon, it would be dark.

With that thought, I heard it, faint, distant but unmistakeable. The engine-sound of military motor, chugga, chugga, chugga. On the bridge, we stiffened, each making eye contact with each other. I could see the twitch of that muscle of Barney's that always flickers beneath his temple when he is nervous. Both he and Tipsy pointed their double-barrelled guns down to where the car would pass and Barney whispered, 'Nearly too easy. It'll be down to timing.'

We heard the chug of the lorry drawing nearer and with it came the sound of soldiers. They took the bend and we saw there were five of them. No sign of Dan and a flood of relief swept through me. Would I ever learn?

The car approached, closer and closer and as it came to the bridge, Barney lobbed a grenade. It fell with a clean arc and seemed to land right in the middle of the vehicle.

'Bull's eye,' he hissed. 'Feckin' bull's eye!'

The soldiers only had time to look down at the bomb before the explosion erupted, blasting them with it. The vehicle, thrown off its steer, hit a wall.

The air seemed to drain of sound, eerily empty. Above gulls cawed as if nothing had happened. I was horrified and yet exultant. I was still alive. They are dead but I am alive.

I looked around and saw the others all looking to me and to each other, all with the same wild and fearful and exhilarated awe.

Barney looked sad and said to me, 'You shouldn't have had to see that.'

He meant well, some sort of chivalry, but the call to blood and sacrifice was mine too.

'Well, it's too late now,' I said, not wanting an argument.

'Come on,' he said. 'The Free Staters are only a quarter of a mile away and they'll have heard that explosion. We're off. In three minutes, all they'll see is their six dead comrades. We'll be long gone.'

Diary 4th September

The raid we've been waiting for came last night. At eleven o'clock they arrived, two lorry loads of them. No Dan, thank God. They started beating down the doors with their rifle butts and every man drinking in the pub was hauled out onto the road while they went through our goods and belongings. Even Mammy who was sick and shivering. I said nothing for the whole time they were there, just let Daddy do the talking for us because I was afraid of what would come out of my mouth.

They gave the place a right going-over. Crockery was broken and the Sacred Heart was taken down from the walls. Locks were busted and wood panelling was broken. It will cost us a fortune to fix.

As bad as the wreckage was, I was afraid all the time they would find my diary. I hid it but they spent so long going through everything as if it was a tip-off. I will give it to Molly tomorrow and find a new place to hide it.

Barney is having a night home, which we're grateful for because he is safe.

Norah managed a small while with him and promised a longer time tomorrow so he went to sleep happy.

Diary 9th September

'Lieutenant' O'Donovan arrived from Wexford with a party and proceeded to set fire to a row of cottages. The Whites own one of those cottages but to be so zealous in the punishment of old friends who once fed him tea and welcomes, is not the Dan O'Donovan I knew.

The Whites said they have a legal right for action against the government and he thinks we should also make a claim for the number of times we've been raided and smashed up, but Mammy says she'd rather be homeless than ask that crowd for compensation.

We got used to robbers holding up banks and post offices under the name of the IRA but for several weeks a band of armed thieves have been terrorising the district late at night with masked faces demanding money at gunpoint. On Saturday, the lads went after them and made an arrest. They were brought before a Republican court and found guilty. On Sunday morning, the lads tied them to the front of the chapel gates and put a label on each of them saying: 'Robbers Beware! The IRA is on your track. Leave the Country within 24 hours!

Diary 15th September

Disaster! Disaster! Disaster! I didn't go to the Redmond's last night as Mammy was feeling poorly and I couldn't leave her alone. Molly and Cat went with a friend of Molly's, a Kathleen O'Brien. I don't think Molly even asked Norah. They were all together with Barney, Tipsy and eight other men when Joe Breen came running in from cycling over the fields to warn them he had heard the Stater troops were headed out there after them. At that very moment, they heard the rumble of lorries and tried to make an escape. Some were lucky, but not all. Not Barney. Nor poor Tipsy, Molly or Miss O'Brien either.

Also captured were sixteen rifles, seven revolvers, twelve hand grenades and hundreds of rounds of rifle ammunition, cables and electric batteries. The best of our stash.

What is worse, what is truly terrible for us all, is that Dan located the papers, every last one I gave Molly a few weeks ago were found, hidden under a stack of hay. I cannot believe her carelessness, hiding them all in one place. Nearly everything was in those papers. A record of all our activities from January up to the end of last month. The names of all our forces throughout South Wexford, our strength and equipment. In short, our entire scheme of operations and plans. I'd never have handed them over to her if I'd known she was so careless. Now we'll all pay the price.

I glanced up at the clock, rubbing the tiredness from my eyes and catching sight of my face in the reflection from the microwave. A dishevelled version of myself stared back at me with dark shadows ringing my tired eyes.

I blinked a few times to clear the fuzziness only to replace it with a stinging of sorts in my eyes. Due to the age of the diary, almost eighty years, the writing was so faded I knew I would damage my eyes if I continued reading by the soft yellow light.

As eager as I was to continue, it would have to wait until tomorrow. Jack was waiting for me at the tavern and we needed to formulate the questions we wanted to ask the captain tomorrow.

Reluctantly, I shut the diary and headed upstairs for a quick shower before heading back to the restaurant for dinner with Jack.

12

It was still early for most of the dinner crowds so most patrons were sitting at the bar, making finding a table by a window relatively easy.

"I'm starving," he stated as we sat down. "How about you?"

I could have waited longer but I went along with him.

"Sure. Let's order the food now with the drinks."

He put his hand up to stop me. "A glass of Sauvignon Blanc with fish and chips?" he asked.

"Am I that easy to read?" I grinned.

He winked. "I've got this one. The next one is on you. But I warn you, I like my food."

I watched Jack walk to the bar and order our meals and drinks with the barmaid. The blush on her face and the coy smile meant Jack was flirting with her. I heard him say, "And proper bread please. Not that sourdough rubbish."

Further along the bar, a drinker sat on a stool studying the form guide. He raised his head and turned towards Jack and the barmaid and grinned before he bent back to the guide.

Jack has never been the most social of people. Most of his life is a mystery to me although I know he was married and has a 15-year-old daughter who is going on 25. I also know there was a woman in his recent past that was murdered by his best friend and the memory of losing them both still pains him. Now he seems closed off, anchored in the memory of her, and seemingly happy on his own. Some people are meant to prevail.

Collecting the drinks, Jack joined me at the table as a whoop went up from across the room where an old pinball machine sat surrounded by teenagers.

He placed the drinks on the table and began removing his jacket before sitting down.

He picked up his pint of beer and said, "Cheers," before taking a long gulp.

"Nectar." He smacked his lips theatrically as he placed his glass on the table.

I took a sip of my wine, my eyes downcast. I was lost in the diary resting in the suitcase under my bed.

"You look a little distracted, Sam. What have you been doing for the past couple of hours?"

"I'm sorry, Jack." I apologised. "I told you Mum left me a letter and a suitcase with photos in it?"

Jack nodded as he sipped his beer.

"Well, I've been reading the diary from my Nana Peg from when she was in Ireland." I shook my head. "It's amazing! She was this feisty old woman in my youth who always had something to say about everything."

I looked back down at the table. "She died a few years ago but I wasn't able to get back for her funeral."

"Couldn't?" Jack knew me well.

I gave a sad smile. "In my defence, there were extenuating circumstances. Family issues that were never resolved."

"Ah," he mumbled. "Go on."

"This diary she wrote in regularly tells of the conflicts we only read about in history books." I sipped my own wine. "And she lived through it. No, she was a part of it. Her and her best friend I knew as Auntie Norah."

"It's got you hooked by the sound of it."

"Hook, line and sinker," I grinned. "I love reading it but more than that, I have a feeling it's leading up to something. Something big."

"Those family skeletons I mentioned a day or so ago?"

"Perhaps," I smiled. "But definitely something. I read a little every day. It's sad somehow that I never knew Nana's history. Sadder still that I never bothered to ask her about her youth. I must have seemed like someone who didn't care about anyone else but themselves."

"Come on, Sam. You were a kid. Every kid on earth is selfish. You're no different from anyone in that regard."

"I know," I mumbled, swirling my half empty glass on the table. I was leaving little wet rings on the table and without knowing it, I'd made Celtic circles with the glass. "Still," I muttered again.

"Don't be so hard on yourself." He rested his chin on his hand, the elbow resting on the table. "Let's talk about today."

I took another sip of my wine then said, "A very productive day, I thought."

His eyes glued to mine but he said nothing.

"What?" I asked.

"She was lying, you know."

"Jessica?"

I hadn't liked her, and the feeling was obviously mutual. But lying?

I blinked a few times before asking, "I'm not questioning your abilities Jack, but why would she lie after all this time? And what did she lie about?"

A basket of garlic bread arrived. He pushed the basket towards the middle of the table after taking a slice, offering me some. I should my head as he polished off the first slice and reached for a second one.

He shrugged as he chewed. "I'm not sure yet if she was actually lying. But there's something off about what she was saying."

He took a sip from his glass, washing down the bread.

"That's the thing about lies. They're easy to tell but difficult to hide. Some people tell them brilliantly but most of us struggle because our minds don't control our bodies completely. There are thousands of automatic responses from a beating heart to a prickling of skin."

He was trying to tell me something but I had no idea what it was.

"These responses," he continued, "have nothing to do with free will. They're responses that we can't control and finally give us away. The problem with secrets and lies is that you can never tell which is which until you dig deep. Some things are buried for safekeeping while some are buried because they're toxic."

"I missed something big, didn't I?"

He nodded and leant back as our meals arrived. Tucking a paper napkin into his collar, he continued eating. As he chewed, he mulled over the interview with Jessica.

"I can't put my finger on what is bothering me, Sam. But there are bells clanging in my head." He chewed some more. "One thing is for sure. Merrell's character will be dissected and questioned."

He hesitated, taking the harshness out of his voice. "Don't look at me like that, Sam. I'm giving you the good news. If you open up this can of worms, everything about Merrell will be dragged up again. Worse this time, if I'm right."

"How on earth do you know stuff like this?"

"I watch people."

"Do me a favour. Don't watch me."

"To see what you're missing, you must step back and widen the angle. Then hopefully the big picture will appear."

I grinned. "Well, thank you Sherlock Holmes."

I hadn't seen Rory enter the pub and I certainly hadn't seen him walk over to our table.

"Hello, Sam."

The soft words were spoken to me, but his curious eyes were directed at Jack.

"My name's Rory O'Donovan." He held out his hand to shake Jack's, his eyes dropping to the napkin tucked into Jack's collar. "And you must be the knight in shining armour who has come on his white horse to help Sam."

The smile he gave Jack somehow looked false.

Jack hesitated before answering, his own eyes giving Rory the once over as he pulled the napkin from his collar and dropped it on the table beside the garlic bread.

"That would be me, Jack Curtis," Jack replied with a nod as he held out his own hand. "And you must be the person who let this beautiful woman slip away from you twenty years ago."

The words weren't meant to have a barb to them but the look in Rory's eyes told me he'd taken them as a slur. Fire burned in his eyes as they dilated.

"We're all allowed one serious mistake in life. I'm not about to let that happen again."

This smile directed towards Jack looked like something from a Grim Brothers novel. A smile I imagined the wolf gave grandma before saying *'All the better to eat you with.'*

"You're a very lucky man then," Jack smiled widely. "You must have a very understanding wife."

In the silence, the two men smiled grimly at each other and while glasses tinkled and cue balls clicked, I felt like I was juggling chainsaws.

"Are you meeting your wife for dinner tonight, Rory?" I said, breaking the silence. "The menu is new apparently."

Rory turned back to me, glancing at his watch.

"Not tonight. I just dropped in for a quick drink with a client before heading home."

He turned to glance at the bar where a man stood watching us, a glass of beer halfway to his mouth. His height and bulk and the scar on his face fit the image of a bouncer. His droopy brown suit, tragic tie the colour of basil pesto and his wash and wear shirt, that had long since been white, didn't.

Rory turned back to Jack.

"I hear you're helping Samantha out with her investigation. How's it coming along?"

"Very promising," Jack replied with a nod. "We seem to be making progress."

Rory's eyebrows raised. "Really? What sort of progress?"

"We can't give too much away at this time." Jack grinned. "It's early days but little steps, as they say."

Rory's eyes held Jack's for a few moments. "Well, that's good news."

Jack looked at his drink thoughtfully before raising his head to look up at Rory again.

Here it comes, I thought.

"We're considering a trip to Hobart prison to visit Sean to see if he is willing to give us a blood sample for DNA. It would certainly help the investigation along."

Rory paled noticeably and blinked a few times.

What was that for? I thought.

"Didn't the police take samples at the time?" Rory asked. He was trying to keep his voice even but a worried frown had creased his forehead.

"They did," Jack replied slowly.

Jack never missed a thing. I could see the concentration in his own eyes as he noted Rory's reaction. "But from our investigations today, there were some anomalies during the initial investigation." He grinned. "Just crossing our t's and dotting our i's."

Rory nodded slowly but said nothing before turning back to me.

"Well, I must be off but if there's anything I can help you with, please just let me know, Sam. Because of my work, I may be able to get you into places you normally wouldn't be able to access."

"Oh? What is it you do, Mr O'Donovan?" Jack asked.

"I'm a lawyer."

Jack's head tilted to the side. "Nice. Criminal law?"

Rory hesitated. "No. Land and titles. Wills occasionally."

"Ah," Jack muttered, non-committally.

Rory nodded stiffly. "Nice meeting you Mr Curtis. I hope we meet again."

For all his bluster, Rory's eyes betrayed his uncertainty, like a man who suddenly discovers that the ground beneath his feet is not as stable as he once recalled. It took me by surprise that Jack had that effect on him.

"Please," Jack said, "Call me Jack."

Rory's nod was almost non-existent.

"Jack," he said quietly, before turning to me. "I'll see you soon Sam. We have things to discuss."

With that he walked away as Jack reached for his beer.

"Why didn't you warn me, Sam, instead of letting me walk into this with my zipper down?"

I dropped my eyes to the table, trying not to laugh.

"I didn't know he was going to be here, Jack. And I didn't exactly roll out the red carpet for him."

"Yeah. Well, you ought to have anticipated such an eventuality."

"I'm not psychic," I grinned at him. "One thing for sure is he'll remember you."

Jack squinted at me. He might have been relatively experienced in matters of the heart but I had a feeling he was way out of his league with Rory.

He shook his head as he sipped from his glass. "I know I've only just met him, Sam, but I get the distinct impression he's a shark in shoes."

"He's of no concern anymore. Can we get back to where we were?"

He grinned. "Sangfroid Sam."

"Sang who?"

"Sangfroid. It's French. Self-possession. Poise. Steadiness. That's you. But remember, you spend too much time alone, you can talk yourself into some rotten ideas."

I knew what he meant. He was warning me to stay clear of Rory. And I had no intention of getting back on that merry-go-round.

"We have an appointment with Captain Marshall in Hobart at 11am tomorrow," I told Jack just as the food arrived. "Let's eat then work out what questions we want to ask."

Two hours later, I was running through a deluge of rain to my car.

13

TUESDAY, 23RD MAY

Through the gaps between the blades of the bedroom shutters, patches of shrubs leading down to the water's edge began to appear as the sun peeked out from the bruise-coloured sky at dawn.

My night had been restless again as I lay huddled in bed listening to water soughing and gurgling down the drainpipes. Water tumbled out over the gutters that needed a clean out, another job that needed to be done by the Germans, along with hinges that needed oiling and taps that needed washers. They had their work cut out for them and I was mildly pleased it wasn't me who had to organise and pay for the repairs.

As I watched through the window, the distant bay fully materialised and the bedroom was striped with light and shadows while the house creaked and groaned as if complaining of being neglected.

I showered and dressed, then went downstairs to make my coffee. I'd just switched the kettle on at 7 am when there was a light tap on the back door.

"Brought you some scones and coffee."

Looking fresh and handsome, Rory stood at the door, a smile on his face and a blanket over his arm.

"Thought you might not have had a chance to go out for supplies yet.

It's a corker of a morning out there. I thought we could go down to the clearing and have these."

He held the box containing the scones and coffee high in the air and before I could think about the stupidity of it, we were walking towards the trees and towards Lovers Hollow.

Oh yes, the irony was not lost on me.

A soft breeze was blowing through the magnolias, throwing shifting patterns across the path, and the air felt velvety soft on my skin. As I looked around at the vast expanse of sky, sea and sand I got a strange hall-of-mirrors feeling. The early hour and the cold wind coming in from the sea meant that few people were around to notice us.

A flash of memory of his wife and children standing hand in hand at the funeral jumped into my mind yet again and for some reason, I remembered one of the last conversations I'd had with my sister.

'Sam. People are selfish. Even if they don't want to be. They are. They might think they're doing the right thing, might make some shitty excuse for themselves, but in the end, they're making the choice based on whatever's going to bring them gratification. Selfish. That includes you. Don't be afraid of being selfish. You can't win in this world if you don't put yourself first. Don't forget that.'

Rory was bent over his camera lens looking out over the bay. "If it weren't for the warning signs and the barbed wire fence, you'd never know, would you? You'd expect there'd be some sign, wouldn't you?"

"Sign of what?" I asked stupidly.

"Of the sinking sands." He slung his camera over his shoulder and lifted the top wire of barbed wire to slide through.

"What are you going out there for?"

He grinned. "I'll be careful. I just want to get a close-up of that grass."

It was only common gorse but I knew he saw something in it that I didn't.

I took the cloth from the basket and spread it across the sand. "Another perfect day," I said taking the coffee and scones out of the basket.

"You're lucky you didn't come last year, when it rained almost every day. We had the heating on all summer."

I laid out the food on plastic plates. A thermos of coffee. Two plastic knives. Four scones along with a small plastic container of whipped cream and another of strawberry jam. I felt like a housewife preparing the food while he occupied himself snapping picture after picture. Click. Whirr. Click. Whirr. His sturdy thighs strained against his denim jeans as he leant in, rapt, every cell focused on his subject. I chewed my bottom lip watching as he slipped through the barbed wire fence to join me on the rug, stretching his legs to the full.

I was hyper-aware of those legs, their closeness to mine, but he seemed unaware of my glances as he reached for a scone.

"I haven't done this for years."

"Which part?" I asked.

He broke a scone in two and reached into the cream with a knife, smearing it liberally before licking his fingers. I couldn't stop watching those fingers.

"All of this" he said. "Breakfast on the bluff. Taking photos. A beautiful woman sitting next to me." He glanced up at me. "You inspire me Sam. I'm over the moon you're back."

All the broken memories that brought me here jostled around inside my head.

"I'm not back, Rory. I'm doing what Mum wanted me to do. Find out who really killed Merrell. That is, if Sean didn't do it. And I'm not convinced that he didn't. Then I will go back to my own life again."

"I thought this time..."

He left the sentence unfinished.

"You made it obvious twenty years ago how you felt."

All my resolve not to talk about the past disappeared. I couldn't help it. We'd never spoken about what happened and finally all my emotions were pouring out.

"I didn't, Sam. I did not. We never discussed it and before I knew it – *fingers snapped* - you were gone."

My mind leapt to the injustice of his statement. "You never spoke to me to," I did speaky signs with my fingers, "discuss it."

"You left without a word! You didn't give me time to discuss it."

"But I did. I so, so did."

"I wanted to. But you were gone by then."

"So why didn't you follow me. Kathleen knew where I went."

"Jesus!" he said. "Women!" He sat up and brushed the crumbs from his shirt with force. "Your entire sex should come with a mental health warning."

I didn't lob back the jab pushing itself forward. Those poisonous little vampires of exoneration and vindication had nestled in my consciousness for so long, I knew them all by heart. What was the point of explaining or defending the viewpoint of a younger me? It was all so long ago. *That* Sam was someone else, with her convoluted desire to be desired, her need to be needed.

I remember the first time I kissed him. Inside I had this small, deep-down fear that I had not acknowledged to myself, that our attraction might only exist in my mind. A reasonable fear, but I had been right to think it.

I remember taking a deep breath and leaning over to kiss the lips that I had yearned for often with my eyes. He pulled me close and I tumbled into forever.

I let out a breath I didn't know I was holding and whispered. "Maybe I should have had more faith in us."

"You should have, Sam." His voice was vehement. "You should have."

But I am my mother's daughter. I had known how it felt to need, to want, to crave what the other person could not give. To be ignored and shoved aside. But was that how it really was? Or was it just the hurt and angry tale that my younger self used to tell herself?

My head began to ache. "Rory, I can't do this."

"I know it's hard, Sam. And I'm not bringing it all up to make a point. It's that I…I…" He sat up. "It's that I've been thinking…about…about what might happen if I left my marriage."

I stopped breathing.

"Sam, I don't want you to think…I haven't decided anything."

As if I'd asked him to.

"And your wife? Have you discussed it with her?"

There. That's the first time I'd mentioned her, this woman who has started spending too much time in my thoughts.

"Not exactly, although we have discussed you."

My eyebrows rose. "I imagine you'd have to, with you packing a picnic breakfast for two and heading out here at this time of a morning."

"She didn't mind."

"She didn't mind?" This seemed astonishing.

"She thinks you might need a friend."

"A pity loan of her husband, you mean."

He looked sheepish. "If I'm honest, that's the way I played it with her. But this morning, she asked me not to come."

"And yet here you are."

"Yes. Here I am."

Out on the bluff, seabirds splashed in and out of puddles. The angle of the sun was making each puddle a small mirror, holding the depth of the sky.

"We haven't been right for a while," he continued as I stared at the birds. "Our relationship was always different to yours and mine. Never as..." He searched for the right word.

"Intense?" I suggested.

"Yes. Less intense. Less passionate, which was what I thought I wanted then. She was attractive, clever and good at everything. She was... she is...a good person. Everybody likes her."

"But?"

"Oh Sam. I'm so confused. All of that stands and then there's the kids of course. But our marriage is not what it was. And for the first time in my life I know what I want. Not what my parents want or what the world tells me I should do, or what the family needs from me. What I want for me. I fantasise about it all the time. At work, while I'm putting the kids to bed, all the time."

"And what is it you want?"

"To leave here with you when you go back to Surfers Paradise. To start over and get it right this time."

I pushed down whatever thoughts I was thinking and kept my voice even.

"Does your wife know what you're thinking?"

"Like I said, she's clever. She knows more than I tell her."

That made me laugh, I don't know why. A small sniggery kind of laugh that I didn't like but couldn't help.

"And of course, there's the kids," he continued without commenting on my rudeness. "You see, so many fathers get shut out when a marriage breaks up."

Another laugh spurts out of me.

"Sam, stop it."

I tried but I couldn't. I was laughing so hard, tears were coming to my eyes.

He grabbed my shoulders and kissed me on the mouth. A severe kiss, full of hard feelings and oh yes, something in me leapt to it. My old self. And what a kiss. On it went, all laughter wiped away now. My half-open mouth pressed all I wanted to say into his. You know me...You know me... I shouldn't have left...I want you...I'm afraid...afraid to let myself love you again...afraid you're not mine after all...afraid this is just a whim...not mine...afraid.

Not. Mine.

I stopped.

He stopped.

We looked into each other's eyes, ribs rising and falling over short panting breaths.

"Be mine," he whispered, echoing my thoughts, as he always used to. "Just for one day."

One day, in a vacuum, sealed off from his marriage and everything else. I loved the words coming from his mouth and I loved the sound of him saying them. And then sanity prevailed.

For one day.

I pulled away and stood up, glancing at the watch on my wrist. Where had the hour gone? In two hours, I'd be sitting with Jack and I had to get everything together before meeting with him. In the back of my mind I thought *Damn you Rory for your dreadful timing.*

"Please, Sam," he said, jumping up too, gripping my arms. "Give me something."

That emotion in his voice, in the clutch of his hands – how can I know whether to trust it?

"I can't Rory," I murmured.

"Why not? Don't pretend. I felt that kiss."

"It's not that. You know I have feelings ..."

"Feelings!" His upper lip curled. "Steady on there. Take it easy. Don't go overboard."

I stepped back, right out of his grip. When I was at a safe distance, I looked into his eyes and said, "Yes. Feelings. And I won't be careless with you."

He shoved his fists in his pockets as if he might use them.

"This friend of yours." The sneer on his face made him look like a spoilt child somehow. Ugly. "I think he's simply a boy scout who wishes he had a badge."

I almost laughed because he had no idea what Jack was capable of.

"Are you happy just to keep playing this little game of, *'will we, won't we?'* Because I tell you, I can't stand much more of it!"

A fat duck, startled by his raised voice, took off from the weeds that fringe the water. For a moment it seemed to walk on water before gaining height and lifting its undercarriage.

My heart shuddered, still trembling from our kiss. It would have been so easy to give in, but what I told him was true. And it bothered me that he seemed so ready to cheat on his wife, whether they were having troubles with their marriage or not. One conversation about how bad he felt and ... BAM. But I couldn't get past my uneasiness. And not just of her but of two others. Two small and silent children.

I stood still for a moment, feeling a tense edge of anger. Or remorse. Or some long-denied emotion I couldn't identify. It has always been like that for me. A hesitation before taking the plunge and making a split-second decision that could mean the end of something and the beginning of something else. In that moment of hesitation, I was picturing the faces of his children and it was that vision that made me start to clear the plates and shake out the tablecloth, to fold up the rug and pack away our uneaten food.

Two children, lying in bed, hearing the sound of their mother, distressed with the loss of her husband. Two children feeling their home fill up with betrayals and humiliation. Two innocent children knowing their daddy had left. Gone off, gone away, and left them.

And I would have to count myself responsible for that.

14

———————

I watched Rory drive away up the rutted drive but the anger that was so palpable on his face was not lost on me. I'd forgotten to even ask him what the argument he had with Merrell on the night of her party was about. Jessica was adamant it was Rory, not Sean, and I kicked myself for not asking him the reason for it.

All I could think was how much I wanted to talk to Jack, to have him comfort me, and the realisation of that need for him sent another wave of shock through my soul.

We had a full day ahead of us, I reminded myself, and the last thing Jack needed was a call from me this early in the morning hoping he would ease my distressed conscience. He needed to stay focused and he needed to help me end all this madness so I could go back to my life in Surfers Paradise. I would see him later which meant another meal afterwards at the pub to discuss our findings. Until then, I had an hour to fill and the diary was luring me in to finish it.

Fifteen minutes later, I was sitting in the small kitchen again with a hot black coffee warming my hands and the diary opened up on the bench.

. . .

The Gaol.
> *Wexford*
> *7th October*
> *Dear Peg,*

Thanks for your welcome letter. To answer your questions, there are between forty and fifty of us here in the goal. During the day we're allowed out of our cells and confined to a large dayroom. We pass the time reading, playing cards and our exercise is one hour walking round and round the yard. I'd give anything for a game of football but we're not allowed.

One of our officers is Lieutenant Dan O'Donovan. He likes the title a lot, I can tell you, and takes his duties very seriously. He's getting himself a name as a right hard man. Lucky I don't have anything to do with him.

Thanks for the offers of help. We know you are always there and thank God we do know it. The only thing I ask is that you look after Norah. She doesn't have your strength.

Hoping you're in the best of health. I'll write again when I get the chance.
Your affectionate bro
Barney

Kilmainham Gaol
> *13th October*
> *Dear Peg,*

Well, you will have heard by now that they got me and how. So I am in Kilmainham where the 1916 leaders were brought to die. Could we ever have believed that Irish men would stoop so low?

I am in a ward of nine and each of us takes turns doing orderly for the room. The girls also take their run serving food, washing-up etc. We are forced to hang our washing over banisters to dry, an embarrassment in front of our male warders.

To keep our hands and minds busy, we study Irish, knit or sew and read.

The Staters grow more insolent and shameless with every passing week.

I hope this letter reaches you. We have been told we will be able to get out a stack of letters by a laundry van in a day or so.

Give my love to all and tell them to remember me and write.

Your affectionate friend
Molly

The Barracks
Newbridge
15th October
Dear Peg,
This letter comes from Newbridge where we are put up in the old British Cavalry Barracks. We were transferred two days ago by train. Conditions are not too bad, about twenty men to each room, and we all have a bed and enough blankets. Food unfortunately is not too plentiful.

It was dark when we got here to Dublin and after a long wait we set off again. They didn't tell us where we were going. A rumour went round that we were all being brought to the island of St Helena, where Napoleon saw out his days. Tipsy is here with me as well as Larry Crean, Joe Duggan, Paddy Doyle and the Redmond brothers. All are in good form. Tipsy sends his regards.

The worst is the slander being put out about us. Tell Daddy never to believe any of the stories that are used against us. I know you and Mammy won't.

Take care of yourself Peg. We know the risks you take for us. God bless you.
Your affectionate bro
Barney

Diary 17th November
Barney is home! Escaped from jail! He turned up tonight while Mammy and I were on our knees in the kitchen saying the rosary. I nearly died of fright when two faces, himself and Tipsy, popped up at the window.

Oh, I haven't been so happy and excited in weeks, and neither has Mammy. Since the Staters executed four prisoners the other day, we've been so worried.

I still can't believe what the Free State has come to. Four men taken out and murdered without a trial, without a word of warning, their relatives not even informed. They found out by receiving a telegram. It was meant as a warning that nobody on our side is safe. That's what they are telling us. Nobody. Thank God Barney's out of their grip. We must keep him safe from them now.

They escaped through a tunnel with six others from various parts of the country and then had to walk the whole way back. It was too dangerous to beg for lifts. So, they walked a distance of a hundred and fifty miles across hills and fields.

They've both lost weight from the long trek and from lack of food and their clothes are hopping with fleas and stink. Worse, Barney says, is the rash that makes him itch all over.

They are downstairs now and Barney will go nowhere until he sees Norah. He wrote her a note and I took it down and put it under our stone. Yes, in the pitch dark. Once I did it, he fell into a deep sleep. Hopefully, she'll get to him somewhere, sometime in the morning.

Diary 26th December

What a miserable Christmas Day we had yesterday. I keep comparing this year with last. The bonfires, the songs and celebrations, the vote on the treaty yet to be taken, Dan and Barney coming home from the English prison. This year Barney is absent from our table. Mammy is doing her best not to let on how sick she is. It's Dan estranged and Norah isolated.

We would probably have taken the chance of having Barney here yesterday only a rumour went around that the Army were using Christmas Day to do a big round-up. The lads broke up into small groups and while we were eating our Christmas dinners, he was eating his in a friendly hay barn. In the event, nothing happened.

And to cap it off, Norah never got down to see me. Dan is home for the holiday and she will have to endure her people fawning over him. It's no wonder she hasn't been herself lately.

Diary 28th December

Still no sign of Norah and it very awkward for me to call up her way. I thought about it, even set out this morning in my hat and coat, but I turned back. I could not face Dan if he's still up there on his leave. That I just can't face.

.   .   .

Diary 2nd January

I finally took courage in hand and went up to the O'Donovan's and how I do wish I'd gone sooner. When I didn't see Norah at Mass on Sunday, I knew something was wrong but I thought only of sickness. Up I went to their place.

Norah's mother saw me crossing the yard and came to the back door and then just stood there with a face on her. Norah's little brother John hid himself behind his mother's skirts as if I were a goblin ready to eat him.

'I've come to ask after Norah, Mrs O'Donovan,' I said.

'Have you indeed?'

'I was worried she might be sick.'

'She isn't.'

'Can I see her for a minute?'

'No.'

'I won't keep her long.'

'She's not here. She's gone away.'

'When will she be back?'

She just looked at me, hard, and when I didn't budge, she picked up the sweeping brush that was standing by the door.'

'Norah's got herself a fancy job in Dublin. She left two days ago.'

'But she never said goodbye. And she never mentioned anything about a job to…

'Enough! Now you listen to me, Peg Rooney. We've had as much trouble as we can take from your family. Go home. I don't want to see you or your brother near any of our family again. You should be ashamed to come near this fine house. Get yourself gone before Norah's father comes home, for if he finds you here, he won't be as light on you as me.'

Oh dear mother of God. Would Norah not have told me? That is what I ask myself. If it was me, would I tell her? Please God. Let me be wrong. Let there be another explanation.

Oh, my poor friend. Whatever the truth, I wouldn't have thought less of you. Never.

Diary 9th January

This morning I was feeding the hens when two cold hands came round my face, covering my eyes. I knew straight way who it was. 'Barney!' I cried, delighted first then fearful.

Did he know about Norah? As soon as I turned, I could see he didn't. He was smiling a smile that broke my heart to see because I knew what I had to tell him would wipe it away.

'Come on inside,' I said to him, wiping my hands on my apron. 'I'll put the kettle on. How does a feed of rashers and eggs sound?'

It's been three weeks since I've last seen him but he is grown thinner. And he is filthy from face to foot. 'Have a wash there in the barrel before you see Mammy. She'll think the devil himself come to visit.'

While he washed, I put water on to boil for a proper soak in the tub and got in food from the shop. Then he went upstairs to see Mammy. They held each other in a way neither would have done six months ago.

Over food, he asked, 'What are we at, Peg?'

He let his head fall onto his hand and I knew nothing I might say would reach him. And then I had to tell him about Norah. I took a deep breath and did it.

'Gone to Dublin?' he said. 'That can't be right. She'd never do that without telling us.'

'That's what I said, Barney. But she's gone.'

When he was leaving, I told him I'd see if I could talk to young John, Norah's little brother. 'I'll get a message to you somehow tomorrow.'

Diary 10th January

What a morning. Tipsy arrived before the dawn with a letter from Barney marked 'private and confidential' which he was told to put directly into my hands and no other. Dear diary, I was never more surprised than I am after reading this letter.

I hadn't time to think properly about it because I had to bring Mammy up her breakfast and next thing, while I was up there, four lorry loads of Army boys went honking up through the village. Mammy shook her fist at the window and shouted after them and I laughed because it's been months since she had a shout in her.

. . .

9ᵗʰ January 1923

> *Dear Peg,*

I'm writing this shortly after saying goodbye to you. It's for your eyes only, this letter. Destroy it when you've read it. You'll see why.

I hope you'll soon have news of Norah for me. You know as well as I do that something must be up. We'll get to the bottom of it, never fear. To think of her having to sneak off without telling us is killing me.

And so, I'm writing because I want you to face the truth. I hate having to say this to you Peg, you who has done more than anyone. When everybody else deserted us, you were there, facing the danger, shoulder to shoulder with me. Don't think what I'm about to write now means I don't know it. Don't think it will ever be forgotten.

But dear Peg, I have to tell you, it's all up with us. It's only a matter of time before surrender is called. I know you don't want to hear that but that's the truth of it. We are going through all kinds of hell with this fight and continuing it is nothing but a spillage of blood. The Enemy now knows every man of us. They know what we're planning to do before we know ourselves. Then there's the lack of money. Our arms are a joke, we have hardly any ammunition.

I have to tell you the truth, Peg. I have to tell it to someone for keeping it to myself is driving me half insane. I'm glad, so I am. Surrender can't come soon enough for me. What exactly will happen to me, I'm not sure. Prison, maybe, for a while but as soon as we can, Norah and I will get a nice little house and get married. That's all I think about now. I'll find her wherever she is, if you haven't found her first. Tell her whatever has happened, she shouldn't have run away from us. Her family won't like it of course, but if we have to, we'll go away. I'd give up everything. Anything. It wouldn't matter. And if there's no work in Ireland, then I'll take us to England, or America. Maybe to the bottom of the world in Australia. We'll manage.

It was good to see you today, Peg, to see you so well. It did my heart good. Look after Mammy and Daddy during the coming weeks. What would they do without you, God alone knows.

Like I said, burn this when you're finished reading. You can imagine the trouble if it fell into the wrong hands. God bless you and keep you safe.

Your brother

Barney.

. . .

Diary 10th January

Was it only this morning I got Barney's letter? It was Tipsy who brought the news to me and he was that upset I was hardly able to get out of him what he had come to say. When it dawned on me what he was getting at, I let out a big scream. 'No, Tipsy. No! You've made a mistake. No. You're not right!'

But at the same time as I was denying what he said, I was starting to cry, admitting with my tears that I knew it was no mistake. I'm crying again now as I write this, hard out-loud crying that gets on my own nerves to hear.

Barney is dead, may the Lord have mercy on his soul.. My darling brother Barney is dead.

No matter how often I say it and write it, I can't get myself to believe it.

Barney is dead. We always knew it could happen but I've learned this morning the wide ocean of difference between imagining something and the real living of it.

Barney is dead and they're saying it was his one-time friend Dan O'Donovan who fired the shot that killed him. God help us. How in the name of all that's holy are we supposed to bear this?

15

I stumbled to the beach, cool air fanning the hot tears on my cheeks as the sun dipped behind trees throwing long shadows. Beyond the shoreline, clouds reflected on the dark waters. There were thankfully no tourists yet. It was too early in the season. I walked by the edge of the water, the soles of my boots clinging to the sand, each step lifting with a small, wet smack. White-winged commotions of seabirds flapped up and away as I approached and let my tears run freely.

I knew the trick to stop them was to close your eyes and imagine something else, anything but what I had read. My head felt as if I'd been smacked with a mallet and my jaw ached from the force of my clenched teeth.

There were so many unanswered questions. The diary said Norah was sent to work in Dublin but she had somehow come to Australia with my Nana Peg. Had they come together somehow?

My family's history jumbled together in my mind. When Auntie Norah died, she had requested to be buried in the Rooney/Neil plot, not with the O'Donovan clan. That means she was definitely estranged from them, even to her death. When had they arrived here in Tasmania? Norah's little brother John, mentioned in the diary, was Rory and Sean's elderly grandfather. He had to be. I was sure of it. The time frame fitted perfectly. But did that mean Norah and her family had come to Australia together on the same boat? Had Nana Peg accompanied them? Surely not, after reading how Norah's mother sent her away.

The answer to some of the questions would surely be in the diary and I was eager to get back to it. But first, I had to collect myself, I had to, and finish what Mum had asked me to do.

Jack would be waiting and we had work to do.

Just a couple of more days.

16

Driving the 25 minutes to Hobart brought back so many memories, more specifically Mary MacKillop College where I boarded for all of my high school years. Across the Derwent River via the Tasman Bridge, it was a short drive through Queen's Domain to Liverpool Street and the Hobart Police Station.

Jack had noticed my puffy eyes from the tears I'd shed. His concern was that I didn't want to go to the police station in Hobart but when I told him about reading the diary, he simply nodded and drove in silence.

Once we parked, we hugged our coats around us while we stood looking through the main door leading to the enquiries desk. The corridor's bilious green paint resembled most police stations I've visited.

"Ready?" Jack asked.

I nodded and he held the door open for me.

We waited downstairs for someone to see us and eventually a tall gangly officer, no older than his late teens, ducked his head through a doorway and walked towards us.

"Captain Marshall will see you now," he said, turning and heading back the way he'd come.

He gestured for us to enter a door at the end of a corridor and sitting behind a simple pine desk was an overweight man of about fifty years old with loose strands of greying hair combed over his shiny dome of a head. His uniform was stretched tightly across his ample stomach and two of the buttons I could see were struggling to keep the shirt from bursting open. In contradiction to the softness of Captain Marshall's body, sharp eyes peered out from his fleshy face.

His office was basically a box, furnished with a desk and a filing cabinet. In front of the desk sat two padded chairs and he waved at them for us to take a seat. The walls were covered with photographs and in every one of them, he was shaking hands with a smiling person.

He noticed our eyes travelling over them as he bit into a sticky bun.

"They're my solved cases," he mumbled as he chewed.

A cup of tea rested on the desk beside some files and he lifted it and sipped between more bites.

"I don't have much time," he said, licking his fingers. "I have a briefing in fifteen minutes. We can go to the conference room and talk there if you like. It's more private."

I remained silent, letting Jack take the lead.

"That would be great. Thank you captain."

He shoved the remainder of the sticky bun in his mouth and walked around his desk to the door, picking up a slim file resting on his desk before leading us back down the hallway to another doorway on the right.

The conference room was a stark windowless room with vinyl seats and strip lighting. I instantly wished we'd stayed in his office.

The chief sat down at the end of the table, dropping the file on the table, and gestured to a group of chairs for us to sit as well.

"Now. From your phone call to the station, Ms Neil, you told my officer you and Mr Curtis here, I assume that's who you are," when Captain Marshall raised his eyebrows towards Jack, he nodded, "would like to see the file pertaining to Merrell Neil's murder. This one," he patted the file. "Is that correct?"

"That's correct, sir," Jack replied.

He sat back in the chair and tented his hands over his stomach.

"May I ask why you would want to see the file of a closed case from over twenty years ago?"

He looked steadily from Jack to me, a smile on his face, waiting.

"You were told my mother died recently?" I began.

"I was, Ms Neil. And I'm sorry for your loss."

"Thank you, captain. After the funeral, Mr Rory O'Donovan, my mother's lawyer from here in Hobart, gave me a letter she wrote for me before she died," I explained. "She believed that someone else murdered Merrill, not Sean O'Donovan. She asked me to look into it." I shrugged. "And here we are."

He looked at me disbelievingly and blinked, his eyebrows high on his forehead. "A letter you say? The lawyer Rory O'Donovan? Would he be a relative of the criminal?"

I nodded. "His younger brother."

"Well, let me put your mind at rest, Ms Neil. The case is closed for a very good reason. Sean O'Donovan confessed to the murder. I know you'd like to honour your mother's last wishes, but it's a fool's errant she has put you on. We got our man," he smiled widely.

"We would still like to see the file if we may."

I looked over to Jack. "You know I'm a detective in Surfers Paradise and until a year ago, Jack was my partner. He now owns a very successful private investigation agency of his own in Surfers and he has come to help me."

Jack looked self-consciously at his hands, trying not to smile.

"Has he now?" the chief muttered. "Be it as it may, that doesn't give you the right to question our investigation. I wasn't here at the time of the murder but let me assure you, every detail," he patted the file in front of him, "was considered before the case was closed." His eyes travelled from me to Jack. "And let me state again, Sean O'Donovan confessed to the crime and we have his fingerprints at the crime scene to back it up."

Neither Jack nor I spoke but I knew Jack was biding his time to step in.

Unaware of Jack's intent, the Chief swivelled his chair from side to side, gearing up for a lecture. A squeaking noise filled the air.

"As you know, fingerprint ridging falls into one of three broad patterns: arches, loops, or whorls. Each ridge shows further individuality in the form of endings, bifurcations and dots. An ending is the place at which one ridge stops and another begins. A bifurcation is the place where a ridge splits, forming a Y-shaped pattern. A dot is a segment of ridge so small it appears as, well, a dot. There are often hundreds of these 'points' of identification on one finger. The relationship between each point and the surrounding ridge detail is so complex it is believed no two patterns are exactly alike. Bottom line: fingerprints kick ass for individual ID."

His eyes travelled from Jack to mine, waiting for a reaction. When none came, he continued.

"Early in the twentieth century a French investigator named Edmond Locard observed that when two objects come into contact there is always some exchange of material. Ditto two people. I touch you. You touch me. We share bits of ourselves. The notion became known as Locard's exchange principle."

"Seems obvious in the age of CSI but back then the idea was madly cutting-edge. Today the concept keeps thousands employed in forensics labs around the globe. Hair, fibres, fabric, rope, heathers, soil, biological or chemical substances, whatever. Trace evidence experts identify and compare materials hoping to tie a suspect to a victim or to a crime scene. And the process can be quite high-tech. Are you with me?"

I didn't want to be rude but it wasn't our first time with trace evidence.

"Sounds like they were very thorough," I said trying to diffuse the situation.

"Yes," he nodded. "That's what I'm telling you. Every one of the prints matched with Sean O'Donovan. There was no error."

Jack had been silent the whole way through the speech, and I knew he was harnessing his frustration. Finally, he ran his fingers through his hair before commencing.

"We had a talk with James Russell yesterday, captain. He was one of the detectives who investigated the crime."

Captain Marshall held up his hand to stop Jack from continuing as he flicked through the file. He stopped at a page and scanned it before saying, "That is correct."

Jack compressed his lips together and I could tell his patience was wearing thin.

"Apparently Tim Logan was the head of the fingerprint lab at the time and it was no secret that Logan was barely sober in those days. James Russell told us that most of the time when he showed up for work, he didn't know one end of the microscope from another. That's a quote. And when Mr Russell began comparing his report and the lifts from the scene, he discovered they didn't all match. They were close. But there were several minute differences in some prints."

"Are you seriously questioning the investigation?"

"No. That's not what we're doing," Jack replied. "We just want to go over the details again to honour the request left by Ms Neil's mother. Most of the information from the investigation is available now to the public but not all of it. We'd just like to see the rest."

Captain Marshall nodded. "What are you expecting to find, Mr Curtis?"

"There is probably nothing to find." Jack looked pointedly at me. "And more than likely we will have to come to the conclusion that Sean O'Donovan did actually commit the crime."

The captain nodded, slightly mollified.

"But the motive for the crime has always been that Merrell was leaving to start a new life in Melbourne and Sean O'Donovan didn't like it. But after talking to Ms Neil here," Jack nodded to me, "I think we should be looking at another angle."

In the silence, phones rang outside the office and muffled voices drifted through to us.

"From my experience as a detective," Jack continued, "there is such a thing as a 'half-life of facts'. Over time we know 'true' will become 'untrue'. New technology will make a mockery of the correct truth."

He made speaky signs with the two fingers of each hand, stressing the words 'correct truth'.

"Smoking was once doctor recommended," Jack continued. "Pluto was once a planet. The earth was once flat. Based on these facts, half of what we know about this crime will be proven wrong." He hesitated. "Sometimes when you look too hard at a scene, it leads to a kind of blindness because the images become burned in our minds."

Jack was talking slowly, trying to tread softly around the captain's ruffled feathers without insinuating anything.

"And sometimes, the images will remain there unchanged even when some new piece of evidence appears that should draw our attention. Similarly, the desire to accept the obvious can cause us to ignore details that don't fit rather than to explain them."

"What new evidence?" the captain snapped.

"There's none. I was just making a point."

Jack sat back, straightening his shoulders before he continued. "But from experience, to solve every crime, murder especially, you must have both opportunity and motive. With this case, Merrill leaving Sean and heading to Hobart has always been considered to be the motive." he stated. "But if you think about it, that's pretty flimsy at best."

Captain Marshall had waited for Jack to finish, but his eyebrows had risen high on his forehead questioningly.

"You're going to have to expand on that but I hope you're not suggesting the police were negligent in their duties, MR Curtis."

His eyes had narrowed as he stressed the MR title, letting Jack know he was no longer a policeman and on thin ice.

Jack looked almost serene. He didn't squirm under the gaze. He hardly showed any emotion at all. But his voice was glacial when he spoke.

"And I hope you're not predisposed to ignoring the possibility of a mistake having been made."

Undisguised contempt filled the captain's eyes. He didn't like having his judgment questioned.

"Mr Curtis. How many murders have you investigated?"

"Upwards of ten, I suppose."

Captain Marshall grinned. "Too many to remember?"

Jack stared at the chief for a few seconds before answering. "I remember every last one of them," he replied quietly.

The words hung in the air, heavy as fog. Captain Marshall's eyes softened slightly and dropped to the file. He sighed and patted it with both hands before looking back up at Jack.

"You have five minutes left, Mr Curtis. What is it you actually want?"

"Can you tell me what solid evidence the police had in their possession?"

He sighed again. "It was mostly blood and fingerprints. Spatters from the window, the blood specimens that were taken from the members of the Neil family at the time, and Merrill's blood of course. The duty police retained plaster castings of the shoe prints in the flower bed, and they fit the brand and size of Sean O'Donovan's shoes. There were also envelopes containing evidence collected from Merrell's room: six different hairs that were gathered off her body as well as several fibres, all of which proved to have been from her clothes. Then there were the tyre prints that were collected down the hill from the house. The tracks matched those of Sean O'Donovan as well."

"You're talking about the obvious."

He frowned. "What do you mean?"

Jack hesitated, gathering his thoughts, before continuing.

"If you see a man in the street in a white coat you instantly think he's a doctor. And then you extrapolate. He probably has a nice car, a nice house, a trophy wife. He likes to holiday maybe in Europe."

"What's your point?"

"What are the odds you're wrong about him? One in fifty? One in a hundred? He might NOT be a doctor. He could be a food inspector or a lab technician who happened to pick up a stethoscope that someone dropped in his lab. He might even be on his way to a fancy-dress party. We make assumptions and most times, we're correct. But sometimes we're wrong and that's when we think outside the square. The obvious explanation is usually the best one. But not always."

"What are you suggesting, Mr Curtis? You now have four minutes."

"Sean visited Merrell's bedroom regularly, possibly the night before. His tyre tracks are bound to be there. Plus his shoe prints. That's not conclusive evidence either."

The chief smirked. "What about the confession? Is that conclusive enough?"

"That is something we'd like to look into because apparently he had an alibi."

"Are you talking about his brother's statement that he was with him fishing and drinking the whole night? Tell me you're not suggesting that we should disregard evidence on the supposition that his brother is actually telling the truth?"

"But what if he *was* telling the truth?"

"Why would Sean O'Donovan admit to murder if he didn't do it? Why would he commit himself to life in prison if he was innocent?"

"That is the million-dollar-question," Jack said softly. "Why *would* he do that?"

Captain Marshall closed the file firmly and stood up. "You may read the file but it must be returned before 4 pm this afternoon. Is there anything else?"

"Yes. Are we able to have preliminary DNA tests done on the fingerprints and blood? Purely to exonerate or confirm."

Captain Marshall snorted. "DNA? On a closed case?" He scratched his ear. "That would be lengthy and you'd be throwing money down the drain."

"What if I paid for preliminary tests?" I jumped in.

I'd been quiet for most of the ten minutes but it looked like we had hit a brick wall. In the back of my mind, I already knew the answer would be *no* so somewhere in my brain, I had formulated the plan to pay for it myself. My mother left me more money than I expected and since it was her wish to exonerate Sean, it may as well be her money that helped to do just that.

Jack turned to look at me, surprise on his face. "Are you sure, Sam? It could be costly."

"Very sure," I smiled. "Absolutely."

He nodded and winked at me before turning back to Captain Marshall.

"Do you have the name of a forensic who can help us, Captain Marshall?"

"If you want to waste your money, Ms Neil, it's of no concern of mine. We have the samples here in our vault so I will give you the name of someone we use regularly. He can have access to the samples and since it is your money, he will be in touch with you personally to organise the payment and any other issues that arise. I am very sure that if there is a discrepancy in the outcome, you will share the information with me and we can progress from there."

He passed the file to Jack. "You may get the contact number of our forensic personnel from the duty Sergeant at the enquiry desk. Dr Wagner is his name. If anyone can help you, he is the one. Is that everything?"

"May we also book an appointment to see Sean O'Donovan in prison?"

Marshall gaped at Jack. "Are you serious, Mr Curtis?"

"I am."

He shook his head and harrumphed. "I cannot see the point to that. You may have the existing samples and the contact details for Dr Wagner but at this stage, the answer to your last request is no. There is no point. You may get the results you need from the existing samples so retrieving more will be unnecessary."

He walked around the desk, hitching his pants up unsuccessfully to his belly.

He hesitated as he came level to Jack. "I cannot allow you to visit Sean O'Donovan in prison, Mr Curtis. But depending on the results of the samples, I will re-evaluate whether I can help you any further in the future."

He nodded to Jack. "Now if you'll excuse me, I am late for my briefing."

17

"There's nothing in here that we don't already know," Jack said.

The midday noise from the alley outside the 'Hope & Anchor' was lost on him as he flicked through the pages of the file. People walked in and out of the pub, unnoticed by him, as he turned page after page, his frown deepening after each turn.

Finally, he slapped the file shut and pushed it across to me. "Maybe you'll have better luck. I can't see anything new in there. The file James gave us had just as much information in it. The only good thing about today is we managed to have the samples sent to Dr Wagner for analysis."

He reached across for his beer as I began turning the pages. As he said, James had already given us all this information.

When I glanced up, Jack was staring through the opened door, lost in his thoughts. I watched him in silence as he frowned, then half-smiled, then sighed.

"A penny for your thoughts," I asked.

His blue eyes shimmered in the dimness of the pub and I frowned.

"Are you okay?" I asked, taken aback.

He nodded and smiled. "I was reminiscing."

He stared outside as he spoke. "Did you know I came from Hobart?" he asked, glancing back at me.

I nodded. "When we became partners, I remember you telling me that you lived here until your ex moved to Surfers. That's why you followed her. To be near your daughter."

"You have a good memory," he grinned.

His eyes turned back to the busy alley. Lunchtime crowds were making their way up and down the alley, most holding takeaway bags of food to presumably eat back at their desk.

"I'm surprised at how little it's changed in all that time. I remember the night time skies of Hobart being bright with a light that only comes from brilliant stars."

His eyes travelled around the dimness of the pub and he smiled.

"When I was young, we used to brag that Hobart had the most Irish Pubs outside of Dublin. My father and brother used to join in a marathon pub crawl on St. Patrick's Day to raise money for local charities. Two beers and two shots of Whisky per bar and then they'd move onto the next bar. The idea was to see which man could remain standing long enough to make the circuit that started in Battery Point at 'Irish Murphy', continued through a couple of small pubs on the way to 'Bridie O'Reilly', and then finally, after a couple more on the way back here to the 'Hope & Anchor', back at the start. My father was a hell of a drinker as were most of the Irishmen who signed up for the pub crawl. But in all the years that my father participated, no one ever made it back to 'Irish Murphy'."

"Are your parents still alive?"

His eyes saddened. "No. They've both gone now. And my brother. Adam died in Afghanistan and my father died of a broken heart not long after. Three years after that, my mother lost her battle with breast cancer."

I watched the shadows travel across his face, not wanting to interrupt.

"People talk about dignity in death," he continued. "I'm not so sure I believe them. There was certainly no dignity in my mother's death. They talk about battling cancer and it's nuanced more like a fight. But with her, it wasn't a win or lose thing. She didn't bother to fight it at all. She simply gave up. Her eldest son had died horrifically in a foreign land, her husband died shortly afterwards, and she felt there was little left for her, despite my closeness to her. Cancer took her so fast that I didn't have time to tell her that I loved her or that she had been a terrific mother. I never told her I had enjoyed my childhood or that I forgave her for loving my older brother more than me. And that I didn't blame her. After all, everyone adored Adam. Even me."

A tic pulled at his left eye and a corner of his mouth.

I reached across the table and put my hand over his, letting him know I felt his sorrow. He looked down at it then up at me. "It's fine. Really."

On a platform near the bar, across from a pool table, members of a band adjusted equipment, directed by a woman in black leather pants and Cruella de Ville makeup. Every few seconds we'd hear the amplified tap of her finger, then a count from one to four. Her sound tests barely overrode the TV and the clicks from the pool balls.

Nevertheless, the band looked like it had enough acoustic power to reach Buenos Aires. I suggested we order.

Jack scanned the room and made a hand gesture to a waitress with an out-of-season tan near the bar where two guys were pulling taps, scooping ice and pouring liquor in front of a dingy mirror. Each had pasty skin and lank hair tied back in a ponytail.

The waitress arrived at our table wearing a plastic badge that said 'Tiffany'.

She glanced from Jack then to me.

"What can I get you both?" she asked, her pencil poised over a pad.

"May we have a menu, please?" I asked.

She sighed, retrieved two menus from the bar and slapped them on the table. Then she looked at me with feigned patience.

My decision did not take long. The 'Hope & Anchor' offered nine types of burgers, four hot dogs, all served with a salad and fries.

I ordered the Aussie Burger, complete with pineapple, egg and beetroot.

"Do you still make killer Chilli here?" Jack showed Tiffany a mouth full of teeth.

"Best in town." Tiffany showed Jack even more.

Tap. Tap. Tap. Tap. One. Two. Three. Four.

"It must be hard to wait on so many people at the same time," he said, glancing around at the lunchtime crowd. "I don't know how you do it."

"Personal charm," Tiffany tilted her chin and threw her hair over her shoulder, resting on one hip.

"How's the Walkingstick Chilli?"

"Hot. Like me." A wink and a grin.

I fought a gag impulse.

"I'll go for that. And another round of drinks for us both, please. The same as before." Another mouth full of teeth.

Tap. Tap. Tap. Tap. One. Two. Three. Four.

I waited until Tiffany was out of earshot, which, given the din, was about two steps.

"Nice choice," I said sarcastically.

"One should be nice to the locals."

He looked at me over the rim of his glass. "So. What about the file? What's your thoughts?"

"I hate to admit it but it looks like Mum was wrong," I admitted. "Sean confessed to the crime because he committed it, no matter what she thought. Maybe Rory put the idea subliminally into her head in the first place and she was swept along with the idea."

I sipped my wine as I thought out loud. "One thing I remember well was she was so convinced of Sean's guilt at the time. So why this sudden change of opinion? If you knew my mother, you'd know it's totally out of character for her. She was never one to admit being wrong." I gave a wry smile. "About anything."

"Well, by this time tomorrow, we should have the preliminary results on the DNA. Then we'll have a better idea of what we're up against. But if you want the full spectre, it'll take a lot more money and you'll have to wait weeks for the result."

He put his forearms on the table and leaned forward.

"But before we do that, we have to have a list of everyone at the party," he tapped the file. "Then we contact every last one of them to request a DNA sample from them."

He shook his head.

"That in itself will be an uphill battle because I'd bet anything there'd be precious few who would be willing to give you one. Especially if you say we're using the sample to compare DNA that was collected from a murder scene twenty years ago."

Tiffany arrived with the drinks and I waited until she'd put them on the table and turned back to the bar for the food.

"Even if I was stupid enough to do that, I don't have weeks, Jack," I said. "I'm leaving in a few days, whether we discover anything different or not. The German couple who bought the pub will be here on Sunday and I want to be gone by Saturday at the latest."

Tiffany came back.

"I gave you extra cheese," she purred at Jack, bending low to give him a spectacular view of cleavage.

"I love cheese." Jack gave her another blinding smile. Tiffany stood watching and waiting.

Tap. Tap. One. Screeeeeeeeeech. Two. Three. Four.

Jack's eyes drifted to the band then back at Tiffany.

"Will that be all, handsome?" she smiled at Jack.

"Tomato sauce," I interrupted picking up a fry. "Please."

I avoided the swinging breasts as she reached over to the table behind me, picked up a sauce bottle and put it down with a thump in front of me.

I smiled widely. "Thank you so much."

As I lifted my burger, a cheese umbilicus clung to the plate and stretched all the way up to my mouth. Tiffany sniggered and left.

Fifteen minutes later, the band's deafening version of Lynard Skyard's, *'Sweet Home Alabama"* began and we were weaving our way through the fully occupied tables towards the front door.

As we passed the bar, Tiffany nudged another bartender with iridescent pink hair and called out "See you later, cowboy!"

Everybody laughed except me.

<h1 style="text-align:center">18</h1>

By the time Jack dropped me off at home it was close to 3 pm. Jack wanted to go through the reports from James again, trying to find some differences. We weren't hopeful but you never know. We planned on eating at the Richmond Arms again at 6 o'clock, which gave me almost three hours to myself.

My first thought was to go back to the diary. I was engrossed in it by now, especially since there seemed so little left to read.

I retrieved the suitcase from under my bed and took the diary from it. Five minutes later, I had a much needed cup of tea in my hands and the diary was opened in front of me on the kitchen bench.

Diary 12th January

SURRENDER WE NEVER WILL!

They didn't want us to wake Barney at home. The doctor at the hospital suggested he be brought direct to the chapel in a lidded coffin, to our great surprise. Mammy would not hear of it. Her boy would be waked in his own home, she insisted. Her will, as usual, won the day.

The ambulance brought him out from the morgue and we had the room all ready for him with clean sheets and a candle lit on each side of the bedhead. A statue of Our Lady rested on the bedside table and a font of holy water sat beside her.

The two attendants carried him onto the bed for us on a stretched, leaving the white sheet that covered him in place. After they left, we stood over him, Mammy and me, and found we weren't able to go on. Mammy looked at me, I looked at her, we both looked at the sheet between us, the lumps and bumps rising on it that we knew were Barney's nose and chin, chest and feet.

And the smell! As long as I live, I won't ever forget that smell.

The military gave us a bag with the things they took from Barney's pockets. Mammy asked me to go through it as she was unable. And am I glad she did, for what was in it was notes and letters from Norah, rolled up in string. I don't think Mammy would have been able to stop herself reading those letters if they fell into her hands, and it was good for Norah that they didn't. I put them away where they would not be found by anyone else and will return them to her when I see her. Whenever that will be. Maybe she'll turn up for the funeral? Or maybe she doesn't know that he is dead? That's the worst to think of.

I didn't know what Mammy was thinking but to me it seemed impossible that I could ever peel back that sheet to confront the remains of what used to be my brother. To my shock, Mammy stepped forward and pulled back the sheet.

I heard a strangled sounding cry and realised it was coming from my own lips. His face was twisted, the eyes bulging, showing too much yellowing-white. His jaw was knocked out of line but it was his mouth that was the worst of it, all curled up in one corner into a leer. What could put such a face on a boy on his way out of this life? He looked like a man possessed. We could do nothing but stare at him in horror with all sorts of dreadful thoughts flying through our minds.

Mammy took a shuddering breath and muttered, 'Strip off that coat. Get hot water and soap and a couple of cloths.' I fell to obeying her and while I carried out my tasks, she kept up a long string of talk to him, mumbling why didn't they close his eyes and straighten his jaw.

In any other mouth, it would have sounded like disrespect but from her, it was a strange sort of comfort. With her matter-of-fact words, she brought me back down, made me see that it was nothing but a turn of the eye, a twist of the mouth. Soon enough, we began to see our boy again.

He was wearing the clothes he had on him that day of the shooting, the clothes I had given him. Under the jacket, the jumper and shirt were stuck together with blood and other excretions that were part of the stench emanating from him and getting worse as we stripped him back to the skin. I turned bright red as we took off the last of his clothes and came to his naked person. It didn't seem right that I should ever see my brother like this, though Mammy wasn't making too much of it. Her eyes were on the job and I suppose she had bigger things on her mind than embarrassment.

An attempt had been made to dress his stomach wound in the hospital, but it was still a raw and bloody sight. Once we cleaned all off as best we could, we bandaged the wound as if he were still here with us, then dressed him. The lads had done us proud getting together as good a Republican uniform as they could to muster. A proper pair of britches. A Sam Browne belt. A tall and shiny pair of boots that Mammy cursed over for the difficulty of pulling them over the stiffness of his feet.

We got the job done, lying on his back, rosary beads looped around his dead hands and a couple of candles lighting either side of him. For all our efforts, he still looked tormented, like he was someone to fear.

I heard a noise from behind me and spun around, scared that it could be the military. It was only Tipsy knowing we'd been up all night. He jerked his head, meaning to meet him outside and when I went out, he said he had something for me. In his arms, he cradled a canvas bag like it was a baby. When I asked him what was in it, he opened it to me much as a mother might allow you to peep under a blanket at her child. It was a gun. A Webley pistol. The minute I saw it, I knew what it was. 'Barney's,' I said.

'I thought you might like to have it.'

'It was a good thought, Tipsy. Thank you.'

He took it out of the bag and handed it to me and I felt the weight of its handle heavy in my palm as I fondled the trigger with my index finger. Outside our family, nobody cared about Barney more than Tipsy. That made him dear to us.

When Barney joined the volunteers, back in '17, he kept this gun and a rifle that Mammy bought him under a loose floorboard in his bedroom. As I stood there, I tried to call up his face the way I remembered it that night and I couldn't. I could recall the bright, bursting expression he had on him but not the face itself. I reached for it in my mind — the arrangement of his nose and eyes and mouth, the real look of him. But they were no longer there. They were wiped out by the image of that leering corpse inside my home. Only dead a couple of days and already his features were going from me.

The tears that were only barely held down were welling in me again.

'It's not loaded,' I heard Tipsy say, his voice a long way off.

I was grateful to him for bringing me the gun, knowing how short they were of arms at this time, but he brushed away the thanks. 'One pistol will hardly be missed,' he said, but I knew better.

It was then I heard Mammy whisper behind me. 'This horror will never happen to you Peg. I cannot allow it. I can't survive two dead children. I have to save you.'

She reached out to Tipsy and gripped his sleeve tightly, balancing herself as she leant in close to him. 'You have to save her, Tipsy. Do this for Barney as much as for me.'

My heart did a double-take at the look on her face. 'What are you talking about Mammy?'

Mammy ignored me. 'Take her to Dublin, Tipsy. Put her on a ship bound for somewhere other than this graveyard. Keep her safe and never let her out of your sight until the ship sails over the horizon. I will give you all the money I have in this world because it means nothing to me now. My boy has been butchered but my girl will not leave this world as he did as long as I have breath in my body.'

Neither Tipsy nor I said a word.

'Promise me!' Mammy begged.

'Mammy. You're not well.' I walked towards her to steer her back in to the horror inside. 'Come with me.'

She shook my hands off. 'PROMISE ME!' she yelled at Tipsy.

'I will.' Tipsy had seen Mammy in a state before but never such as a fit like this. 'I will, Mrs Rooney,' he repeated.

Her chest rose and fell, her breath rasping in her throat.

'Well then,' she murmured. 'That's settled.'

'No it's not! I have a say in this and I am not leaving you alone!'

'You will, girl! And don't be talking back to your mother in that fashion. One day, you'll be grateful I saved your life. I've thought this through and it's the only way for you out of this mess.'

The colour was up in her face again and I kept my mouth shut because I didn't have the heart to say anything else to her with her only son lying dead inside our house.

'I have some money put aside and it will be for your passage to Australia. Tipsy will take you to Dublin in a couple of days and you will get on that ship, to be sure you will. You will have a new life and I can go to my grave knowing that I have done my duty as a mother and done everything I could to save you.'

She looked at Tipsy. 'Now you young man, help us take Barney to the chapel. He will lie there for the rest of the day in front of the altar, giving those who wish to see him their last chance to pray for him. Please God the Free Staters will allow us to bury our dead unhindered. If not, you will have a ring of men surround the village, Tipsy, on all roads in case they get any ideas about calling by.'

Mammy was back to herself again. Bossing us all around and taking over. There was nothing left to do but to follow her orders. I will talk to her tomorrow after the funeral.

Diary 13th January

We've just got rid of the last of them from after the funeral. Lama and Andy White were the last to go as usual – I thought they'd never shift.

Never in my life have I felt as tired as I am in this moment but I still can't sleep. Everything that has been said today about Barney is buzzing around in my head as if the words themselves were living things. And buzzing even louder is what's not being said. Nobody mentions Dan O'Donovan, though we all spent the morning wondering whether he would show up.

We are not the only ones spinning from the shock of how my brother died. Many you wouldn't expect to be there at all turned out to honour him. We held our heads high, didn't let our sorrow overcome us, even when Father Ryan made that speech. Who'd have thought he'd turn up so forgiving? It's true what he said. Some things are bigger than the man.

Mr and Mrs O'Donovan were at the church, standing at the back with their younger children, John and Martin, but no Dan, thank God. And no Norah. People say to each other (not to us) that it was brave of the O'Donovans to come, given the circumstances. Behind their fists, they talk about the two who couldn't be there, the two who had most reason: Barney's sweetheart and his old comrade, Dan.

The secret of Barney and Norah's love affair is known to all now, common knowledge, passed around like an unaddressed parcel, together with recollections of what happened to James Tracey and Nellie Shiels two years ago, when the Shiels boys tarred and feathered James' private parts and Nellie was sent away to England to an aunt. They're saying it's not unusual for the menfolk of a family to set upon a young man, if he's thought to be interfering with a girl of theirs. That it's not unknown for such a young man to have the life near beaten out of him. That such might have been in Dan's mind when he fired the shot that killed my brother.

The burial was the worst. Desperate altogether. It was I who let the volley off over the grave, using his own gun, three shots of promise and warning. I didn't flinch from the task. I kept my eyes open as I let the fire and didn't screw up my face to one side as I have seen others do. Oh, the sounds. The three loud cracks from the Webley. The cry Mammy let out of her as the coffin went into the ground. The thud of the first sods of clay hitting the wood. The chant of the prayers, breaking over the headstone to meet the sound of the sea itself below.

Diary 15th January

I'm shaking so hard I don't know if I'll be able to write this and it's more than a day since it happened. He came down to us, down to the shop and into the grocery. What he would never do in the days we were supposed to be courting. Today he did, without a by-your-leave. I was in the shop when the shopbell went. When I turned and saw it was him, in his hateful uniform, the weight and width of him filling the whole doorframe out, I nearly dropped the bottle of milk I was holding. My heart did such a wallop. Mammy was behind me, bristling like a feral cat so I stepped back and took my place beside her.

In fairness, he didn't enter with any bullyboy tactics, just took off the military cap and said all formal: 'I'd appreciate five minutes of your time.'

What he wanted quickly became evident: that we would, as Rooneys, influence the Republican troops – tougher than ever since Barney's death – to call a halt to activity. Mammy said immediately we'd do no such thing and launched into an explanation, which he responded with the evil intentions of The Free

State Army, how they intended to execute all those who go against them, especially ringleaders.

Mammy said it should fill him with shame to stand there in that uniform and say such things and then they were off, both yelling about the sorry year we've all just put in, the rights and the wrongs, the ins and the outs, with one of them saying black was white and the other the opposite.

The next thing I knew Dan was putting his hat back on and retreating. 'You're right, Mrs Rooney. Of course you are. Everything you say is right. You must be happy with the outcome thus far and you'll be only over the moon with what's coming. Enjoy it all, then. I bid you both good day.'

And out he went.

'Yes! Get out!' Mammy shouted after his back, so loud I'm sure the men in the bar heard her. 'And don't show your face in here again.'

I ran for my coat.

'Where are you going?' She looked alarmed.

'He needn't think he's going to get away with that,' I said to pacify her, but that wasn't my thought at all. He had come to us and Mammy had blown it. He had come to us, and that felt like an opportunity to me, though for what I wasn't sure. Norah? Persuasion? Resolution? Maybe, maybe. I wasn't sure. All I knew was I couldn't let him go like that.

When I caught up with him by Duggan's, he didn't look at me, just carried on walking in a temper down towards the sea, but I knew it was okay because he slowed his pace a small bit so I was able to keep up. We took the old way down to the back strand, across to the shoreline, then westwards where fewer people go. We needn't have worried, only two crazy people would be out on the day that it was, freezing cold and with a sharp wind that didn't look too strong but would whip the ears off you.

We met no one and were up nearly as far as the old cemetery before he'd calmed down enough to say, 'Thanks for following. It was you I went to see anyway, not her.'

'Nobody wants any more bloodshed, Dan. But that will need both sides to give in, not just one.'

'You had the power to prevent all this from the start, Peg. Do you never stop to think on that? God Almighty, Peg, it wasn't like you didn't know where lazy talk of honour and principles led. You saw that young lad in Enniscorthy.'

Denis Heffernan, with the sky in his pale eyes. The cry of his mother up to the same dead sky.

Dan was still talking. 'You were a good person, Peg, I thought that would stop you in your tracks. That was your warning from God. But no. Hyenas in petticoats.'

'Hyenas? What?'

'That's what the men call you. Even on your own side.'

'Hyenas in petticoats?' I repeated.

'A woman's job is to care and nurture. It's the greatest calling there is on this earth, but Republican females want to be men instead.'

Hyenas in petticoats. He'd shocked me to silence with that one. Were we as misguided, as ugly, as ridiculous as that? Every bit of my body was enraged by this slur. I wanted to think about it, what he was saying about goodness and nurturing and caring, which I did think of as the finest calling, which was what I had thought I was doing with Barney and the boys. But if that was right, why had it all gone so wrong? I couldn't think it all through in front of him and his certainty.

What I didn't want was to get into an angry argument. That, I was positively sure, would solve nothing.

So I swallowed the insult. I let it go. 'Dan, I would like to see Norah,' I said. 'I'd like to visit her, wherever she is and let her know that we have not deserted her.'

'Jesus, you've a nerve, woman. I'm not going to bargain over peace using my sister.'

'That's not what I meant.'

'Norah is where she can come to no more harm from the Rooneys or anyone else. That won't be changing no matter what happens with the Irregulars.'

'Dan, it's me. I would never, ever hurt Norah. You know that.'

'Do I?' he said, in a voice I'd never heard from him before, soft and quiet as a flick knife.

'What's that supposed to mean?'

'You won't even admit to how your family has hurt her already.'

Was he saying what I thought he was saying?

'And,' he went on quickly when he saw I was about to speak, 'that lying story of yours that's making the rounds, that'll be remembered long after you

and I are gone, that make out that I killed Barney. Do you think I don't know what those boys of yours are claiming? Only it's all twaddle. And you lap it up and spew it back out, though...'

'Oh God,' I groaned, but he went on.

'Though you weren't even there so how do you know what happened. The truth is, if they had surrendered that morning, as they said they would, there would not have been one shot fired. And the shot that killed him was not fired by me. I never even saw him.'

'Oh God,' I whispered.

'What you can't face is that you are the ones to blame for his death, not me. You and your mother and my sister, twisting his head round till he didn't know what he thought himself.'

'Stop Dan.'

'You're at fault as much as the man who shot him.'

'Please.'

'Your mother especially. She knows it too, under her bluster. She'll see her last days out in torment over what she has done.'

'Dan. Stop.'

'As if you are the only one with feelings.'

'Do you mean you grieve him?'

'Jesus, girl, he was my best friend.'

Eyes the colour of a summer's morn, two big jewels of blue, looked at me like I was some class of a dunce.

'I bowed my head. 'I'm sorry, Dan. Truly I'm sorry.'

He let off then. 'Thank you Peg. It means a lot to me, so it does, to hear you say that.'

We did more talking but that was the gist of it. He explained how my determination to accuse him of Barney's murder had gotten back to his commander. And now he was in trouble and not sure what was to become of him. Unless I wanted more anguish to come to him and Norah, I was to leave them alone and try to make amends. He turned and walked away while I swallowed the tears.

My eyes felt tired and scratchy from reading the faint print. I glanced at my watch. 5 o'clock. I had enough time for a shower and a hair wash before meeting Jack again.

I put the diary back in the suitcase and pushed it safely back under the bed. There was very little left to read but the rest could wait until tonight.

Right now, I needed a drink and something to eat.

19

WEDNESDAY, 24TH MAY

The next morning, while I walked to the supermarket for coffee, Dr. Wagner's assistant left a message to say they had concluded the preliminary tests and he wanted to talk to me this afternoon at 2 pm. I called Jack and suggested he meet me at the house, offering to put together something other than the usual fish and chips we'd been consuming most nights at the pub. He was happy to meet me and suggested we meet at midday.

Right on time, he walked through the back door into the small kitchen carrying a bag of groceries.

"I come bearing food," he grinned.

I looked down at the items as he emptied the contents onto the kitchen bench. Sliced ham, potato salad, a green salad mix with a punnet of cherry tomatoes and a bottle of wine. Nothing I could ruin. My ex-husband told me many times I could make anything look like dog food and that Gordon Ramsay would have a fit if he witnessed anything I cooked.

"I assumed you wouldn't have much in the way of food in the house since you plan on leaving this weekend so I bought a couple of things just in case."

I looked down at the items, annoyed with myself for not thinking of this.

"This is perfect," I smiled. "But I warn you, I can ruin anything."

"It only means emptying the food onto plates but let me do it, just in case. You open the wine and find some glasses. Do you have any plates?"

There was very little left in Mum's pub and I suddenly wondered who had removed most of the items. Probably Kathleen, being endlessly efficient.

I turned to an overhead cupboard where I knew there was an assortment of crockery and found two chipped dinner plates.

"This is the best I can do. And as a bonus," I grinned producing two forks and two knives, "we don't have to eat with our fingers."

An hour and a half later and one empty wine bottle resting on the table, my phone rang. I handed it to Jack as I removed the plates to the sink.

"Good afternoon, Dr Wagner. This is Jack Curtis and Samantha Neil is here with me. You are on speaker."

"Good afternoon, Mr Curtis and Ms Neil," came the voice over the phone.

Jack was almost sitting on the edge of his seat. "Were you able to make use of the samples provided by the police?" he asked.

"Oh, most definitely, Mr Curtis. We were provided with small amounts but that's all we need these days. Technology has progressed amazingly over the past ten years or so."

Jack nodded. "And you had enough time to produce some results for us?"

"Indeed, I did."

Jack nodded. "Then please, go ahead."

"I have quite a bit to tell you," Dr Wagner said, "but it will probably make the most sense if I explain my results in order in which I performed the tests."

He cleared his throat. "Remember, Mr Curtis, I described a very basic testing protocol. The first step in order to do things properly, was to confirm that the blood at the Neil home had come from Sean O'Donovan. Given the age of the fingerprints and the blood samples and the likelihood of contamination, we said we would try a more involved testing. All of that takes time and money. Authorities are always reluctant to spend money on cases that have had convictions, such as this. What I have done is a very basic test."

"We understand, Dr Wagner. Thank you." Anticipation oozed from Jack. "Do you have anything to tell us?"

"Yes. In this case, the specimen contamination was a considerable risk. That's one of the many reasons to look first at the Y chromosomes because females at the scene present no chance of contamination. We know Sean O'Donovan had spent time in Ms Neil's room so I thought it would be helpful to have the X chromosome, the female, sequenced first. Then we sequenced the Y chromosome. When you do a DNA analysis, you don't know precisely what cells you are analysing. It may look like a blood drop to the naked eye, but even a single skin cell from someone else can show up in the results."

A glass tinkled over the line in the break, and I realised Dr Wagner was taking a sip of water.

"Ok. If we have a specimen large enough to test in several regions, it's very helpful to understand what the DNA of a possible contaminating cell looks like, to understand a variation in results. With a father and son, you expect the same Y sequence. And it was fortuitous that we did because our results how that Sean and Merrell are in fact genetically linked."

Linked? What did he mean 'linked'? In the silence, the veins at my temples throbbed and my vision wavered.

Beside me Jack looked as stunned as I felt. He was the first one to recover but even so, his voice sounded shaky.

"This is from the broken glass, is that correct?"

"That is correct," Dr Wagner assured. "We matched it to the prints on the glass beside the bed with Merrell Neil's prints. There is no doubt. There is a definite link. But there is one more item to add this report."

"I hope it's not as stunning as the first surprise," Jack muttered.

Dr Wagner laughed softly. "I'm not sure. There were more than two samples of blood collected at the scene and looking solely at both chromosomes, I got another result. Both Sean O'Donovan and Merrell Neil have blood type O. But this other blood collected is blood type B. It was only a speck and was easily missed because of that reason."

Dr Wagner stopped for a second, before continuing. Paper rustled in the background and I assumed he was turning pages.

"Despite the small sample I have, I am positive it's not from either of the other samples taken. You can be sure that we examined all samples many times to be absolutely certain. But we found the same result each time. All the blood on the broken window came from Sean O'Donovan but the small splatter of blood on the wall came from a woman. And not Merrell Neil. Another woman."

I felt icy cold.

"Are you certain?" I asked, stunned.

"As sure as Madonna's lost virginity."

"There was another woman in her room that night?" I repeated stupidly.

"There was," he replied.

20

"Kathleen?"

I still couldn't believe it! My heart was pounding and the reflection in the mirror showed a shocked face with dark circles surrounding the eyes.

A link, Dr Wagner had said. But how close? And if there was a link between Sean and Merrell, the logical conclusion was there had to be a link between all the O'Donovans and the Neils.

Sean and Merrell. Rory and me.

There were so many questions to ask and the only one who could possibly know the answers was Kathleen.

My head swam in confusion. What link? Was this the cause of the rift between our families for all these years?

"A first!"

Kathleen's words were light enough and I imagined I could hear a trace of her smile. "You calling me instead of the other way around. Can you imagine?"

There it was. The usual barb buried in the softness of her voice.

I ignored it and went straight to my question.

"Kathleen, did you know of the link between the O'Donovans and the Neils?"

The sharp initial intake of breath said everything I needed to know.

"You knew!" I stated.

"Was it in the diary?" she whispered.

"YOU KNEW? You actually knew and didn't tell me? Was I the only one who didn't know?"

"Calm yourself, Samantha. You would have been told on your 21st birthday like we all were. But it was you who chose not to be here with your family on that occasion."

"Don't you turn this around, Kathleen! Don't you dare! This isn't some trifling thing."

"As well I know."

I heard a sigh from her end.

"I was told on my 21st birthday as was Merrell. She was told the morning of the party."

I was shaking my head in denial.

"Merrell knew? It's true? We're related to the O"Donovans?" I whispered.

There it was again. A hesitation from her.

"We share blood. Yes."

In the background, Jack was pacing back and forth between the sink and the fridge. Three paces, turn, three more, turn. It was like watching a guardsman on a battlement.

Suddenly, he stopped pacing and walked to the door.

"I'll see you at the Richmond Tavern for dinner," he called out as he opened the door, ready to leave. "I need to think this through."

I nodded and turned back to Kathleen. Outside, the sound of gravel hitting the side of the house sounded like a machine gun as Jack sped down the road.

"How, Kathleen?" I dragged my attention back to the phone. "Where is the link?"

"How did you find out, Samantha?" she asked, ignoring my question. "Rory told me at the funeral you would be given a suitcase with photos and letters to sift through. For the life of me I have no idea why Mum thought to give it to you and not me. I was the one who stayed with her until her dying breath. I was the one who supported her and helped in the pub. Where were you? Off to Queensland. Oh but no. She had to give it to you."

"You can have the bloody suitcase if that's what you want! I never wanted it in the first place."

I was shouting now. All the anger and pain welling up inside and spilling out in a rush.

"I don't want it, Samantha. It's yours."

The petulance that was usually mine could be heard now in Kathleen's voice. Was she jealous? The realisation stopped me short.

"How did you find out, Samantha?" she asked quietly, her anger spent.

"From the Pathologist." My voice cracked with emotion. "He found blood splatters on the glass door which were Sean's. No surprise there. But his comparison between all the blood came up with this blood link between Sean and Merrell. As well as that, he found another small drop of blood on the wall that came from someone other than them both."

"Another person? On the same night?"

"Yes. With a different blood group."

"What does that mean?"

"It means someone else was in the room that night and it's enough to put doubt on the verdict."

"But he confessed. Sean O'Donovan said he did it."

"And he may have but there's this other drop of blood that clouds the issue."

I wanted to get away from this and return to the link.

"Kathleen, what did Mum say to you on your 21st birthday?"

She sighed. "She told me the blood link comes from Nana Peg's days. Nana Peg had died by this time but Mum was still reluctant to say too much."

She was being deliberately evasive. She knew something she wasn't telling me.

"Surely there's more to it than that. There has to be."

"I can't talk now. I'll come down on the weekend and we can talk about it, face to face. I can't now. Rianne is due to be picked up from school and I look a fright as it is."

"I want to be leaving by this weekend, Kathleen. The Germans are coming to pick up the keys."

Her voice was firm. "I can't talk now, Samantha. I'll see you on Saturday. In the meantime, read the diary. Nana Peg put everything in that diary apparently. If there's anything to be learnt, that's where it will be."

Then she hung up and was gone.

I ran upstairs, grabbed a coat, and headed back downstairs. I needed to talk to Jack about this.

21

JACK

My phone rang and Frank Fitzroy's gravelly voice greeted me when I answered.

It was a little early for diners in the restaurant so there was no problem with people at close tables being disturbed by his booming voice. Even though it was over the phone, his voice still reverberated in the relative quietness of the room.

I'd decided to sit quietly and think in the restaurant with a pint of Boags in my hand rather than sit in the cramped confines of my hotel room. I'd only walked in the room when my phone rang.

My eyes swept the room, looking for a secluded table, and I walked over to the table where Sam and I sat last night. I pulled out a chair and sat down while I talked to Frank and waited for Sam to arrive.

"How've you been, mate?" he asked.

His voice was still throaty as if his larynx had been damaged for years. Despite our obvious differences, Frank and I have become friends over the past couple of years. One of my few friends, if I was being honest, and I'd learned to ignore his ears that stuck out like handles, his crooked teeth, his piggy eyes and the scars from stitches across his jawline. Frank was a rough diamond who had helped me when I really needed it.

"Hanging in there, Frank," I replied, not bothering to hide the smile in my voice. I was surprised at how happy I was to hear from him.

"How are you and the animals getting along?" I asked.

Frank was staying in my house and looking after the dog I'd only just adopted and Sherlock my cat. The dog I knew would be easy. But Sherlock. Well, that's another matter. He was a rescue from the RSPCA and he came with the attitude of Paris Hilton.

"We're bonding, mate. I've got a talent for it, by the looks ov it. Did you fink that would 'appen when you aksed me? I found me forte." He drawled the word *forte* out, making it sound more like *four tay*.

"Funny the way things work out, ain't it?" he said. He gave a snort that I imagined was supposed to be a laugh.

Everything about Frank was relaxed. But from experience, his brain was firing. He had a reputation for violence but I'd never seen it. He was the kind of guy to whom other lowlifes refer to as having 'smarts' but I'd never subscribed to the theory of comparative intelligence where petty criminals were concerned. So the fact that Frank's peers considered him a sharp operator didn't impress me much.

"So to what do I owe the pleasure, Frank?"

"Ooh. La-di-da," he snorted again. "Going all posh are ya with that policewoman? Trying to impress 'er, are ya?" He tasked a couple of times. "You're taking your time about it, mate. But maybe you're just not as pretty as me."

He snorted again and added, "Don't go telling 'er about Sandra Burton up 'ere, will ya, or you'll be right screwed."

Don't get the wrong idea. Sandra Burton is a heavy-set woman with greying hair pulled back into a ponytail with eyes the colour of freshly brewed coffee. She is the secret I'm keeping from Sam because Sam was on the money when she asked if my new occupation was to do with vigilantism.

Sandra ran a secret organisation with people working for her who handled situations involving degenerate men who abuse children. She and her people take matters into their own hands when the police have their hands tied. She actively works to uncover these men, people high up on the food chain, who think they are so smart they can lure young boys into online chat rooms with nothing but perverse and disgusting intensions.

I'm not a hit man. But I know how to destroy careers. And so does Sandra. In a secret room behind a video game parlour, she has four men who infiltrate chat rooms disguised as young teenagers. They sit behind monitors and participate in the chats and more often than not, they uncover someone who is doing the same, only their purpose is to harm not defend.

And Sandra asked me to join her organisation.

I'm not one for theatrics or even feeling much of what might be labelled astonishment. I have seen a lot in my forty-plus years. I have killed and I've nearly been killed. I have seen depravity that most would find difficult to comprehend and I have learnt over the years to try and control my emotions and reactions during stressful and volatile situations. These qualities have saved me from time to time. But when she asked me, I was shocked. Not just because she asked *me*, an ex-policeman, but because I was considering it.

What I did know was it would change everything for me forever if I accepted. My principles. My morals. My rules. My life. And I would have to keep it a secret from everyone I knew. Especially Sam. Not just because she was a policewoman but because I didn't want to lose her presence in my life. I instinctively knew she would not be able to accept my new line of work.

In the end, after much thought, I accepted and I have never regretted that decision.

A hissing sound bounced through the phone as Frank sucked air in through his crooked teeth.

"And talking ov Sandra Burton. She rang me and aksed if we were innerested in a job she has goin'. I said I'd call you and get back to 'er. So, Jack, me old darlin'. What do you say? You wanna do this job for 'er or do still want to consort wif prostitutes. Do they give you vouchers to redeem later instead of payments these days?" he chuckled. I had to stop myself from laughing as well.

I could see him sitting in my lounge room brushing dandruff from the shoulders of his badly-fitting suit as he guffawed and rearranged himself via a trouser pocket.

Thankfully he interrupted my visions. "How long are ya gunna be down there with sugar lips?" he asked.

That was my dilemma. I'd promised Sam I'd help her find the person who murdered her sister, if in fact it turned out that Sean O'Donovan was innocent, and I didn't want to leave until we'd done that. This DNA result put a definite spanner in the works.

"I'm not sure, Frank. Another couple of days, at a guess. Sam wants to leave here by the weekend in any case and we're close to a solution," I lied.

I filled him in on what we were doing, explaining about Sean O'Donovan who had spent twenty years of his life in prison for a crime he may not have committed. I explained about the slipshod initial investigation and about the findings from the DNA lab.

"A blood splatter from anuver woman, you say? How many people did she 'ave in the blasted room with 'er that night? Sounds like the party up there, not just downstairs." He snorted. "Know wha' I mean?"

He coughed, a phlemy sound that sounded like Sherlock coughing up a fur ball.

"And all of this happened, wha', twenny years ago, you say?" he continued as if he hadn't coughed up a lung. "How does anyone remember fings like tha' from so long ago? I suppose if it's important like, but jeez, twenny years?"

I blinked, thoughts crashing around in my head. A thrumming sound echoed in my ears as my heart began to race. My breath suddenly caught in my throat and my stomach felt like there were 100 snakes in there and all of them fighting to get out.

All of a sudden, I knew.

Memories can be distorted. Memories can change the colour of a car. Or change the shape of a room. They're like clouds you can't see through. Like smoke in the air obscuring everything.

But this was different. I was absolutely positive I knew. Why hadn't I seen it before? It was all there. Disparate facts jostled. Pieces. Photos. Evidence.

But proving it was going to be the problem.

22

SAM

Jack was on the phone when I walked into the restaurant. He was sitting at our regular table, drumming his fingers on it, his face serious.

I walked over and he put his hand over the mouthpiece and mouthed, 'Frank'.

I pulled a face as the tinny voice of Frank drifted over to me from Jack's phone.

"Do you want a drink," I whispered.

He mouthed, "You're an angel," and nodded. "Boags."

By the time I got back to the table, Jack was finishing up his call with Frank.

"I'll call later tomorrow, Frank. Take care."

He pressed the stop button and placed the phone on the table, face down.

"Sorry about that. Frank checking up on me."

"I seriously don't know how you get along with that man."

Jack smiled. "He's alright when you get to know him."

He lifted the beer, muttered his thanks, and took a long drink.

"Ah. I needed that," he muttered. He wiped the froth from his top lip and said, "My shout for dinner."

"You're on," I grinned.

"So, what did Kathleen have to say?" he asked.

I frowned angrily. "She knew about this link. She was told on her 21st birthday as was Merrell. But she's not saying anything else. She's hiding something, Jack. I know it. I know my sister and there's something she's not telling me."

Jack put his beer down on the table slowly.

"I know this evidence of a link between Sean and Merrell," he hesitated, "obviously means there's a link between you and Rory. And it's like a bomb dropping on your world. I understand that."

His gaze was intent, watching my reaction.

"But the other issue you should be looking at is the fact that there was a drop of blood from someone else in that room. That means someone else besides Sean was there that night. A woman. And perhaps it was that woman who killed Merrell, not Sean."

I felt like the roof was falling in on me. It was too much to take in.

"So why did Sean confess to the crime?" I asked bewildered.

"Maybe he thought he *did* kill her." Jack shrugged. "He was there, no doubt about it. His blood is on the glass from the broken window. And we know he hit her hard enough to leave a bruise on her cheek. Maybe her head hit the bedhead when he hit her." He shrugged again. "Then the next day, he hears that Merrell was found dead in her bed from a head injury. And he assumes he did it. What else was he to think?"

Jack leant his elbow on the table with his chin resting on his fist. I'd seen that look so many times when he was my partner. His concentration was incredible and legendary.

"Let's go over this from the start, okay?" he said. Deep creases were making furrows between his eyes as he concentrated. "From the party onwards."

I nodded. "Okay. From what Kathleen told me this afternoon, Merrell was told this family secret on the morning of the party. Her 21st birthday. Kathleen was told on her 21st as well but I missed out because I left home at eighteen."

My voice cracked and I cleared my throat before the rising tears filled my eyes.

Jack spoke softly. "Can we assume that, at the party, Merrell told Sean?" he asked.

I nodded. "I'd say that's a given. They had some sort of falling out, so Jessica says, and Sean and Rory left the party while Merrell spent the rest of the evening dancing with everyone and anyone. She basically ignored him the whole time he was there. Which was strange now that I think about it. Because she was seeing him on the sly. Much like I was seeing Rory behind every one's back."

Jack nodded. "That backs up what Jessica said as well. And let's not forget Rory in this, Sam," Jack reminded me. "According to Jessica, Rory and Merrell had an argument at the party as well."

He took a sip of his beer and looked at me over the top of the glass.

"I'm going to say something you won't like."

"I don't like any of this," I scoffed.

"I know, but this…" he began, then he sighed. "What if Rory knew this secret? Sean could have told him. Then he confronted Merrell. She confirmed it and they argued. Jessica was a witness to that argument."

Memories of Rory suddenly popped into my mind. He avoided me for weeks after the murder before I finally left home for good. I'd tried so hard to contact him but he dodged me every time. In the end, I left Richmond and my family behind without even saying goodbye to him. There just wasn't an opportunity. I'd assumed he was ashamed of his brother killing Merrell. But what if it was because he knew about this link?

I blinked in shock and murmured quietly, "That fits."

What was even worse about Rory knowing is the fact that he is still hiding it, with his hair-touching and his 'never say never', and 'you haven't changed a bit routine.' He'd had time to come to terms with this link but it was fresh and raw to me and it seemed almost like yet another betrayal from him. Giving him the benefit of the doubt, perhaps he thought I knew. But if that were true, then why hadn't he at least mentioned it? He'd had opportunities. He'd tried to seduce me over scones and coffee but still there no mention of a secret. Not even testing the waters to see if I knew.

This 'new' Rory was someone I'd never seen before. And it shocked me. This man, the one I thought I would die loving, was willing to cheat on his wife and use me with no consequences afterwards on his part.

In my head, I heard his words from that morning. *'Be mine, Sam. Just for one day.'*

Just for one day.

'My wife doesn't understand me.'

What a cliché! How stupid could I be? Jack was right. Rory was a shark in shoes.

Jack's voice brought me back from my reverie.

"Rory must have had some idea that Sean was guilty. He supplied Sean with a false alibi for two weeks until Sean's conscience got the better of him and he confessed."

I could only agree. "He won't want that to get out, even though it was twenty years ago."

I sat in silence, spinning my glass on the table but I could feel Jack's eyes on me.

"I've been doing a lot of thinking, Jack, since I came back. What with this diary and Merrell's murder and Rory," I gave a wry smile. "I've realised what I felt for Rory was just puppy love."

I looked up at Jack. His eyes were still on me, travelling all over my face. Suddenly, I couldn't stop talking. Words poured out and everything I've been feeling tumbled out.

"My feelings were so strong, it actually hurt," I smiled wryly. "And I've held that emotion in my heart for twenty years as a guideline to what love is. It kept me from having a real relationship with my ex-husband James." I shook my head. "That marriage didn't stand a chance, which is why it only lasted a couple of years."

I swallowed noisily, trying to rid myself of the lump in my throat. I'd done so much crying since coming home.

"In a way it's good I've come back. It's opened my eyes to a lot of things. Love isn't all about passion. Love is being there for someone when you need them. It's the arms that hold you when your world feels like it's falling apart. It's about comforting words that soothe and calm and it's the strong, silent support you give to someone who means more to you than life itself."

As I spoke, my heart gave a little jolt. I suddenly looked up at Jack.

His gaze, which had not wavered from me, held the gravitational force of the moon and the tides. And I couldn't look away.

Then suddenly, it hit me. He was feeling the same as me. He always had. And he was as scared as I was. If I continued, within a few seconds, our lives could change forever. Falling in love had such an element of mortal terror for both of us. It had never worked out for either of us in the past and I didn't want to lose the best, the only good friend, I had.

But I knew Jack. He would never make the first move. Never be the one to cross that boundary. Maybe because he didn't know what was on the other side but maybe because his life now, as it was, was as uncertain as mine.

For most of my life, I'd dreamed of Rory in my arms. When the angry voices in my home became unbearable, it was Rory who had comforted me. He was my sun, my moon and my stars. But twenty years ago that ended and as Jack had said, you can never go back. Especially now. And if I was truly honest with myself, I didn't *want* to go back.

"What satisfies you, Jack?" I whispered.

His forehead creased in a frown and he hesitated and sighed before answering. His eyes never left mine.

"My life is very simple, Sam. My satisfaction comes from having dinner with someone special. I am satisfied when a project I am working on is completed and I'm happy with the result. Satisfaction is knowing that I am making a difference when there seemed to be no hope."

His chest rose and fell. "My life is smaller now than it was and in that simplicity, I no longer feel committed to any grand enterprise." He blinked slowly. "I can't be disillusioned anymore."

"Are you happy with that simplicity?"

"It keeps me sane, Sam."

The weight of the world came through in his sigh.

"I've had a wonderful career but it took me to places I never want to go again. Dark places where evil people walk around doing evil deeds that never go punished."

He turned to look out the window, and I could see he was uncertain if he should continue.

"When I was little, my mother used to read nursery rhymes to my brother and me. One of the ones I hated the most was Humpty Dumpty. It's a very scary poem. Humpty falls over the edge and breaks into a lot of pieces and no one knows how to put him back together again. Not all the king's horses or all the king's men. No one. Nobody wants to think there's anything in the world that could fall apart as badly as that. Right then, I was Humpty Dumpty. I felt broken beyond repair. And when you feel yourself begin to go over the edge, all you can do is hang on as hard as you can to your mind."

He swallowed loudly as he turned back to me, his eyes showing a depth of sadness I'd never seen before.

"I am trying to fix all that, Sam," he almost whispered.

I wanted to touch his face to comfort him as he'd comforted me.

"This new venture you're speaking about, is it the one you mentioned a few days ago?" I asked.

He nodded. "That's right."

Thunder rumbled in the silence.

"And this is what brings you satisfaction?"

He hesitated. "It does."

"Are you lonely, Jack?" I whispered.

Did I want an answer?

His eyes focused on me as they shone silver in the dim lighting.

"Given enough time," he began, "you convince yourself that loneliness is something better than a dismal relationship. It's even a kind of freedom. Once convinced, you are reluctant to open the door and let anyone in. You risk the equilibrium and tranquillity you call peace."

The words were spoken softly and carefully.

"But yeah," he nodded. "I'm lonely. But I bury myself in my work and that's enough to push the loneliness away." He smiled sadly and winked. "Sometimes."

He slapped his hands on the table. "Come on, let's eat," he said, changing the subject with a smile. "My shout, remember."

I wasn't feeling hungry. There'd been too much emotion in one day for me. The report in Hobart was disappointing and the diary entries were leaving me drained and delated. Plus we were no further along into the investigation than when we'd started. The only new piece of information was the DNA results from Dr Wagner and that was the only thing holding me back from suggesting to Jack that we stop.

While we had one last drink each, I moved a Caesar salad around my plate while Jack half-heartedly ate a burger.

The last I saw of him, he was walking towards the units at the back of the hotel at 9.15. As I started my car, black-green clouds were rapidly gathering and the first fat raindrops began to fall.

23

JACK

When I saw the drunk lying beside the wall, my first thought was to just keeping walking. This had nothing to do with me. There was no logical reason to get involved.

I managed two steps. If the passageway had been a little cleaner, there's a chance I might have kept on going towards my unit. Or if the guy had been left with a little more dignity, the scene might not have bothered me so much. But the way he'd been left after being mugged, like a piece of garbage, I couldn't let it pass. I thought if I could get some sort of information about him, I could get someone to come and pick him up. If I was a Good Samaritan for this helpless guy now, perhaps someone would do the same for me if I was ever stupid enough to get in a situation like this.

The body was four metres away from me in the alley, lying in a puddle of water on his back with his feet pointing towards the sky. His hands were partly obscured by the debris that covered the ground.

In the distance, I could see the brightly lit parking lot for the motel units that was connected to the Richmond Arms. So close. I could keep walking and no one would know I'd even been there. Instead, I moved into the alley and crouched down to examine the guy. He was breathing, even though it was only shallowly. So still alive, thank goodness.

The best I could tell he was five years either side of fifty. There was no way to be more precise with the amount of hair covering his face, both beard and head. His face was greying and his nails were manicured and his hands were smooth. His clothes were those of an office worker – a grey single-breasted suit, a fine-weave white shirt and thrown to the side was a cashmere overcoat. I had a picture in my head of a down-and-out lawyer or an accountant.

I went through his pockets, working slowly, because he was covered in blood and I didn't have gloves. I started with the coat. At first I thought it was empty but as I pulled it open, I found that a hard rectangular object had slipped through a hole in the lining. A flat flask I sniffed. Scotch. There was nothing else hidden in the pocket. He'd obviously been robbed.

I stood up and went to pull out my mobile from my pocket, ready to call OOO, but I realised I'd left it in my room when I was having dinner with Sam.

I silently cursed just as I heard a sound behind me on the street. A vehicle. Moving fast and towards the passageway. There had been no traffic all the time I'd been in the alley and now this?

Sometimes you know something bad is going to happen. You can feel it in the air and in your gut. I put it down to the abundance of bad decisions I've made in my life of late.

Instinctively, I moved into the shadows and looked down towards the street. Instinctively, I knew I couldn't risk being found at the crime scene with the body of a mugged man feet away from me.

A large dark Ford sedan with white lettering on the side and a lighting bar on the roof turned into the passageway. Police. As the car surged towards me, bouncing over the curb, I had to step back or be hit.

The car doors opened and two policemen climbed out. The driver drew his pistol, holding it two-handed, pointing it steadily at my chest. The other had his gun pointed at me while he rested it on the door. Given the width of the alley, it didn't matter where they pointed it.

"Stand still with your hands in the air," the driver yelled out. "Don't move!"

Both officers were around five-ten, solidly built and in good shape. Neither seemed fazed by the situation as they moved calmly towards me.

"Hands where I can see them," the driver yelled again. "Slowly! Do it now!"

You can see where this is going. They had the wrong end of the stick but I knew there was no point trying to change their minds. I was in the wrong place at the wrong time and I silently cursed my Good Samaritan deed.

I raised my hands to shoulder height, fingers extended, palms towards them and said, "It's not what you think. I didn't do this. I saw the guy and stopped to see if I could help."

"Shut up and put your hands on the car," he said reaching around to push me between the shoulder blades with his right hand.

I fell forward on the front of the car as he jabbed at my ankles with his right foot. I shuffled my legs a couple of inches farther apart while he patted me down. He started with my left arm, running both hands all the way down from my shoulder to my wrist. He did the same with my right arm, then checked my body, my waist, both legs, both ankles and the pockets of my coat and pants. He found nothing.

"Clean," he said from behind me. "No gun."

"Of course I don't have a gun," I muttered as I turned my head towards him.

My eyes saw the muzzle of a gun pointed at my face. Apart from the muzzle, I glanced his name on his badge. Baxter.

"I said SHUT UP!" he bellowed unnecessarily.

He pulled my left arm around behind my back and I heard the snap of a heavy cuff on my wrist. Cold metal bit into the skin as he grabbed my right arm, pulling me upright at the same time as he secured the second handcuff.

"What's your name?" he asked.

Answering would do me no good at all. They weren't listening. So I didn't answer.

"Where's your ID?"

I had nothing on me. No wallet, no phone. Everything Sam and I had eaten at the restaurant had been put on my hotel tab, ready to pay when I finalised everything when I left in a day or so. Silently, thanking my lucky stars, I knew I could cover my tracks for the past couple of hours.

The cuffs were digging into both my wrists. He'd tightened them far more than he needed to.

"What happened here?" Baxter asked.

"I told you," I said. "I saw him from the street and came in to see if I could help. He was like this when I found him."

"OK. I've had enough. You're coming with us to the station. The detectives will sort this out."

Baxter took my left arm just above the elbow and dragged me to his side of the car. He opened the back door, reached up to put his hand flat on my head, and shoved me inside. He made sure I was clear, then slammed the door behind me. All routine except for the attitude.

The seat was square and hard with very little room for my legs because of a thick glass screen that rose up from the floor isolating the rear of the cabin. Overkill for a small country town like Richmond, I would have thought.

The air in the back of the car was warm and stale and I could detect the acrid smell of industrial disinfectant but it wasn't enough to cover the lingering odour of vomit from dirty, sticky humans. I started to breathe through my mouth, wishing I could keep my hands off the upholstery.

After ten minutes of waiting while the two officers kicked rubbish around, another car arrived, parking carelessly at a crazy angle next to the entrance of the alley. Two men got out and moved slowly and deliberately towards the body, joining Baxter and his partner. So far, no ambulance.

I leant forward, talking loudly so I could be heard through the closed window.

"Is anyone going to call for an ambulance?"

Baxter turned around and spoke over his shoulder. "Shut up!" he snarled.

I watched Baxter and his partner, and the two new arrivals, talk for a couple of minutes as nerves skittered across my stomach. One pointed towards his car, then to me, then back to the prone man lying in the alley, all very animated. Then the group moved to the front of the car I was sitting in.

What the hell was going on?

They kept gesturing and pointing at me but I couldn't make out what was being said. Just then, an ambulance arrived and I breathed a sigh of relief.

Baxter brought the conference to a close as the two paramedics ran to the body. One stayed behind, checking vitals while the other ran back to lift a stretcher from the back of the ambulance.

As they loaded the body into the ambulance, Baxter came back and sat down in the front passenger seat. His partner sat behind the wheel. Without a word passing between the two men, the car pitched forward as we sped out of the alley.

24

———

SAM

There had been no mention of any family link in the diary. Nothing. And flicking through the remaining pages, there was very little left to read. I'd left Jack at around 9.15 pm and my watch said it was only 9.30 pm now and far too early for me to head to bed. I was eager to finish the diary and reading the faded writing in the diary was a sure way of making me tired enough to sleep.

I pulled a stool over to the bench and opened the diary where I'd left off the night before.

Diary 16th January

Dear Diary.

Help me. I sit before your empty page as the tears run down my face. Mammy has sent me away as she planned. She thrust a small package into my hands and told me it was all the money she had in the world but she wanted me to take it and start a new life. The parting was terrible. I begged and pleaded for her not to send me away but she never flinched. Tipsy held me close as he helped me into the cart and when I looked back at Mammy through the veil of my tears, I could see her chest heaving too. But her resolve was strong. I was on the first part of my journey to a strange land. Alone. If only Norah was here.

Finding her, making up to her for all she's been put through, feels like the best way to commemorate Barney and make amends. But how, that's the question. How?

Diary 17th January

I am in Dublin. Tipsy has me in a small dark room with a single bed and little else while he buys my passage. When he returned, he held the ticket out to me and told me I had a two-day wait before the ship sailed. There was bread and cheese in a potato bag he held out to me and it was to last me until my journey. And since it wasn't safe in Dublin for me, I was to stay inside my tiny prison. He would come for me in two days' time to take me to the ship.

I am bereft and have nothing to say. I have so much I want to write but as soon as I put pen to paper, the chaos of nonstop sorrows and angers, a horrible sucking swamp of blackness, is pulling me down into it. Help me, Mary Mother of God. Help me and pray for me.

Diary 18th January

I can't write.

Diary 19th January

I want to, but I still can't write.

Diary 20th January

My ship sails this day and Tipsy is due here at any moment. I will myself to put the events of what happened two nights ago behind me but they will lay buried in my heart forever.

I never expected to see Dan standing at the door after I had gone to my bed for the night. His silhouette stood in the door when I cracked it open ever so carefully. No one knew I was here. Tipsy said that to me as he left. So how was it that Dan knew I was here?

'It's running away you do now is it, Peg? Without so much as a by your leave to me?'

My hand went to my heart. 'What are you doing here Dan? I whispered.

I heard trepidation creeping into my voice and I wasn't sure why I should feel this way. I'd known this man all my life. I strained to look behind him but there were no soldiers waiting behind him to arrest me. He was alone. Then he pushed me, shoved me, inside the room, and my heart fairly jumped into my throat with fear. I let out a cry but his hand covered my mouth as he kicked the door closed behind him with his foot.

Diary, I can't write about the terrible thing he did. Words cannot express my agony. He violated me in that small room and I don't remember him even saying a word as he ravaged me, leaving me bruised and weeping when he was finished.

As long as I live, I will never forget the look on his face when he turned to look back at me from the door. Contempt. From the very man who was expected one day to be my husband, if all this madness hadn't happened.

I wait now for Tipsy to come. I don't care what happens to me.

I stared at the diary in shock. Had Dan O'Donovan actually *raped* Nana Peg? Then another shocking thought popped into my head. If that was true, and Nana Peg had been on the ship bound for Tasmania, had she fallen pregnant from that dreadful encounter? In those days, a journey from Britain to Australia would have taken roughly six months. Did that mean that my mother was his child? My own mother?

My head swam. I couldn't believe it! Sean and Rory's father, John O'Donovan, was surely the John from the diary, Dan's younger brother, only a child at the time. Which made Dan their uncle. But he was also my grandfather!

The final night with Mum suddenly resurfaced in my memory.

'This is a fine time of night to be coming in,' she said.

Mum was not asleep even though it was 2.43 am. She'd been sitting in the fireside chair and waiting through all the hours, stirred into a high temper and I could see the disgust that was spilling out of her eyes. Her daughter, out God knows where, doing God know what with God knows whom. Loathsome.

'I'm almost eighteen,' I said. 'When Merrell was eighteen, she used to come home this late.'

'You can leave your sister out of this. I always knew where Merrell was. Merrell could be trusted.'

I remember taking in a sharp, pained breath. 'Good old Saint Merrell,' I remember saying, instantly feeling guilty.

'That's enough! Your sister has nothing to do with this.'

'Except that what was OK for her is not OK for me.' I couldn't stop myself.

'If you're trying to imply favouritism miss...'

'I'm not implying. I'm saying. That's what it is. That's what it's always been.'

'If you weren't always thinking of yourself, you'd see that...'

A bitter red stain tracked up her throat and I found myself feeling almost sorry for her. Nana Peg always pointed out that Mum had had a hard life, full of bad things done to her.

But before I knew it, the anger swelled up in my chest and I remember thinking, 'Here goes.'

'I might as well tell you. One of the things 'I get up to' is seeing Rory O'Donovan.'

She stopped dead. 'Rory who?'

I remember smirking. A cruel twist of my mouth, it must have been.

'You know who I mean. John O'Donovan's grandson, Rory.'

'No!' she gasped.

'Yes.'

I didn't have time to say any more. Her hand, clenched into a fist, swiped towards me. I ducked to avoid it but it was too late. Her knuckles caught the upper part of my cheek, just under the eye. I heard the crunch of bone on bone, then a wave of shock and ringing pain.

She had punched me. Not just a slap but a punch. A punch in the face. The acid rage seared through my centre and flared into my head. I wanted to box her back. Box her in the face as she'd boxed me.

But I couldn't. I didn't. No sound came out except shocked tears gurgling in my throat.

She was shocked herself. Her hand, her punching hand, covered her mouth and guilty words blasted through her fingers. 'What have you made me do?'

I held my swelling cheek with both hands just as the door opened. We started to turn and it was Nana Peg in her dressing gown, her grey hair down.

'Maeve. Samantha. I thought I heard...Good God. What's happening here?'

Mum tucked her fists under her arms and when I saw her face as she turned to Nana Peg, my fury chilled.

'You hate me,' I said almost in wonder, as if I had just had a revelation. 'You actually hate me.'

My mother's eyes swivelled back to me and Nana cried out, 'Samantha!'

'You do!' I had crossed the point of no return. 'But you know what, Mrs Neil?' I let the name linger in the air before continuing. 'It's all right. You can let it out now. Because I hate you too.'

There it was. All the hurt over the years had exploded from my mouth. And in that moment, it was almost true.

'Samantha!' Nana Peg's eyes were wide with shock. 'Samantha, stop it!'

I took down my hand to reveal my face and shock jolted Nana Peg when she saw the damage. She turned to Mum and then back to me, a question mark hanging between all of us.

'Ask her what she's been doing!' my mother screamed. 'Go on! Ask her!'

Poor Nana, who didn't deserve any of this, held her breath.

Mum shouted, 'She's only gone and taken up with young O'Donovan.'

Nana Peg gasped. 'O'Donovan? You mean...'

'Yes. Yes! Him! Yes!'

Nana's eyes spun towards me. 'Oh no, Samantha. No.'

'She picked the one thing that would hurt us most,' Mum shouted again.

'Now Maeve, stop it. Stop. Of course, she didn't. These things happen. Samantha doesn't know...'

She shot Mum a look, a warning, like 'Don't say too much.' And that finished everything off for me. It was the trapdoor opening up under me. That one look and down I plunged. Forever.

Mum started to cry, fingers splayed across her face.

'No, no, Maeve, pet. Don't cry.' Nana Peg enclosed her in loving arms. 'Come here. Don't cry love.'

. . .

There had been nothing for me to do but leave them to each other, wrapped around their precious, protected secret, whatever it was. I turned and hardened my heart to both of them.

I left the next day and never saw my mother or grandmother again.

I gulped back more tears, dreadful regretful tears. Why hadn't she tried to explain this to me before I left? But then Kathleen had just told me that I was to be told on my 21st birthday and I was only eighteen when I left. I was still three years from knowing the whole truth. Still, I was walking out the door with my suitcases in my hands so why hadn't she tried to stop me?

I glanced down at the diary and saw there were still a couple of entries to read before the end of the diary. I couldn't stop now.

Diary 23rd January

I have been on this ship for two days now and the motion of it has me leaning over the side heaving even though I have not been able to hold down a single thing. To be sure, my insides will be floating back to Ireland where I long to be.

But one thing shocked me to the core. My first day and there on the deck, heaving as well as me, was Nora. Dan had lied to me about her being in Dublin and I don't know why I ever believed a single solitary thing that man told me in the first place. But it was not just Nora. Mr and Mrs Donovan and wee John were there as well. They had all boarded the ship, bound for a place called Tasmania, at the far ends of the earth.

They were as shocked to see me as I was to see them and when Nora caught sight of me, she ran in to my arms. We held each other so tightly, I thought for sure our ribs would break. I haven't had the heart to tell her about her brother and the terrible secret will die with me. I feel so humiliated, I want no one to know of my shame.

Diary 18th February

We have been on the ship now for three weeks and the heaving is no better than it was when I came on board. Nora is eating a little now but the seas are so rough, it still turns my stomach. I keep tea and dry bread down but not much else. My clothes are swimming on me.

I have precious little paper left. In the rush to leave home, I forgot to bring another book to write in. I will need to be careful from now on if I am to have enough paper to reach this new land.

Diary 20th March

I thought life could not deal me another viscous blow, but it has. I am with child. Dan's child. And I have no one here with me. When I finally realised, I had to tell Nora my secret and she was in shock. She is ashamed of her family and has vowed never to join them again once we land. She will be my rock, she told me, and I am ever so grateful for her love and care. I will be almost seven months along by the time we land and I can only imagine the looks on the faces of the people who will be waiting to take me in. Tipsy organised everything before I left but this was not something that was planned.

I am disgraced.

Diary 30th April

I am showing now. A tiny bulge stretching my skirts and bodice. I can no longer hide this.

I am also running out of paper and the ink is almost at an end. This will be my last entry, I fear. Nora has been true to her word and she stays with me every day. Her family also knows now what their precious son has done and they hide their eyes from me when I walk around the deck for my daily exercise with Nora. I don't care. I don't want their company anyway.

I have been told we will land in three more months. If I am able I will purchase more paper and ink and continue with my diary. But I have no idea what awaits me.

At least I have Nora by my side.

. . .

I stared in shock at the final entry in the diary. Auntie Norah. Mum's best friend who asked to be buried with the Neils and not with the O'Donovans, was truly my great aunt. Not just an honorary one as I'd always thought, but a real aunt. And I'd never known.

I shook my head in bewilderment. It also meant she was Rory's aunt.

I picked up the phone and pressed Jack's number as I glanced at the bedside clock. 10.15 pm. Would he be asleep?

The phone rang for five times and went to voicemail. I pushed the hang-up button and redialled. The same thing.

I had to talk to him. I grabbed my car keys and ran out the door.

25

JACK

I knew where we were going and the journey didn't take long. It was the same little building they called a station house I'd been to a couple of days ago for information on Merrell.

Inside, the reception desk was vacant and the small area still smelled of dust and floor polish, like a school. Baxter approached the desk and rested his elbows on the wooden counter as another unformed officer emerged from a back room. They leaned over to talk quietly and spoke for a minute, the officer glancing over at me and running his eyes up and down my body. I was guessing I was the first person Baxter had dragged in at the dead of night and I was also guessing I was the cleanest and soberest. Finally, the officer laughed and slapped Baxter on the shoulder as he pushed a shiny metal dish across the counter.

Baxter walked over and said, "Empty everything into the dish."

"All I have is my watch," I replied.

"Then put it in the dish," he sing-songed.

Baxter stepped forward, a frown on his face, and searched me all over again. He pinched his fingers along the seams of my clothes, squeezed the edges of my collar, and inspected the inside of my boots. It was a much more thorough job than was necessary and it still turned up nothing.

He took the dish over to the desk and the officer tipped the watch into a clear plastic bag. He sealed the top and held it to the light to emphasise how little my possessions amounted to. Then he stuck the label on the bag and dropped it on the counter.

"You could save yourselves all this trouble by listening to me," I called out. "I didn't do anything. I found him like that just before you guys turned up."

"Shut up. I only want to hear you speak when I ask you a question." Baxter snarled again.

I shook my head and smirked. "You guys have been watching too many crime shows on Netflix."

He loomed over me, pulling a pained expression as though I were a dim-witted acquaintance who was trying his patience.

"How about my phone call?" I asked. "That'll clear this up."

Without a word, Baxter pressed a button to the side of the desk and a glass waist-high barrier to our right slid open.

He pushed me through, then led the way down the corridor to the last room on the right. It was white-washed with only a table and three chairs, inside one for me on the far side and two on the near side of the table, closest to the door.

I was shoved towards the chair on the opposite side of the table.

"Sit down," Baxter growled. "The detectives will be here soon."

"Can you just answer me one question? Why?"

He smirk was lop-sided. "A crime was committed, genius. And you're the only suspect we have."

The detectives took their time coming. In the silence, I kept glancing at the clock on the wall, as the hands moved slowly. It gave me plenty of time to run things through my head. What was going on here? Without sounding paranoid, it was almost as if I was being set up to take the blame for the crime. But if that was the case, why? And who was setting me up? For what purpose? I know I'm not the most charming of people but three days in town was my all-time record to piss off someone to this degree.

It was close on an hour before the door opened and two men walked in. Apart from wearing suits instead of uniforms, the detectives reminded me of the two officers who had picked me up in the alley. They were probably both in their forties and capable-looking at around five-ten tall.

The younger-looking one was the first to speak.

"My name's Detective Matt Gibson," he said. He pointed to the other detective. "This is my partner, Detective Damian Harris."

"Got any coffee?" I asked.

Gibson turned to Harris and said, "Three cups, Joe."

Joe left and Gibson sat down in the chair, smiling at me.

"Mind if we record this?"

"I insist on it," I replied.

He pushed a button on the underside of the table then opened a notebook, scribbling on the top of the page without saying a word. In the silence, the clock on the wall ticked loudly. I saw him glance up to the corner of the room above the door. I turned to look over my shoulder and saw a tiny CCTV camera mounted on a metal bracket where the walls met the ceiling. A red light next to the lens was blinking steadily.

Harris returned to the interview room carrying his own notebook under his arm and three white polystyrene cups with lids in a brown cardboard carry container.

"No doughnuts," he said as he sat down.

"Just don't tell me you put milk in my coffee," I said.

"No. For you, tough guy, I guessed no milk, no sugar."

"That's a relief."

The detectives were silent as I took a sip of the coffee. It was surprisingly good. A little cold, but I allowed myself a moment to enjoy the strong bitter taste. Gibson left his cup on the table and watched me sip while Harris emptied his cup in a single gulp and wiped his mouth on his sleeve.

"Okay," Gibson said. "Let's not waste any more time."

"Fine with me," I said. "I'm not looking to drag this out."

"The boys down the corridor said you don't have ID, so maybe you can start with your name."

"Jack Curtis," I said.

"Where's your ID and phone, Jack?"

"In my room back at the Richmond Arms."

"And where are you from, Jack?"

All very polite.

"Surfers Paradise," I replied, just as polite.

"And what are you doing here?"

"I'm visiting a friend."

"And you were out by yourself without this friend?"

"I had dinner with her and I was on my way back to my room."

Harris was looking at me for the first time since handing me the coffee. "If you know anything, now would be the time to tell us."

"You need to work with us, Jack," Gibson said. "If you're straight with us now, maybe we can help you. But if you keep lying to us, we'll make sure this whole thing falls right on you."

I sat and looked from one to the other and I felt insulted more than anything. If I had been lying, there was no way anyone would know about it, least of all either of these guys.

"You should be looking to get out in front of this, Jack." Harris said. "Be smart. This is your last chance to do yourself some good."

"We'll find out later, anyway," Gibson said. "But then it'll be too late to help. You need to tell us now."

"Look, I don't believe you're a bad guy, Jack," Harris said. "But if you didn't mean what happened, you need to let us know now. Stop wasting our time."

I took another sip of coffee.

"Maybe the guy attacked you first?" Gibson said. "Forced you into the alley?"

"Yeah," Harris said. "But if that's how it happened, you need to tell us now. Then we can help you with your statement and make sure it shows you in the best light."

"We're just trying to help you," Gibson said.

I waited for the good cop/bad cop routine to finish.

"I appreciate that," I said. "So listen to what I'm telling you. I found the guy as he was. Nothing else. And while we're at it. How come the police car arrived at the scene so quickly?"

I looked from one to the other.

"I was barely in the alley for a minute when they arrived."

Both men sighed audibly.

Harris reached into his pocket and pulled out a tape. It was a tiny handheld one people sometimes use for dictation. He held it up so I could see it clearly, then stood it upright on the table in front of Gibson.

"There's something you should know," he said. "Someone saw you."

"Saw me find the guy?" I asked.

"No. Saw you hit the guy."

"Rubbish," I muttered.

"No Jack, it's true. They called ooo."

"That's how the unit arrived so fast."

"Maybe they saw someone but it wasn't me."

Both detectives were looking at me intently.

"Anything to add, now's the time."

"Nope," I replied.

Harris scowled. "Okay. This was taken from the ooo voice recorder," he said, reaching out to the tape machine.

A synthesised female voice gave out a date. May 23rd. She gave the time and asked, "Which service do you need?"

"Please just help me," a man's voice said. It was high pitched and trembling. *"I've just seen a guy get mugged."* He was breathing hard, and I could hear some light traffic noise in the background.

"I understand that, sir, but I need to start with your name, telephone number and address."

"Okay, it's Andy Ne..."

Harris leaned forward and pressed a button. The voice on the tape squealed and jabbered for a moment, so I couldn't make out any more details. Then Harris let go of the machine and I heard the operator speaking again.

"... what you saw?"

"Ok. Well. There was this guy. A big guy. He went into the alley and up to this other guy. The other guy saw him and held out his hand. It looked like he was drunk or something. He started moving back. Kept going. But this big guy moved in and hit him hard with a pipe of some sort."

"What happened next?"

"The drunk was on the ground. The big guy leant down and started

rummaging through his pockets. The drunk was bleeding everywhere and this guy still robbed him. Jeez! I didn't want him to see me so I ran."

"And where were you when this happened?"

"Right there, on the street."

"Did you get a good look at him?"

"Yeah. I got a good look."

"Can you describe him?"

"Sure. He was white. Tall. About six foot, six foot one. Black leather jacket. Black jeans. Black boots."

Harris switched the machine off.

"Jack. I notice you're a white male," he said. "You're about six-one tall, wearing black boots, black jeans and a black leather jacket."

I'd only bought one coat. This black leather one. It wasn't quite the jacket I should have bought with me because it didn't keep the cold out. It was perfect for a Surfers Paradise winter but not here in Tasmania with winter just around the corner.

"Your point is what?" I asked.

"You see now that we have a witness, it's going to be bad for you. You see, we have a description of the assailant, and it matches you exactly, and this witness can be brought in at any time and he can pick you out of a line up."

"Only if I did it," I replied. "Which I didn't."

Gibson sighed. "I thought you were a smart guy," he said. "You look like a smart guy."

He looked at Harris. "Doesn't he, Joe? He looks smart?"

Harris nodded. "Real smart."

"What do you do for a living, Jack?" Gibson asked.

"I'm a detective. Ex-police detective. Private now."

Both heads and eyebrows raised at the same time, as if they were synchronised.

I nodded. "I was a police detective with Surfers Paradise Police Force for five years and before that, I was a detective for ten years with Hobart Police Force."

In the silence, they stared at me as I smiled at them.

"Yep. So I know your officers have broken so many rules tonight concerning my rights."

I put my coffee cup on the table and sat back conversationally.

"Firstly, before I proceed, how is the man from the alley?"

Gibson hesitated before answering slowly. "He's in the hospital with concussion and a head wound. Five stitches. He'll live."

I nodded. "Good to know." I nodded again after thinking for a few seconds. "So you've seen him?"

Gibson glanced up at the CCTV camera and nodded slowly after another hesitation.

"Before coming here to see you," he replied slowly.

"And did he fill you in on anything that happened? Did he see the guy who hit him? Is he pressing charges?"

I looked from one to the other while I asked the questions but neither said a word. It was like pulling teeth. They didn't want to part with any information and I was wondering why.

Gibson glanced down at his notebook and shut it slowly, placing his hands on top of it and lacing his fingers together, before looking up at me.

"We're asking the questions here, Jack. If you have nothing to hide, why didn't you explain yourself at the crime scene?"

I raised my eyebrows. "I tried on several occasions but Officer Baxter was in a hurry to bring me in here. I explained why I was in the alley but he chose to ignore everything I said. In fact on many occasions, I was told to 'shut up'."

I glanced up at the blinking light and spoke directly at it. "I was thoroughly, and quite roughly, searched on two occasions and I was refused my one phone call when I asked for it."

The clock ticked loudly in the silence.

"Here's a question," I asked, turning back to Harris. "If I was the one who robbed and beat the guy up, where is his phone and wallet and his credit cards? Because I certainly didn't have them on me. I didn't even have my own."

Even if I wanted to, I couldn't have called Sam. My phone was in my room and her number was on speed dial. But I continued pushing.

"And why was there no weapon on me if I was supposed to have hit him with a pipe, hard enough to give him a head wound needing five stitches?"

I looked down at my hands, then held them out. "See. No injury to my hands."

I leant back in the chair with my elbows on the arm rest, linking the fingers of my hands together. My eyes moved from Gibson to Harris who didn't seem to be paying any attention anymore to the conversation. He was just leaning back in his chair vaguely smiling and staring into space. I looked back to Gibson again.

"I know for a fact your officers searched the alley because I waited for about ten minutes in the police car, with hand cuffs secured tightly by the way, while they searched the alley."

I harrumphed. "They kicked rubbish around if that's what they call 'searching' these days." I did speaky signs with my index fingers when I spoke the word searching. "And as you know, they turned up nothing."

Again the detectives were silent. Harris chewed his bottom lip while Gibson simply stared at me.

"So, gentlemen. If your officers arrived at the scene so quickly, where am I supposed to have hidden his wallet and phone and the weapon?"

I leant forward and picked up my coffee cup. I sloshed the dregs around for a bit, then drained the last of it before putting the cup slowly back on the table. I was taking my time so I could gather my thoughts for the final thrust.

I glanced up at the camera again. "My one phone call tonight was to be to Samantha Neil, Detective Samantha Neil of Surfers Paradise Police Force by the way, who is here to bury her mother. She is looking into the death of her sister twenty years ago and has asked me to help with her inquiries. I was with Ms Neil in the restaurant until 9.15 pm, and you can check that with the bartender because I bought the last round of drinks and I signed for them to be added to my hotel bill at around nine. We left directly afterwards and I came upon the gentleman in the alley about two minutes after that."

I grinned smugly at them. "I'm not doing your job for you, but have you checked to see when the injured gentleman left the Richmond Arms?

Because my bet is he left a good half hour before I did and was lying in the alley for that half an hour before I got there."

Without saying a word, Gibson looked across at Harris and nodded. Harris then rose from his chair and began to walk from the room.

Before he did, I called out, "Hey Joe."

Harris hesitated and turned to look at me over his shoulder. "My one phone call, please. I'd like you to call Samantha Neil." I grinned. "I'm sure you know where to contact her."

Harris glanced at Gibson, then up at the blinking red camera light in the corner before walking out.

I tuned back to Gibson and continued unfazed.

"My rights have been violated here tonight and I have a right to know if the gentleman in the hospital is pressing charges on someone he knows nothing about. If he isn't, then my friend, why am I still here?"

Then it suddenly hit me. "You had no intention of ever charging me, did you?"

I blinked a few times letting my jumble of thoughts merge together.

"This was all a set up from the beginning, wasn't it?"

I was thinking out loud, almost in shock, vocalising my thoughts as they popped into my head. As I spoke, Gibson was quietly twisting the pen in his hand, just listening.

"That was why the police car arrived so soon. The call to 000 was a fake. They were waiting close by for me to walk into the alley. They knew the guy was lying in there injured."

I sat back in the chair in shock. "Did those policemen hit the guy over the head and leave him there for me to find? Tell me they didn't actually cross that line?"

Gibson stopped spinning the pen in his hand and glanced up at the blinking light again.

"You've been led down the proverbial garden path here tonight, Gibson," I continued. "I don't blame you. You've been called in here on false pretences and on a wild goose chase. You're a victim as much as I am."

Gibson's right eye twitched.

"But why? Is someone seriously trying to make me turn tail and run as soon as you free me? Do I look like I scare that easily?"

Without a word, Gibson scraped his chair back and stood up, picked up his notebook. He leant down to press a button under the desk and as he did, I glanced up at the CCTV camera. No red light.

"Who set this up, Gibson?" I yelled as he opened the door, ready to leave. "I don't have to tell you that I have every right to press charges and you'll be up to your armpits in paperwork for a week."

The door slammed shut on my final words.

I stood up, scraping my own chair on the wooden floor, and walked over to the door, turning the handle. I had every intention of walking out of the station, with or without Sam's help. What I found was Gibson had locked the door behind him and I was trapped in here until someone came in again.

I walked slowly back to the chair, anger surging through every pore of my skin.

In the silence, the clock continued to tick loudly.

26

—————

SAM

I drove with the windows down, the cold, moist air buffeting my face. I knew the wind would soon be whipping the trees and rain would wash across the pavements, but for the moment, the fresh air felt good as I sped towards the Richmond Arms.

Pulling up outside the Reception area, I saw only two other vehicles in the parking area besides Jack's rental. I tried his mobile again and it went straight to voicemail. Now I was worried.

Think! Where could he have gone at this time of night? Without his car and phone?

The foyer had the same feel as the restaurant: knotty pine, lacy curtains and a smell of jasmine. A plaque above the reception desk welcomed me.

A man with a Hobart Hurricanes cricket jersey sat at the reception desk, leafing through a copy of *Mechanics World.* His blond hair was thinning and his skin was a pale pink and shiny.

He looked up when I walked in and smiled at me across the wooden floor.

"May I help you?"

"My name is Samantha Neil. I'm a friend of Jack Curtis," I said.

He nodded. "Okay."

"Mr Curtis has been staying here for the past three days."

"He has."

"I've been trying to contact him but he isn't answering his mobile. Is he in?"

"I can ring his room if you like."

"Please."

He dialled, listened, replaced the receiver.

"Mr Curtis is not answering the phone. Would you like to leave a message?"

"Has he been back tonight?" I asked, getting more and more worried.

"I can't possibly keep track of all our guests," he said with a smile.

I raised eyebrows. There were only three cars in the parking lot but stating this fact was bound to make it even more difficult than it already was.

"I'm concerned about him," I countered. "I had dinner with him tonight and he said he was heading back to his room. Could you please tell me what room he's in?"

"I'm sorry," he said, shaking his head. "I can't do that." The smile widened. "Policy."

"He may be ill."

"The maid will report it in the morning when she cleans. Or he can ring me here if he is unwell."

He was being as polite as a policeman on a traffic stop. OK. I can do polite too.

"This is really important." I placed a palm lightly on his wrist and looked into his eyes. I don't do coquettish but I tried. "Can we go together to check his room?"

"No."

"Will you go while I stay here?"

"No ma'am."

Pulling my hand back, I tried another tack.

"Is there anyone else here who might know if Mr Curtis came back this evening?"

Blondie laced his fingers and laid his hands on the magazine. The hair on his forearms looked pale and wiry against the calamine-pink skin.

"You are asking the same questions the other man asked. I will give you the same answers as I gave them. Unless served with an official warrant we will open no room or divulge no information about any guest."

His voice was buttery smooth.

"What other man?" My mouth had gone suddenly dry.

Blondie drew a long, patient breath.

"Is there anything else I can help you with?"

I honed my voice to scalpel sharp.

"If Jack Curtis has come to any harm because of your *policy*, you'll wish you'd never sent away for that hotel-motel management course."

Blondie's eyes narrowed but the smile held firm.

I leant over and snatched up a pen from the desk and wrote my mobile number on the magazine.

"If you have a change of heart, give me a call."

I turned and strode towards the door.

"You have a nice night, ma'am."

I heard the flip of a magazine page.

Revving the engine, I raced from the lot and sped around the corner of the building and parked on the street out of sight. If I knew human nature, curiosity would drive Blondie to Jack's room. And he would go there immediately.

Hurriedly locking the car, I sprinted back to the corner of the building and peeked around the edge, careful not to let him see me.

My intuition was right. Blondie was just arriving at unit four. He checked to his left, then his right, unlocked the door and slipped inside.

Minutes passed. Five. My breathing slowed to normal while I waited. The sky darkened even more and the wind picked up. Overhead, pines arched and swayed.

I waited. Lightning streaked from an eggplant cloud, illuminating the world like a million-watt battery. Two counts later, thunder cracked. The storm wasn't too far away.

Finally, Blondie emerged, pulled the door shut, jiggled the knob then hurried back towards the office. When he was safely inside and out of sight, I began circling around the corner of the building, using the trees in the garden beds for cover. I moved through the trees to a point I estimated was opposite unit four, then paused to listen.

Boughs swished madly in the wind and the thunder was louder now. My heart was beating way too fast.

I crept to the edge of the tree line and peeked out. Only five yards of grass separated me from unit four.

I took a deep breath, darted across the gap and reached for the screen door. I yanked it and it opened with a grating squeak. The wind had suddenly calmed and the squeaking sound seemed to shatter the heavy air. I froze.

Stillness.

Sliding between the screen door and the main door, I leaned close and peeked through the eye hole. It was impossible to see anything. I tried the knob hopefully but it stayed locked.

I eased the screen door closed and inched towards the window, looking inside. Curtains covered in green and white roses blocked my view. I placed my palms on the window and tried to slide it open. The window slid open slightly and again I froze. In my mind, I imagined an alarm ringing and seeing Blondie burst from the office with a rifle.

What I was doing was illegal. I knew that. Breaking into Jack's room was precisely the wrong move given our present situation. But I needed to assure myself that he was alright. Later if it turned out he wasn't, I needed to know that I had done what I could to help him.

I was just about to try and move the window further open when the first pitta-patta of fat raindrops slapped the concrete at my feet. The drops multiplied and merged around my boots. I tried to open the window again but it was then that the storm broke. Lightning streaked, thunder cracked, and rain fell in torrents, turning the small area I was standing on into a shimmering pool.

I abandoned the window and pressed my back to the wall, hoping for protection from the overhang. Within seconds water soaked my hair and dripped from my ears and nose. My clothes moulded to my body like papier-mâché on a model's dummy.

Millions of drops cascaded off the roof and bit into the lawn, meeting up and coursing in channels between blades of grass. They formed a river in the gutter above my head and overflowed on top of my head as the wind slapped leaves against the wall and my legs. It carried the scent of wet earth and wood and countless creatures burrowing to escape the deluge.

Shivering, I waited it out, my back glued against the stucco, hands under my armpits.

Suddenly, my mobile shrilled, the sound so unexpected I almost jumped into the rain.

I reached around to my back pocket and took the phone from my pocket.

No caller ID.

I glanced at my watch. 10.45 pm. No good news comes at this time of night.

27

———————

JACK

Fifteen minutes later, the door opened and Rory O'Donovan walked in, surprisingly alert and fully dressed in jeans, a collared shirt and a woollen coat.

I looked up at him and slowly nodded.

"Rory O'Donovan. Why am I not surprised?"

His mouth twitched in a half smile as he watched me.

I watched a wildlife show not so long ago and it explained how some animals have the power of super scent. The wolverine, a thickly furred snow mammal, is bearlike in strength and somewhat in appearance. But it is the biggest species in the weasel family, and it has the strongest sense of scent in the animal kingdom. It can smell food up to a kilometre away even buried in the snow. If we were to spread out all our human olfactory sensors, ours cover the size of a bottle top whereas the wolverines cover the size of a dinner plate. Despite my casual words, he could sense my apprehension.

The look only lasted for a few seconds, but I could have sworn it was longer. The intense scrutiny was there and then it was gone but for that length of time I felt my scalp recede.

"Detective Gibson called me in to sort this out."

"Bullshit, O'Donovan! You orchestrated all of this."

He looked down at his feet and chortled. "That's some imagination you have there, Jack."

"The name is Curtis to you."

He looked back up at me and nodded. "Whatever. But I'm here to smooth your ruffled feathers and do you a favour."

He spread his arms wide and grinned. "I'm your 'get out of jail free' card."

"I'd have been gone long before you arrived if the door hadn't been locked from the outside." I was trying hard to keep the anger under control. "Why was that, do you think?"

"I think you must have been mistaken." He spread his arms wide again and shook his head. "You could have left at any time."

I stood up, the chair making a scraping noise on the wooden floor. "So I can leave now, then?"

He nodded to the chair. "Sit down, Mr Curtis. Make yourself comfortable for a few more minutes. Let's have a chat."

"There's nothing I have to say to you. I'm leaving."

I made to leave when he put his hand up, palm outwards, stopping me, then pointed to the chair again. He pulled one out for himself and sat down, lacing his fingers behind his head and crossing his right ankle over his left leg. It gave me a good view of his red socks the colour of blood and his ankle-high Nike trainers. My eye was attracted to the heel where a small thumbtack lay imbedded in the muddy tread, possibly picked up from the front reception area after walking inside from the rain. He hadn't limped when he came in the room, so it wasn't deep enough to cause discomfort.

"This investigation of yours. Truly?" he harrumphed. "Visiting Sean in prison?"

He shook his head slowly. "You are **not** to do that," he continued. "He does not want to see you. Final."

I frowned at him. "Is that what this is all about? Visiting Sean in prison? What are you hiding, O'Donovan?"

I've always believed that no matter what, I can see through any lie or deception and come up with the truth. And without sounding egotistical, my instincts have always worked for me. But this time, I wasn't sure. Was it deception I sensed or was it simply my dislike for the guy?

He snorted. "I'm not hiding anything. I'm just telling you Sean doesn't want to see you. He has almost served his time and he wants nothing more than to return to his family and start afresh."

I glanced up at the camera in the corner of the room and wished it was still recording.

"Are you admitting to concocting this whole scam tonight to scare me off?" I asked. "Because I'd already worked that out with Laurel and Hardy out there," I jerked my head towards the door and the corridor beyond it, "were talking to me. I just hadn't joined all the dots together yet with you in the mix."

He unlaced his fingers and uncrossed his feet, sitting upright in the chair. He squirmed a little to make himself more comfortable and grinned, showing me a full set of pearly white teeth in the process.

"You forget we have a witness who saw you."

I laughed. "You have the voice of someone on the phone who said he saw someone. That's it." I let that statement hang in the air before continuing. "But that 'someone' wasn't me."

He watched me for a few seconds, his eyes blazing into mine.

"I've done a little research into you background, Jack. Sorry. Mr Curtis." He grinned again. "I have to admire someone who can go through what you did without seeing a psychiatrist." He looked down at his fingernails. "Perhaps you should have."

I felt my scalp recede because I knew where this was going.

He looked back up at me. "Everyone wanted you to see one, I hear. So maybe you just snapped in that alley?"

The air crackled around us and I found myself holding my breath. Almost instantly, I felt sweat pop out on my top lip and my stomach clenched, threatening to release the undigested remains of my dinner. Unwanted visions from my last case as a police detective jumped into my head and my stomach turned a bit more, followed closely by an unpleasant taste in my mouth. Myriads of images bubbled up from my sub-conscious. Images shot through with violence and I steeled myself against them. I could almost smell the sweet, cloying odour of eucalyptus on Mount Tamborine along with the musky animal smells as body after body of young boys were discovered under the dappled light filtering through the trees as the cacophony of birds sung in the background.

I had been the lead on the case and as such, I took the full responsibility for the failure to apprehend the murderer of five 10-year-old boys, all runaways and all homeless. Not that anyone blamed me for the outcome. In fact, it was the opposite. But it hit me hard and I lost all faith in my ability as a policeman. It was why I left the police force. Everyone said I needed time to heal. But in fact, I was scared. Scared that the same thing could happen again and my mind would not be able to cope the next time.

"So you looked into my past." I tried to look unconcerned, despite the smell of sweat filling the room. "It's old news now, O'Donovan."

We glared at each other for a few minutes until Rory stood up from his chair and sighed.

"I'm sorry. That was out of line." He ran fingers through his hair, the first sign of uneasiness I'd seen tonight. "What I'm trying to tell you is that I have taken matters into my own hands and no charges will be laid against you."

It was my turn to snort. "That's very generous of you but I'm up to here," I put my hand high above my head, "with this unprofessional organisation you call a police force. It's me who will be pressing charges against you. If you think this is bad, I'm just playing catch up."

I heard activity in the hallway outside and footsteps approaching. Then there was a pause before the door was flung open and a male voice yelled, "Sam. You can't go in there!"

"Just watch me, Matt," Sam yelled back over her shoulder as she stepped into the room.

Her hair was plastered to her head and shoulders, her clothes saturated and clinging to her body. As she stood panting at the door, a small puddle of water formed on the polished floor at her feet.

She instantly picked up on the tension in the room.

"What the hell is going on here?"

28

SAM

As I stumbled angrily into the room, pulse racing, both men turned towards me, their eyes travelling up and down my body in unison. I knew I looked bedraggled. I'd been running in the rain from the car park and the torrential rain had not abated. I glanced across to the two-way mirror and saw the reflection of a woman with lank, wet hair dripping on to her shoulders and a heavy woollen jumper clinging limply to her body.

Normally, I would have been embarrassed but I was too angry right now.

"What the hell is going on here?" I demanded.

I wasn't even trying to keep my voice calm.

I'd seen Jack angry before on a few occasions but they were nothing like this anger. Now that his fists were clenched tightly by his side and I realised just how large they were.

Jack was giving Rory one of his long steady looks that frightened children and strangers but it wasn't working on Rory.

"You shouldn't be in here, Sam," Rory stated, his eyes shifting between me and Jack. "This is an official interview."

"Like hell it is!" Jack almost spat at him. "You've no right to even be here! In any case, we're finished." Jack hesitated, "For now at least, O'Donovan."

Jack turned to me. "We're leaving, Sam."

"Oh no we're not." My voice sounded strangled. "Not yet. I'm just getting started here."

As I turned to Rory, I could feel my face burning with anger. I had so much I wanted to say, and perhaps this wasn't the time or place, but I couldn't stop myself. I unleashed everything that was building up.

"Have you ever wondered why your Auntie Norah lived with us, Rory?" I began. "Why she never wanted to be buried with the O'Donovans? Why she hated her own family?"

For a moment, no one spoke. In the silence, Rory's eyes widened.

He has to know, I thought. *He knew back then and he knew when he tried to seduce me. Was that only yesterday?*

The realisation hit me hard and I couldn't stop the anger rising.

"Of course, you know."

I was trying to keep control of my emotions but I almost spat the words at him.

"It's because she knew the dreadful secret that everyone else knew, except for me!"

Beside me, Jack frowned, his eyes travelling from me to Rory and back again.

"Your great uncle, Dan O'Donovan, RAPED my grandmother."

Rory visibly paled as Jack's eyes widened.

"That's right, Rory. And Nana Peg fell pregnant because of it. Almost seven months she was on board that ship from Ireland. Seven dreadful months of trying to hide her shame from the other passengers when she had nothing to be ashamed of. She was all alone, except for Auntie Norah who never left her side, when they landed in Hobart. She was never able to marry because no one would have her. Tainted, she was. And the two of them, Nana Peg and Auntie Norah, kept the secret to themselves all those years."

My chest gave a series of heaves as I pulled a ragged breath.

"And your grandfather!" I spat the words at him like they were venom. "As young as he was, has known his entire life what his elder brother did. And despite that, he has always made the Neils feel like trash."

I was working myself up even more. I could feel my face glowing and my eyes blazing as I watched Rory's chest rise and fall.

"Trash!" I shouted, as my eyes glared at him. "When in fact it is *your* family who are the trash."

Rory said nothing. A deep frown had creased his forehead as he breathed heavily but he listened to me rant in silence. I wanted him to say something, anything, to proclaim his ignorance. But nothing. Just that stony look as he watched me, his eyes twitching.

Deny it, I felt like screaming.

Jack stepped over to me. "Sam. Enough."

"It'll NEVER be enough, Jack," I spoke through gritted teeth.

"You've made your point," he whispered. "Enough. He knows and you know. And there's nothing to be done about it. Leave it alone now."

But I couldn't leave it alone. I turned back to Rory.

"Sean *did* kill Merrell, didn't he, Rory?" I yelled. "He went to her room that night after she told him the truth and he killed her. He hit her head so hard on the bedhead that she had a haemorrhage and died. And to make matters worse," I was shrieking now, "if it's at all possible to be worse, you tried to cover it up by giving him an alibi."

Rory looked as if he would be visibly sick but I was out of control.

"WHO'S THE TRASH NOW?!" I screamed at him.

I will not cry. I will not cry.

"Sam." Jack was holding me by the shoulders and trying to stop me. "Sam, stop."

Twenty years of built-up pain and hurt came spewing out, banshee style. I couldn't stop. A red hot rage was building up inside me.

"WHO'S THE TRASH NOW?" I screamed even louder, trying to make eye contact with Rory by leaning around Jack as he held me firmly.

"SAM. STOP!"

I was shaking so violently, I could feel my head bouncing on my shoulders.

"Ssshh. Sam. That's it, love. Calm yourself," Jack whispered.

I lifted my head, my chest heaving, my eyes searching his. I swallowed hard, forcing Jack's word *love* from my mind. At the tenderness in his eyes, all my pent-up energy evaporated. I collapsed against Jack, exhausted. My forehead rested on his chest as he brushed my damp hair back from my forehead while I quietly sobbed.

In my peripheral vision, I glanced Rory standing as still as a statue, pale and shaking as he watched.

The door leading to the corridor opened slowly and Gibson stuck his head in.

"Any dead bodies in here?" he asked quietly, his eyes sweeping the room.

"Leave us, Matt," Rory said just as quietly. "We're good."

Gibson nodded and shut the door softly behind him.

"That's it love," Jack repeated to me. "Calm down and listen to me. I have a theory you both might want to hear."

Behind him, Rory's head turned, a frown forming on his forehead.

Jack turned to look at Rory over his shoulder, still holding me tightly.

"Tell the truth, O'Donovan," he said. "Do you know what happened that night?"

I reluctantly pulled away from Jack, wiping the back of my hand under my nose, still sniffling, as my chest heaved, so I could watch Rory's face as he replied. He was trying to make up his mind which way he would go.

The clock on the wall ticked loudly in the silence.

"Oh for fu..." Jack began as Rory started talking.

"I gave Sean an alibi but I knew he left home at some stage during the night."

The words exploded in the room, almost sucking the air from it.

Rory breathed heavily, his nostrils dilating. "I gave him a false alibi," he said softly as he nodded.

I pushed Jack away, ready to deliver another onslaught as Rory held up his hand to stop me.

"Let me speak, Sam," he said softly. All the fight had gone from him as well.

I glared at him but said nothing. Seconds ticked by before Rory began to talk.

"God, where do I begin?" he said quietly looking at his feet.

"I think we all need to sit down," Jack mumbled.

He pointed to a chair for Rory to sit in as he pulled one out for me and another for himself. As he sat down beside me, his eyes never left Rory's face.

A scraping noise filled the room as Rory pulled the chair out from the table and sat down heavily.

"This goes no further than this room," he said shakily.

He looked from me to Jack. "I'm serious. I've spoken to Sean and he doesn't want another investigation into this. Confessing was his choice and he is standing by that choice."

Jack and I nodded in the silence and Rory breathed out heavily.

"Merrell told Sean at the party what my great uncle had done," Rory began. "She'd just been told by your mother and she was still in shock." He blinked as he thought where to go with his story. "I'm not excusing Sean but Merrell was harsh with him."

I snorted loudly and he held up his hand again.

"Hear me out!" Rory said. "She was so spiteful. She told him to never see her again and at first, he didn't know why."

His cobalt blue eyes searched mine and I suddenly remembered why I fell in love with him twenty years ago. You could get lost in those eyes and believe anything you're told.

"You know how close they were," he said, his eyes sad now. "Almost as close as we were." His chest rose and fell as he turned to me, sadness radiating off him. I knew he was remembering those stolen nights we'd spent together away from our family's prying eyes.

"They'd only been seeing each other for about a month but they were close," he continued. "But that night," he shook his head, "there was no talking to her. She was in some sort of shock."

"She told him the story as she was told and he was in shock as well. Everything we'd thought as a family, this stupid feud, became a terrible reality. We always wondered why our families hated each other but no one would explain. We were just meant to do as we were told. But as you said, Sam, it was us who was the trash."

He shook his head in anger and I could see him fighting back his emotions.

"He came and told me and I couldn't believe it."

He was visibly shaking now as he ran his fingers through his hair.

"So I went over and spoke to her and she told me she was going to tell you."

He looked at me and I could see the fear in his eyes.

"I loved you, Sam. I truly did. No matter what you think now, my love was real. I was just too young to process this new information properly. When I should have talked about it, I shut down."

I felt like I was holding my breath. *What was he saying?*

"The alibi was real, up to a point," he sighed. "I grabbed Sean and we left the party. That part was true. But he did go back to Merrell's bedroom that night. I saw him come back with his hand bleeding and he told me what he'd done."

I said nothing, waiting for him to finish.

He took a shaky breath. "He hit her and he smashed the window in his temper before leaving but he never thought he'd hurt her badly. Not till the next day when he heard the news that she was dead."

Tears began to fill his eyes as he shook his head.

"Then he was inconsolable." He ran his hand through his hair angrily. "That's when I decided to lie to protect him."

I'd almost forgotten Jack was standing beside me in the room while Rory told the story.

"So Sean didn't think he'd hurt her?" he asked.

Rory shook his head. "He knew he hit her pretty hard, but he said she was alive when he left. Or so he thought. She even told him again that he was going to tell Sam the next day."

Jack smiled wryly. "That's motive for *you*, O'Donovan."

"Except I didn't go to her room." He held up his hands. "No fingerprints in the room, remember?"

Jack nodded. "So why did Sean confess to the murder?" Jack asked.

Jack had turned to face Rory now and I knew he was leading up to something. I'd seen that look in his eyes so many times. The look of concentration on his face. The rigid shoulders. The shallow breaths.

Here it comes, I thought.

"Who was Sean protecting?" Jack asked.

I knew Jack was correct by Rory's reaction. His eyes dilated and he leant backwards. He swallowed and exhaled air through his nostrils.

"Who was he protecting?" Jack repeated. Then he added, "It was Jessica, wasn't it?"

My head spun to face Jack. He'd never mentioned anything about Jessica to me and we'd had dinner together only hours beforehand. Okay, we'd been distracted by our emotions at the time. But Jessica?

Rory's chest rose and fell as he stared at Jack. Seconds passed before he nodded. "How did you guess?" I thought I could hear grudging admiration in Rory's voice.

"When we spoke to Jessica, she was pretty angry at Sam," Jack began. "For no good reason except Sam was Merrell's sister. In itself, that's not a good enough reason. But to Jessica, the scorned woman, it was more than enough. Then as we talked, she knew every detail of the day of 21st birthday party. Who she spoke to, what was said even down to what she wore. That's pretty amazing considering it was twenty years ago. To remember the details so accurately, the day must have meant something very special to her. It was when she held a hand over the spot where her womb was, I began to have suspicions."

I just stared at Jack. In my peripheral vision, I saw Rory nod.

"It was a mess," Rory said. "She had just realised she was pregnant a couple of weeks after Sean had dumped her for Merrell," he admitted. "She told Sean, but he was smitten with Merrell by then. There was no way he was going back to Jessica."

"Then, almost a week after Merrell's death, Jessica told Sean she'd gone to Merrell's bedroom that night to confront her. Sean realised she must have gone there *after* he'd left that night because Merrell made no mention that Jessica had been there. Jessica even said Merrell was wiping blood off her mouth when she walked in so Sean knew she wasn't lying."

Rory looked at me sadly. "Jessica told Merrell about the baby and she laughed in her face."

I snorted loudly. "Oh sure. She'd say that, wouldn't she."

"She did, Sam," he said firmly. "No matter what you thought of Merrell, she was cold-hearted."

I gritted my teeth and leaned closer to Rory, my hands clenched in my lap, ready to give him more backlash. Jack put his hand on my arm to restrain me.

"Let him finish, Sam," Jack said softly.

Rory's chest rose and fell as I glared at him.

"She told Jessica she could have Sean," he continued. "She had bigger fish to catch in Melbourne. She told Sean he was just a nobody with no future from a small town in Tasmania. She didn't want him anymore." He sighed. "That's when Jessica grabbed her by the hair and slammed her head against the headboard."

"What about the noise?" Jack shook his head, his eyes squinting suspiciously.

"Everybody was downstairs cleaning up, Jessica said. She escaped through the broken window."

"And the baby?" Jack asked.

"She miscarried a week later. And Sean never forgave himself."

"Did Jessica think she'd hurt Merrell badly?" Jack asked. His gaze was intense as he spoke to Rory. "Enough to kill her?"

I knew Jack. Something was bothering him.

"She said she hit Merrell's head hard enough for her chin to bounce forward onto her chest. But she thought Merrell was alive when she left her." He shrugged. "But I've seen the same reports you have and Merrell died sometime later from a haematoma. So that sounds right."

Jack nodded slowly before he spoke again.

"And Sean doesn't want this to go any further? He's happy to have wasted his life in prison for a crime he didn't commit?"

"He felt guilty about the baby Jessica lost. His baby. It was *his* fault she went back to Merrell's house that night to confront her. It was *his* fault Jessica hit Merrell and killed her."

Rory shrugged sadly. "You have to realise that he felt he had nothing left to lose. He'd lost Merrell, who he adored, and he felt it was basically his fault that Jessica killed Merrell. And later caused the miscarriage."

He hesitated for a few seconds, his eyes downcast. "Jessica was a mess at the trial, which is why she miscarried soon after." He looked up, his eyes pools of misery. "After that, she just fell apart. She even tried to kill herself."

Rory saw the surprise in my eyes. Was I so self-centred at my own pain that I couldn't see someone else's pain? I'd drawn away from everyone by then and left Richmond, consumed by my own aching heart.

He was watching me closely. "No one knew," he continued. "Her father hid it from everyone. But he told my family," he grunted softly, "in no uncertain terms. In those days, he was a very strong man, not like the man he is today, and Jessica has always been fragile. He blamed my family for everything that happened." He blinked a few times. "And maybe he was right. Our family has done some dreadful things."

His eyes held mine as I watched him in silence. His chest rose and fell in time with the ticking of the clock.

"He confessed because he believed he was the catalyst and he should suffer the consequences. If it wasn't for him, none of this would have happened."

Jack stared at Rory for a few seconds. "That's a stretch."

Rory shrugged. "It's what he felt. Still feels. And I stood by his decision." He looked directly at Jack. "And I will continue to stand by it."

Rory moved in his seat, leaning back a little.

"You've spoken to her, I assume," he asked, his eyes travelling from mine to Jack. "How did she seem?"

I watched as Jack's eyes deepened, a sure sign his brain was firing up.

"What do you mean?" Jack asked, his head tilted to the side.

Rory shrugged. "Well, it's a secret she's kept hidden for twenty years. No one has ever questioned her about it. All of a sudden, two detectives turn up and begin asking questions about the murder." He shrugged again. "She's bound to be nervous."

Jack gave a slow half smile. "Fragile and nervous were not the words I would use to describe Jessica. I'd say feisty. Spirited." Jack nodded in my direction. "Almost aggressive towards Sam. But certainly not fragile."

Rory smiled. "That's good then."

I suddenly realised I was shivering. Not from anger anymore but from the cold, possibly the afters from my emotional outburst. I was holding my arms around my chest, hugging myself to keep warm, but I was freezing. Still, I wanted to continue my rant at Rory.

Jack glanced at the clock on the wall, then stood up, his chair scraping loudly on the wooden floor.

"It's 11.30. There's not much left to say here. And it's late."

Without hesitating, Rory stood as well, his hand halting Jack.

"Let's just call tonight a case of over-zealous constables and put it behind us. No charges have been laid and no harm has been done," he said.

Jack shrugged off Rory's hand roughly and glared at him as he guided me towards the door.

"There's nothing more to be done here tonight, Sam. Let's go before I say something I'll regret later."

I watched his broad back as it disappeared out the door. He was right. Which annoyed the hell out of me.

29

Jack was right. You can't go back. I had two days left before I needed to leave here and return home. Maybe we should just take the time and do some sightseeing together for the remainder of the time.

We were both sitting in my car outside the Richmond Arms as Jack explained the events of the night to me. My anger and confusion built the more he talked until he finally said, "It's over, Sam. Don't stress about it."

"How can we just let this go?" I asked. "That's a total manufacture of facts. You were taken in there under false pretensions. That's a crime in itself!"

"There was a crime, Sam," Jack interrupted. "I saw the ambulance arrive and load the man into the van."

"A crime that was not committed by you!" I almost yelled.

My voice sounded fierce in the confines of the car and the front windscreen began to mist up.

"They certainly know that now," he grinned.

I was shaking my head, trying to calm myself. All this was on me. He'd come down to Hobart to comfort and help me and in doing that, he had been insulted by Rory and then brought in for questioning on a false accusation of a crime. I'd had enough. I wanted to go home.

I turned to Jack. "What about we forget about all of this?" I suggested.

"I've done what my mother asked me to do and I'm finished. Sean was happy to take the blame and he's almost due for parole. Let's just leave it at that and enjoy the last two days here."

Mum always said, when sorrow sours your milk, make cheese. It was a very Irish way of saying count your blessings and move on.

Jack's eyes opened wide. "You're sure?"

I hesitated momentarily. I'd had enough. I came to help bury my mother four days ago and I'd only stayed on because of the letter she wrote. I'd looked into Merrell's murder and I now knew the truth. But there was nothing else we could do and I couldn't bring Merrell back. I was more than ready to put Richmond behind me.

"I'm sure," I answered. "Let's head down to Port Arthur tomorrow for the day. Perhaps Mt Wellington and the Mount Field National Park the next day. Two days left and two amazing sights to revisit. We can leave here on Sunday afternoon after I say goodbye to Kathleen. What do you say?"

"You don't want to go and see Jessica? Let her know that we know the truth but we won't be doing anything about it? Just to put her mind at rest?"

I turned to look at him, a shocked look on my face. "What? And get another serving of the same from her? No thank you."

He turned to look through the windscreen. The last few drops of rain were running down the windscreen as he blinked and chewed his bottom lip.

"What's wrong?" I asked.

"I don't know. Something doesn't feel right. I can't put my finger on it but there's ... something."

He shook his head as he stared out the window. "Maybe it's just me but Rory's concern for his brother is negligible while his concern for Jessica's well-being was totally unexpected. He seems quite at ease with his brother having lost twenty years of his life for a crime he didn't commit."

He shook his head again. "I'd have liked to have had a talk to Sean about this, just to confirm what Rory said tonight."

I turned in my seat. "And how will that change things?"

His surprised eyes turned to me. "We'd know for sure," he stated.

I took a deep breath.

"I wished terrible things for Sean when he confessed. And I'm sorry for that now. I hate the person I was back then." I sighed deeply. "But I want this over with, Jack."

I looked at his face, softened by the shadows, as his eyes held mine. I knew it would be a struggle for him to let go of this, especially if he was feeling doubtful. But I wanted to go home.

The lines on his face tensed. "Is there a reason you don't want to follow up on this?"

I knew he was referring to my feelings for Rory. His question should have been, was I disregarding his instinct and blindly believing Rory's story instead?

For a long moment, I just stared down at my hands, lying clenched in my lap. I could feel Jack's intense eyes watching me. When I raised my head eventually, the face that stared back at me was somehow disconcerting. Not the expression, but something in the eyes. There was something there – a kind of hunger.

I've absorbed enough from Dr Phil to know that bereavement affects everyone differently. I have been through the bewildered stage, the denial stage, the angry stage, and I am now in the resigned stage, ready to move on. Without Rory.

"No reason, Jack. I'm just ready for the next part of my life," I whispered to him.

30

Thursday, 25th May

I lay in bed for what seemed like hours trying to sort my feelings out while I stared at the ceiling.

Jack and I had talked for another hour in the darkness of my car, his body close enough for me to reach out and touch him. But I held back, still unsure, although I wanted to fill that gap with every ounce of my being. On one hand, he wanted us to pursue the matter and talk to Jessica, but on the other hand he was more than happy to spend the next two days alone with me and follow my original plan to do some sightseeing before heading back home to Surfers Paradise.

Finally, and reluctantly, we knew we had to get some rest.

Eventually, I fell asleep only to hear my mobile ring at 5.37am. Shivering and gritty-eyed, I threw back the covers and scurried across to the dresser to retrieve it before hurrying back to the warmth of my bed. I tucked my head under the covers to keep warm and pressed the answer button without looking to see who was calling, fully expecting it to be Jack.

"Hello?" The covers made my voice sound muffled.

"Sam? It's Matt here."

"Matt?" I sat up, hugging the covers around my shivering body. "Matt Gibson? Why the hell are you calling me at this time of a morning? If this is about last night…"

"It's not, Sam."

In the background I could hear people talking. Matt spoke to someone then came back on the line.

"Are you there, Sam?"

"Are you in the station?" I asked.

"No." He hesitated. "I'm at the marina on the Coal River."

I heard a hesitation in his voice. "Look, I shouldn't be calling you but, well, I heard what you were saying about Jessica last night and I thought you should know."

"You heard what was said about Jessica?"

I was repeating his words like a parrot.

"All of Richmond heard what was said about Jessica last night."

I had a mental vision of myself, screaming at Rory, my face as red as fresh sunburn.

"Matt," I almost sighed, "it's too early for puzzles. What are you trying to say?"

"We've just found the body of a woman at the marina. I believe it to be Jessica Danvers."

I shot up out of bed, my eyes wide. "What! What happened?"

I heard voices in the background, then the crackle of a police radio.

"It's looking like a suicide. She took her shoes off, left them, her handbag and her car keys inside the car and walked down to the pier and jumped in."

"Oh God," I mumbled in shock. "When was she found?"

"Glen and Iris own the lease on the marina and their usual routine is to rise before dawn to prepare for the early morning rush for bait, ice, drinks and sandwiches. That sort of thing."

Again a voice interrupted and after a mumbled reply, Matt came back on the line.

"Iris went to check on the boat that came in late last night and heard an odd sound from the end of the dock. She looked down into the water and saw a floating body bumping against the pillar. She called the police and here I am."

"Why call *me*, Matt?"

"I need someone to identify the body. I'm pretty sure it's her but it's been a while since I've seen her. You, on the other hand, saw her a few days ago. I don't want to call her father. He's a cranky old codger and if it's her, it's going to be hard enough telling him as it is. So you're it."

I agreed and said I'd be there in half an hour. Then I called Jack and repeated what Matt had said and told him I'd pick him up in ten minutes.

We drove in silence, both caught up in our thoughts, over the Sorell Rivulet following the coastline overlooking Dunalley Bay across from Fulham Island. When we were past Murdunna, I followed Matt's directions along the highway, turning left into Flinders Bay Road and crossing Duck Creek, onto a narrow dirt road that led to King George Sound. The rain had stopped, though the leaves overhead were still dripping. I wound through puddles toward the bay, my tires throwing up a spray of mud and water.

As the marina came into view, I saw an ambulance, a police car bathing a parking area in oscillating red, blue, red, blue light and a couple of other cars, one of which I assumed was Matt's unmarked police car from the police pool. Parked under a tree, I recognised Jessica's blue Datsun. There was mud splashed along the sides which meant she had driven here around the time of the storm last night.

The marina catered to local fishermen and stretched along the shore but was basically just a dilapidated bait-general store with a wooden pier jutting into the water. One policeman was searching the area around Jessica's car while another was interviewing an elderly couple in jeans and sweatshirts, their arms hugging themselves as they shuffled their feet near the pier. Even from where we were in the parking area, I could see they were upset, their faces the colour of putty.

"Why would Jessica come here to commit suicide?" I asked, bewildered. "Why not just take some tablets and go to sleep?" I looked over to Jack. "Isn't that what all the manuals say women are supposed to do when they commit suicide?" I asked. "Take the easy way out with as little pain as possible?"

Jack was leaning forward, his hands resting on the dashboard, his eyes moving from side to side taking in the crime scene.

"Park over there, Sam." He pointed to a small dirt area away from the office and the other cars. "Away from everyone else."

He shook his head and frowned. "They should have sealed off this area," he mumbled, more to himself than to me. "The place is a mess."

Matt and the other detective I knew to be Damian Harris were standing near the office steps talking to a tall, elderly man with sparse white hair combed straight across his crown.

They watched us as we walked towards them, the white-haired man squinting at us as we approached. As we got closer, a smile broke out over his face.

Matt came forward. "Morning Sam." He looked over at Jack. "Morning Mr Curtis." Damian Harris just nodded.

Jack nodded at both detectives but his smile was directed to the elderly man standing beside Matt.

"Is that you, Jack Curtis?" the man said.

Up close, the elderly man would have been in his late sixties. Despite his age, his back was straight and his gait was solid. He walked forward to greet Jack with his hand outstretched, a wide smile stretching from ear to ear.

"As I live and breathe I never thought I'd see your handsome face again. How have you been, young man?" he chirped.

The two shook hands firmly, the older man clapping Jack on his shoulder.

"Hello, you old ghoul," Jack replied with a smile. "I thought you'd have given up autopsy work by now and retired. What a treat to see you again though. Wish it was under better circumstances."

He nodded sadly. "What are you doing down here, Jack?" he asked.

"I'm visiting with Ms Neil, here." Jack turned and smiled in my direction before turning back. "For more details, Detective Gibson will have to fill you in."

"He already has, Jack. I just didn't realise you were here as well." He shook his head as he glanced towards the ambulance. "What is happening in the world these days?"

He turned to Matt. "You're in luck, Detective. Jack Curtis here was the best damn detective Hobart has ever had the sense to groom. It was a sad day when he left for Queensland. It was Hobart's loss."

As a slow blush rose from Matt' throat to his face, his eyes met Jack's, while Harris was finding something interesting to look at on his shoes. I knew they was remembering last night's fiasco.

"This is Thomas Kirkman, Sam," Matt said to me as he turned to the man beaming at Jack. "The Medical Examiner. And this is Samantha Neil, Tom. The woman I was telling you about."

"Good morning. Samantha. I believe you knew the unfortunate young woman."

He tipped his head in the direction of the ambulance. The doors stood open, revealing a white body bag lying on a collapsible gurney. Bulges told me the body bag was occupied.

"Jack and I met Jessica a couple of days ago," I said, "but I hadn't seen her for over twenty years."

He nodded again, his hair falling forward on his forehead. He brushed it back and said, "We've only just pulled her out of the river. Are you ready for a quick visual to identify conclusively?"

NO. I did NOT want to do this. I didn't want to see her lifeless body.

I swallowed hard. "Okay."

Jack put a restraining hand on my arm, "I'll do it, Sam."

There was no argument from me. I watched them walk to the ambulance and climb in the back. Kirkman unzipped the bag releasing a nauseating cocktail of stagnant mud, seaweed and lake creatures. Holding my breath I watched Jack look down at the body and nod his head.

The dress she'd chosen to die in was blue and I could see fish or eels had nibbled at her mottled cheeks and nose. I'd seen my fair share of dead bodies in Queensland but this body was someone I knew and it grabbed at my heart. I was happy I hadn't had my usual cup of coffee this morning because it would be in the bushes right now.

"Detective Gibson told Sam it was a suicide." I heard Jack say as he leant in closer.

Kirkman hesitated before he answered. "I'll know for sure after the autopsy."

Even from where I stood, I could hear the evasiveness in his voice.

Jack hadn't moved away from Jessica's body. His eyes were still focused on her face, a frown on his face as he looked at the bulging tongue and cracked lips.

"Are those red dots in her eyes?" Jack asked, leaning closer.

How can he do that?

Kirkman nodded. "That's called petechial haemorrhage."

Matt squeezed in and leaned in close as well to have a look, then moved back again, his hand covering his mouth.

"Is that normal for a drowning?" Jack asked, his eyes riveted on Jessica's face.

"Not always. Sometimes. Petechial are minute blood clots that appear as dots in the eyes and throat and are a strong indication that aspiration has been affected."

I turned and hurried away from the end of the pier, standing with my arms wrapped around my stomach, listening to anything but Dr Kirkman's voice. Birdsong. Wind. The scurrying of a small animal. A boat whining in the distance then disappearing. Waves lapping below my feet and frogs croaking in the reeds lining the shore.

I thought about Jessica and pictured her the last time I'd seen her. She'd been angry at me but I think she was angrier at her life. A 40-year old woman with nothing to show for it. No job, no children and no husband. Just a cantankerous father to look after. I imagined her father's face as he was being told the terrible news of his daughter's death. Blank at first, confused even. Then with understanding, grief and pain.

I closed my eyes as I thought of his crushing despair. What would happen to him now? A nursing home obviously, but who would comfort him and help him understand his dire circumstances?

My chest gave a series of heaves as Jack walked up behind me and placed a soft hand on my back.

"It's over Sam," he said rubbing softly. "The medical examiner will do the autopsy this morning."

I turned to face Jack. "Why would she come here at that time of night, Jack? It was so late. It had to have been, because of the mud around her tyres. It rained late last night."

I took a raged breath before continuing.

"This is on us, Jack. Our investigation. I know she killed Merrell." I held up my hand as Jack began to interrupt. "I know that. But from what Rory said last night, it was unintentional. She was angry and lashed out. She never meant to kill her." I almost sobbed. "And she'd attempted suicide before."

Jack stayed silent as I continued.

"I'm not exonerating her." I shook my head. "I'm not. But we both know the circumstances. She felt safe up until we spoke to her. And in doing that one simple thing, she felt threatened by us. She was scared of being found out, Jack. And she panicked."

The sorrow was almost a physical weight on my chest.

"It's called having a guilty conscience, Sam," Jack said, glancing over at the wooden slats of the pier.

He lapsed into silence as his head swivelled from side to side, his eyes scanning the many muddy footprints leading up to it.

"This area should have been sealed off, even if it was a suicide," he muttered. "It looks like half of Richmond has been here."

I glanced around as well. "At least two ambulance drivers, two policemen, the owner of the marina who found her body and Matt's and Damian's." I nodded. "A lot."

Suddenly, Jack stopped. He squinted at the area around the entrance to the pier, a frown forming as his head tipped to one side. His head lifted and swivelled, craning his neck to follow the prints leading on to the pier, and his frown deepened.

Behind us, the ambulance slowly drove away, avoiding the mud puddles. Matt stood beside his car, talking to the medical examiner, who nodded then turned to walk towards his own car. He hesitated before opening the door and beckoned to me.

"Dr Kirkman wants to talk to us, Jack."

Jack dragged his eyes reluctantly from the pier when I spoke but I could see his eyes were troubled.

"What?" I asked.

He shook his head but I could see that something was bothering him as we walked back towards Matt and the medical examiner.

"The autopsy will be this morning in Hobart so we'll know for sure this afternoon," Dr Kirkman said when we approached him, "maybe before lunchtime, depending on how soon I can get an available room. If we're lucky, elevenish. Detective Gibson here is doing a preliminary report stating suicide but I'm not ruling out foul play as yet."

He glanced over to Damian Harris who was studying the ground around the Jessica's car and the area leading down to the pier, his hands on his hips. After the rain from last night, and the amount of people who had been walking around the area, I knew it was a long shot to find anything. Glancing over at Jack, I could see he was still frowning.

Dr Kirkman cleared his throat. "Because this is Detective Gibson's, er, first crime scene," Dr Kirkman said tactfully, "he is new to procedures." He looked back at us. "Without stepping on any toes, he has agreed that you are both authorised to meet with me at the morgue after the initial autopsy, if you so choose, Jack." He looked at me. "And you too, Samantha. It will commence as soon as I set up, perhaps in a couple of hours. It will take me a few hours to complete, so shall we say, eleven?"

Jack turned to Matt. "You're okay with this, detective?"

Matt hesitated, his chest rising and falling as he looked at Jack. Finally, his shoulders drooped as he said, "I could use the help."

Jack looked at me. "And you? Are you up to it, Sam?"

"I think we owe it to her," I replied.

Jack nodded, then turned to Dr Kirkman. "We'll be there. Thanks doc."

Dr Kirkman smiled, clapping Jack on the shoulder. "It'll be like old times."

He chuckled softly and walked to his car, leaving the three of us standing beside Matt's police car.

"You need to stop any more people walking on the pier," Jack said bluntly to Matt.

In unison, we all glanced towards the pier.

"There's been quite a few people on it this morning but as you just heard, Dr Kirkman's final report won't be until later this afternoon." He pointed to where Jessica's car rested under a heavy canopy of trees. "In the meantime, you need to tape this area off."

His gaze held Matt's. "That's the first thing that should have been done when you arrived this morning."

Matt blushed. "It rained last night and we had to do our jobs." He shrugged. "We left shoe prints in the mud. That couldn't be helped."

His voice sounded defensive but I knew it wouldn't bother Jack.

"I'm not criticising you, Matt. It's just for future reference. But I'm serious when I say, you need to seal this whole area off, including Jessica's car and that pier, right now. Let no one on there until after the autopsy report."

I glanced at Jack. *I missed something,* I thought.

"And then, you'll need to contact her phone provider and get a list of all the calls she made yesterday and the calls she received."

"You know something," I stated.

Matt's eyes widened and travelled from mine to Jack's and back again.

"I'm just telling Matt the procedure. It goes for 'state of mind'."

Jack put his hand out to shake Matt's. "We'll be off now. We don't want to miss the autopsy report." He hesitated and nodded. "Thanks."

As we walked to the car, I could feel Matt's eyes on us.

31

JACK

You can add morgues to the list of things I hate. Maybe it's the formaldehyde. Maybe it's the blood. But whatever it is, it permeates everything. The room was all white and cool, clean and odourless with overhead microphone, a wall of steel lockers and steel tables complete with a ridge running all the way around. A drain basin was connected to the foot of the tables into which water, blood or any other matter was channelled. Hanging from the ceiling over each table was a large set of scales. The mixed odours of blood, alcohol, disinfectant, and death permeated the cold air in the room. Most people would recognise all of it from TV shows, but television rarely offers a glimpse of what lays inside the lockers. Dead people on TV were intact, clean and bloodless.

On one table in centre of the room, waiting quietly, lay Jessica. A white sheet was pulled up to her neck hiding the Y section I knew was underneath.

Sam was standing with her arms folded across her chest dressed like me, in white disposable overalls with booties to match, watching Dr Kirkman.

"You look very Madonnaesque, Sam," I whispered, trying to lighten her mood. And for some reason, a morgue gives me the impression I should whisper.

I saw the doctor smirk. I knew I looked like a tubby snowman with a two-day growth.

"Which Madonna?" she asked with a tight smile.

"Your pick," I grinned.

"Okay," Dr Kirkman began. "I've done a preliminary once-over while I was waiting for you. The full autopsy can wait until you've gone." He glanced at Sam. "You don't need to see that."

She nodded and swallowed hard as he glanced back down at Jessica's face.

"All you need to know right now is my initial report on whether it was suicide by drowning." He looked up at me. "Am I correct?"

"Absolutely," I replied.

"Okay. Let me say first, it takes a lot of will power to drown yourself. Your body will resist, and it will fight you for breath. She would have had to have taken a certain amount of drugs, or alcohol, to relax her body enough. The toxicology report will show whether there was either in her system but that will take a day or so to come back."

Sam and I both nodded, waiting to hear what his findings were.

"But," he looked at us over the top of his glasses, "why take drugs then drown yourself? Why not just go to bed and sleep your life away?"

Sam had already raised that question when we arrived at the scene, and I could only agree with them both.

"And why take your shoes off to protect them from the mud if you're going to commit suicide?" I added.

"On closer inspection of the body," he continued as he pointed at Jessica's neck, "I found a thin line around her neck. Very thin, in fact, but I glimpsed it in the folds of her skin."

All three of us leaned in closer, peering at the area Doctor Kirkman was indicating.

He pulled the skin upwards to her chin, giving us a good view of a thin line that scored the flesh around her neck. There were scratches visible around the line mark from where her nails had clawed, struggling for life. The line was almost obliterated by the folds of her skin.

"Garrotted?" I asked.

He nodded. "I would say the bastard wrapped a fishing line around her throat. Very effective in cutting off the windpipe."

He took his hand away from her chin. "If the body had washed down the river instead of getting snagged on the weeds near the pylon, I wouldn't have found the mark. We may not have even found the body. Fish would have nibbled on the flesh and her body would have decayed. After a few days in the water with sea creatures, you'd never find the mark. The person who did this must be the unluckiest man in the world. It could have been the perfect crime. He would have thought the body would wash out to the ocean. Instead it got snagged on the weeds and rushes at the base of the pier."

He looked at me. "And then there was the petechial haemorrhages you noticed this morning. Burst blood vessels."

Some vague memory had surfaced in my mind this morning about a drowning many years ago in Hobart. I'd only been new to the force at the time so I'd taken particular attention to the case, trying to soak up as much information as I could. One of the things that stuck in my mind was the haemorrhages.

"It takes a lot of strength to suffocate a woman, right? A woman fighting for her life for instance?" Sam asked.

She'd been silent since we'd come into the room, and I knew she was feeling the same as I did. Guilty as hell.

Doctor Kirkman nodded. "Looks like she put up quite a struggle. I'll get a sample of the tissue under her nails and send it away for DNA. But don't hold your breath. She's been in the water for over six hours so much of the tissue will have disappeared. But, if some remains, and we get the sample sent away, the killer may already have a record. If so, you might be lucky and get a match."

I wasn't going to hold my breath for that to happen. My guess was this guy didn't have a record. And these days, criminals are getting smarter. They know to wear gloves and to use condoms. It comes from too many crime shows on television and the movies. All our tricks are all over the movie screens and most of the time these days, the police come up empty-handed when it comes to collecting evidence.

"Was she raped?" I asked. Even in an idyllic spot like Richmond, Tasmania, killers lurk disguised as everyday citizens.

Doctor Kirkman shook his head. "No, she wasn't. Her clothing was on, and underwear was in place. I tested for semen anyway but being in the water for so many hours, I didn't expect to find any. But this wasn't a rape and kill. Whoever killed her came from behind with the fishing line and garrotted her. I will need to have a look at her hyoid bone when I do the full autopsy. That's a small horseshoe shaped bone embedded in the soft tissue of the neck, high up behind the lower jaw. When compressed, strangulation occurs. I won't know for sure until I do the autopsy."

"Can you give us a time of death, doc?"

"My guess is she died around one o'clock last night," he said, "maybe a little after, maybe a little before, but I can't be sure until I do the full autopsy this morning. It will just be an estimate in any case since she has been in the water for so long. That will distort the decomposition rate. But between midnight and two o'clock will be a close estimate."

Sam frowned as she looked at me and asked, "What the hell was she doing at the marina at that time of night?"

Doctor Kirkman was pulling his notes together when he said, "I can only assume it was someone of great importance at that time of night." He shook his head. "On a purely personal level, I hope you find this son of a bitch who did this. He deserves everything you can throw at him. And then some."

"Have no doubt, doc. We'll find him," I muttered. My voice was soft but there was no mistaking the resolve in my voice.

"You know, it doesn't make me believe in a God that could let this happen. It makes me believe in creatures that live somewhere in the bowels of the earth not fit to walk around with the rest of us."

I didn't speak. What could I say? I already knew this killer was someone I couldn't reason with. A predator. Someone whose mind was incapable of normal human emotion. And this would make him dangerous.

My mother used to tell me there were no monsters in our world, no real ones. They only existed in movies. She was wrong. They're all around us and if we give them the opportunity, they'll crawl out from under their rocks. From experience, I knew this guy wouldn't look like a monster. He'll look very average. He'll have a demeanour that will not provoke suspicion. He'll be the sort of bloke you wouldn't look at twice, and certainly wouldn't suspect of being a monster.

Kirkman stopped talking and as I looked at him in silence, I realised that his eyes looked haunted. They held a softness I'd never seen before in him and somewhere deep inside, I realised like me, his casualness was merely a detachment from the horror he saw every day and was no different to mine.

"So, not suicide?" I asked, fighting to keep my voice even.

After a moment, he took a deep breath and continued in a voice that was full of pity.

"No. Not suicide. My report will state she was murdered. And by someone she knew. Women are conditioned to be wary from an early age. They walk faster at the sound of footsteps. They stand close to the controls in an elevator. They fear the dark."

He sighed as he repeated, "It was someone she knew. She felt safe enough to disregard all her instincts. She turned her back on him and then he struck from behind. If she had any doubts about him, she'd never have done that. She knew him and trusted him."

Sam blinked a few times and looked at me. "She was wearing a blue dress, Jack. Do you remember her saying when she wants to impress, she wears blue?"

I nodded in silence as my heartbeat raced. I have a theory on time. Fear expands it but panic collapses it. I suddenly understood what the medical examiner was telling me. My mind was suddenly alert and yet everything in the room had the stillness of a hot Sunday afternoon while you slept in the shade. Even the second hand on the clock seemed to hesitate between ticks, unsure whether to go forward or backwards. Nerves skittered across my stomach and a tremor of apprehension ran through me.

Someone she knew and trusted.

My breath suddenly caught in my throat. The world suddenly went deathly quiet and all sounds were obscured by the emotions roiling inside me.

There's a moment in film and television shows when the penny drops. Sometimes, it's like a click when everything falls into place. Something triggers in our memory and we remember where we left the keys or the name of that someone we've been wracking our brains to remember. For me, it was a darker revelation. When comprehension dawns.

The certainty hit me like a cricket bat. I felt a bead of sweat on my top lip, and I felt sick to my stomach as if a hundred snakes were in there and all fighting to get out. Even as I felt my heart turn to ice, I managed to detach as something inside hardened.

What I felt was that old surge of adrenaline rushing through me when pieces start to join up. My blood starts to spark as the pieces of the puzzle come together.

Sam must have seen the expression on my face and asked, "What?"

My heart was racing and my skin crawled. Bells were ringing like crazy inside my head. Dozens of pieces of information were clamouring to the front of my brain.

Focus. Focus on the facts.

Memory is an amazing thing. Sometimes it's something as obvious as a photo that triggers the memory. Other times, it's a scent or a gesture. What I was seeing was the pier with dozens of muddy footprints leading down to where Jessica's body must have been thrown. And then another memory surfaced and I almost gasped. The banging in my ears told me my pulse was going apeshit.

But memory is not reliable. Memory can change the size of a room. The colour of a car. They can be distorted because they're just your brain interpreting. They're like clouds you can't see through. Like smoke in the air obscuring everything.

But this was different. I was absolutely positive. Why hadn't I realised it before. It was all there. Disparate facts jostled.

Time seemed suspended as I stared disbelievingly at the far wall. I blinked a few times. I know I did. But I had to make sure I was right. This could go terribly wrong. Not just for the case but for me.

Sam's voice brought me back to reality.

"Jack. Are you alright?"

Her voice sounded concerned as she stared at me. Doctor Kirkman moved quickly to his desk and brought a chair over. "Sit down, Jack. You're as white as a ghost."

I shook my head, too agitated to sit, and raised my eyes to meet Sam's.

"I think I know."

Sam grabbed my arm, her hands like talons. "You tell me what you're thinking!"

Thoughts were crashing around in my head.

"I need you to call Matt Gibson."

"What? I don't have his number." Her eyes were bright as she suddenly stopped. "Tell me what to do."

She'd been my partner for five years when I was on the force and she knew everything about my thought processes. She was on alert and that was exactly what I needed.

"He called you this morning," I reminded her. "You can find his number from recent call list on your phone. Do it now! I need to talk to him."

Sam hobbled to Doctor Kirkman's desk in her white booties and fumbled out of the white overalls, almost tripping on one leg as she wriggled out of it in the rush to find her handbag. She rummaged around in the bag, pulled out her phone and handed it to me. I held it up to her face for the face recognition before searching through the list of recent received calls. I touched the screen on the last one and the phone instantly began to process the call. It rang three times before the familiar voice of Matt Gibson answered.

"Sam?" he asked.

"It's me, Gibson. Jack Curtis. We're at the morgue and the preliminary report will state that it was not a suicide." There was no time for niceties. "Jessica was garrotted by fishing line."

I heard an intake of breath before I continued.

"Have you taped up the pier and the area around Jessica's car yet?" I asked.

"I organised it as soon as you left. I have a policeman on guard at the marina making sure no one goes anywhere near any of it. Just like you told me."

"Well done, Gibson. Like I said, we're at the morgue but we're just about to leave. Stay where you are at the marina. We'll be there in say," I looked at Sam and shrugged, "half an hour, Sam?"

"Tops. Depending on traffic."

"Half an hour, Gibson. Make sure no one goes near any of the crime scene. It's vital to leave it exactly as it is now. And protect those footprints with your life. While you wait for us, start making a list of all the people who were on it this morning. Don't leave anyone out."

"Right," he muttered as I hung up.

I glanced over at the autopsy table where Dr Kirkman stood. He had a smile on his face as he watched me. "It's nice to see you in action again, young man. I've missed that."

If I was being honest, I'd say I missed this like hell as well. It had been my life for so many years and there wasn't a day that went by that I didn't regret listening to Inspector Grayson when he told me to get some counselling. But one of my biggest character flaws is I never listen to anyone. Instead I resigned and I've regretted it ever since.

"Thanks doc," I nodded.

"Before you leave for Queensland, let's have a drink. I'd like that."

"Your shout?"

"Absolutely."

"Then you're on," I smiled. "But we have to go now."

I handed the phone back to Sam and began taking my own overalls off. A minute later I was almost running down the corridor leading to the exit. I could hear Sam's heels behind me, clicking on the tiles like horse's hooves.

SAM

The drive back to Richmond was excruciating. There were so many thoughts running around in my head. As soon as we were clear of the city centre, but still ten minutes out of Richmond, I felt more comfortable talking to Jack. I could sense the tenseness washing off him in waves as my wipers squeaked against the windscreen and thumping at the end of each smeared arc as the first few splotches of rain fell.

"Bloody hell. Let's hope this is it. Rain will wash away those footprints and we'll be back where we were this morning with nothing," Jack muttered.

Ten minutes later we were pulling into the parking area of the marina near the office. Thankfully, Matt had marked off the area around Jessica's car with crime scene tape as Jack had instructed. The rain had stopped but the mud looked damp which meant a shower had gone through recently. Thankfully, Jessica's car was parked under a canopy of trees so it looked relatively unchanged. Even so, Jack muttered a curse and snorted angrily through his nose.

Gibson was waiting beside his car while two police constables were standing at the entrance to the pier, their arms crossed in front of them. What made my heart sing was the tarpaulin thrown over the end of the pier, protecting the prints.

We parked and squelched our way toward Gibson as he pushed himself off his car, our soles leaving shallow depressions in the soft mud. Beside me, Jack's breath was coming out in sharp gasps.

"You're a bloody genius, Gibson," Jack called out. "Well done!"

Matt beamed and I could swear he puffed out his chest. I remembered that exact stance from when we were in school twenty years ago. 'Goody two shoes,' we called him.

I grinned at him as well. "Great work, Matt."

He nodded thanks before adding, "I've called forensics and they'll be here any minute to work on those prints. I've got the list of names here as well." He waved a notebook in front of us. "Two ambulance drivers. Two constables. Me, Harris and Iris. Seven sets to sort out."

"You've been paying attention," Jack grinned.

As he spoke, the muted wail of a siren told us the forensic team were seconds away. A van rounded the corner just as Iris came over with a plate of sandwiches, potato chip packets and three cardboard cups I hoped contained strong coffee. The van parked under another tree near us and two men in white bio-hazard suits stepped out from the front while a third stepped out from the back seat and moved towards the back of the van. They began collecting cameras and a box I knew would contain rulers and tools to measure the prints.

Neither Jack nor I had eaten anything this morning and as I looked at my watch and saw it was almost midday, my stomach grumbled loudly.

"Sounds like you could use something to eat," Iris smiled. "These are yesterday's sandwiches but they've been in the fridge overnight so they'll be okay. They're better than nothing, at least. The coffee is fresh though and I'm guessing you could use it."

"You're an angel, Iris," I muttered, taking the coffee cups and passing one to Matt and another to Jack. Jack took a sip and tipped his head back in appreciation.

Matt sipped his quickly and said, "I won't eat anything." He glanced at Iris. "I'd like you to come with me Iris so the team can take a photo and measure your shoe prints first before you head back to the office." He turned to us. "Will you be waiting for the team to finish or do you want me to call you later?"

He was directing his question to Jack, as if Jack were in charge. Jack didn't blink an eye, doing what he had always done.

"We'll wait, Matt, to see the count. Before they start on the pier, get them to take photos of the ones around Jessica's car, if they haven't been destroyed, before heading down to the pier."

Jack glanced over to the area around Jessica's car. "You said Jessica left her shoes, bag and keys in the car. Is that correct?"

Matt nodded. "That's correct. Did I miss something?"

Jack jiggled his head from side to side. "Just something to put in your report. You can see her bare footprints around the car where you've sealed the area off, but then they get jumbled because of the amount of traffic coming into the area. But if you take a closer look, you'll see there are none of hers leading down to the pier after that." Jack hesitated. "Which means the murderer garrotted her here and then carried her body down to the pier. He came prepared with fishing line which means it was not a crime of passion. He planned this. It's premeditated murder."

I was slipping. I hadn't seen that and both Matt and I stared at the area in silence.

"If they find there are an extra set of prints from the others on the pier," Jack continued, "and I think you will, you'll need to get a warrant signed by a judge as soon as possible. While forensics are processing, you can have that warrant ready for a name to add to it."

Matt nodded, then harrumphed. "I missed that. Seems like I'm missing a lot." He glanced at Jack. "Thanks again. I'll head down to the pier and watch forensics work if you're both okay to wait up here."

We watched Matt walk away but I had so many questions of my own. Jack was in overdrive but hadn't filled me in on anything and I was wondering why.

As Jack and I made our way towards a folding table and the two chairs outside the office, a breeze swayed Iris's flower baskets and black shadows danced on the bannisters. It was blissfully warm in the sunlight but when we moved into the shadows, the temp dropped appreciably. While I am awed by the beauty of flowing rivers and towering trees, I have become accustomed to being near the sea and I suddenly realised how much I missed Surfers Paradise and my home.

Minutes later, we were seated, a takeaway coffee, a triangle of sandwiches and a bag of crisps in front of each of us.

"Squashed sandwiches and pulverised chips," Jack noted with a smile.

"My usual order," I smiled back. "You know how to treat a woman."

I took a sandwich out of the plastic container and upended the crisps into the empty area where the sandwich had rested.

I waited until we were sipping our coffees before I asked, "Why have you shut me out, Jack? You know something but you're not saying. Don't you trust me?"

"Of course I trust you," Jack said placing his cup down on the table.

He sighed before continuing.

"What if I told you a powerful person was involved?"

"Who?" Annoyance hardened my voice. "The Dalai Lama? The Prime Minister?"

"Don't be mad at me, Sam. If problems develop, no one is going to own up to the mistake. It'll be you and me who will take the weight of it. I don't matter. But you," he shook his head, "you still have a career. That's the real problem here for me. I'm trying to protect you."

He stared off towards the forensic team, an odd expression on his face.

"Do you really want to know what I suspect?" he asked.

"Yes, I do."

He picked his coffee cup up and took a sip, obviously weighing up how to tell me.

This is big, I thought, beginning to feel apprehensive.

He put the cup down again and sat back.

"Okay. This morning when we were near the pier, I saw there were footprints everywhere. A mess. But in that mess, I noticed something. Amongst the footprints there was one that was different from the others. There was a distinctive mark on one set that was close to the end of the pier. That same mark was also on a shoe print around Jessica's car."

As he spoke, the pier creaked and settled against the lap of the waves. A cold breeze blew off the water carrying the scent of fish and gasoline. Closing my eyes, I centred myself and waited for Jack to continue.

"I've seen that mark before," he stated simply.

I was on full alert. "And you know who the print belongs to?"

"I'd rather wait until forensics give us their findings before I tell you. If they find seven prints and they can match them to Matt's list of people who were on that pier this morning, then I'm wrong."

"And if there's one extra? The one with the mark?"

"Then I'll know who murdered Jessica."

"And you can't tell me now? Why not?"

He sighed as he watched me closely, his mouth compressed into a hard line. "Because if I'm wrong, there's a chance you'll take it the wrong way and see me differently."

I frowned and shook my head. "How is that possible?"

"Trust me. It is." He hesitated for a second as his eyes held mine. "I can't risk that."

I couldn't take my eyes off the muscles on his shoulders. They were bunched and tight, as if he was steeling himself against something. His knuckles looked hard and white as a row of pebbles.

He blinked, leaned back and ran both hands through his hair just as Matt approached.

"Forensics are finished."

We both stood up, pushing our chairs back on the soft soil.

"That was quick, Matt. What are the results?" Jack asked anxiously.

"The bad news is there's too much damage for them to separate them all. They're all mixed in together and there's no way they can differentiate one from the other."

Jack muttered *damn* as Matt held his hand up.

"But," he grinned. "The good news is they were able to photograph a good set of shoe prints leading from Jessica's car onto the pier, and alongside the prints from Jessica's bare feet." He waited. "How did you know?"

"A hunch," Jack said. The words were spoken casually but I could see the agitation on his face.

"Were they distinctive in any way?" Jack asked.

Matt frowned. "Again. How did you know?"

"I'll explain it all when you've done with the matching. And you still need to do that to make sure there's no mistake. Someone on that list may have forgotten they went over to her car, so we have to be totally sure of our facts. Forensics still need to photograph all their shoe prints and compare them with this one here," he pointed to Jessica's car. "One of the people on the list may have that print on their shoe but if not, then I'll tell you who I think it belongs to, and why, but only then."

Matt nodded and turned to watch the forensic team walk towards their van. He called out, "Wait up, guys."

All three turned and nodded as they continued to pack up.

Matt turned back to us. "I've already had men at the station rounding up everyone on the list. They'll all be at the station by now waiting for forensics to take their prints. Damian and I will go in now as well and have ours checked and it might not be a bad thing for you both to have yours done as well. Just for elimination purposes."

We both nodded.

"Do you want us to come in with you?" Jack asked.

He nodded. "It won't take long. I'd like you both there when forensics finish up." He looked at Jack. "Whatever you have to say about that print, I want it as soon as possible."

He nodded at us again and walked over to the forensic van.

I turned back to Jack. "You know," I stated.

He nodded. "I don't think anyone has that mark on their shoe, expect our murderer."

"Please tell me," I pleaded.

"This afternoon, once we're sure."

33

———————

Jack and I had been waiting for almost an hour, both of us nursing another cup of coffee in an interview room while we waited for the results to come back from forensics. I felt so wired with caffeine, my skin was tingling.

The look on Matt's face said everything as he walked into the room.

"Okay. The print is definitely not from any of the people who were at the crime scene this morning." His steely eyes stared at Jack. "It's your turn now. The warrant is ready to go and all that's needed is a name to put on it. We have a judge waiting to sign it. I want this wound up within the hour so we can process this warrant."

"Let's do it," replied Jack.

"I've briefed Inspector Brooks of everything and he wants to be in on this as well. He's waiting for us in his office."

Matt held his arm out directing us to an office along the corridor on the right and we all clip-clopped along behind him.

Sitting at a desk facing us was a man in his early fifties with greying hair and black framed glasses that Roy Orbison could have passed on to him. He raised his head from some papers that littered were scattered across his desk and nodded.

"Ms Neil. Mr Curtis," he said in a brusque, no-nonsense voice. "Please take a seat,"

It was obvious he was expecting us because two chairs had been assembled on our side of his desk facing him. We both sat down as Matt stood on the Inspector's side of the desk, off to the Inspector's right, all uncertainty gone from his face.

"I'm Inspector Brooks. Detective Gibson here has informed me you've been helping us this morning," he began. "First off, I'd like to thank you for that but from now on, it's our investigation."

Jack raised an eyebrow beside me but said nothing.

"Now," the Inspector cleared his throat as he looked down at the spread of papers around his desk. "I have here the preliminary report from the medical examiner," he moved the report to one side and picked up another sheet of paper, "and the report from forensics."

He raised his head to look at us over the top of his glasses. "Detective Gibson has filled you in on these reports, I gather?"

We both nodded. I felt like I'd been brought into the headmaster's office for some misdemeanour.

His eyes travelled from Jack, to me, and back to Jack again.

"Detective Gibson also says you have some information you'd like to impart to us, Mr Curtis. Is that correct?"

"That is correct," Jack said.

Inspector Brooks leant back in his seat and stapled his hands across his ample stomach. "Now would be a good time," he stated bluntly.

Jack nodded, his head dropping to his chest as he thought. In the silence, I could hear his foot tapping on the wooden boards. Seconds ticked by before he raised his head.

"Okay," he began. "This morning, Ms Neil received a phone call from Detective Gibson informing her that a body had been found off the pier at the marina. Detective Gibson was asking..."

Inspector Brooks sat forward suddenly. "Yes. Yes. Yes," he muttered impatiently. "The body was that of Jessica Danvers. Like I said, I've read the report from Detective Gibson and I've seen the autopsy results and forensic report."

He glanced down at his watch before continuing.

"What I want is the information you have regarding the shoe prints. I have a judge half an hour away, waiting in a courtroom in Hobart, ready to sign a fully prepared warrant based on what is said in this room right now. It is my job to deem if this warrant goes ahead to be processed."

I've known Jack a long time and I could sense his annoyance. His shoulders tensed and his nostrils flared as he tried to breath slowly. His eyes were riveted on the Inspector.

"Forensics," Jack drew the word out slowly, deliberately slowing the conversation down, "have ruled that the shoe print in question is not from any of the people on Detective Gibson's list."

"Like I said," the Inspector began, patting the two reports on his desk, "I've read the reports and..."

"I know who owns the shoe that will match that print," Jack interrupted abruptly.

The Inspector nodded slowly. "And you know that how?"

Jack glanced up at Matt standing with his hands behind his back, the way he used to when we were in school. *Old habits,* I thought.

"Last night," Jack began, "I was brought into the station at around 9.30 pm on suspicion of a mugging outside the Richmond Arms. I was interviewed here by Detective Gibson and Detective Harris and not long afterwards, Mr Rory O'Donovan entered the room to talk to me as well."

Matt shuffled his feet embarrassingly as the Inspector glanced up at him, surprise on his face.

"Why was that Detective?" the inspector asked.

Matt hesitated. "We were given certain information..."

"Why was Mr Rory O'Donovan allowed into the interview room at all?" he asked slowly.

"He had given us information regarding a crime and we sent out some constables to investigate. We found the suspect at the scene of the crime and brought him in to the station for questioning."

Matt glanced quickly over to Jack. "Mr O'Donovan came into the station during the interview and asked to be allowed a few words with the suspect when we were finished."

Inspector Brooks blinked a few times. "Where is the report on this...incident?"

Matt hesitated, his eyes flashing nervously to Jack again before answering. Beads of sweat had begun to form on his top lip.

"I haven't had time to write one up yet, sir," he replied nervously. "The body of Ms Danvers was found the next morning and I believed it should take priority."

The Inspector nodded slowly. "And the suspect at this mugging, I presume, was Mr Curtis here?"

"Yes, sir."

Inspector Brooks breathed in and out slowly as he thought, never taking his eyes off Matt.

"Was there in fact a crime committed by Mr Curtis, Detective?" he finally asked.

"It was a misunderstanding, sir."

The Inspector eyebrows raised high on his forehead. "A misunderstanding, you say?"

"Yes sir."

"By whom?"

Matt blinked a few times. "Excuse me, sir?"

"A misunderstanding by whom, detective? Your misunderstanding or Mr O'Donovan's misunderstanding?"

Matt's nervousness was palpable. There was no way he could talk his way out of last night's fiasco and he had no idea how to start explaining.

"Inspector..." Jack began.

The Inspector held his hand up to silence Jack as he glared at Matt.

"I want to see a full report on my desk before you leave this afternoon, Detective. I don't care what time it is. A full report. Do you understand me?"

Matt chewed his bottom lip and nodded.

The Inspector turned to face Jack. "If an apology is due Mr Curtis, be assured you will get one in writing."

Jack nodded. "It wasn't my intention to bring this up for an apology, Inspector. I brought it up because it was while I was at the station last night that I saw a shoe with that particular mark on the sole."

The inspector frowned. "Here? At the station?"

Jack nodded. "That's correct."

"And you know who that shoe belongs to, I assume?"

Jack glanced at me before looking back at the Inspector. I'd been sitting in silence, letting Jack lead the way, while he and the Inspector spoke.

"Yes, I do." He swallowed before continuing. "While Mr O'Donovan was talking to me, he crossed one leg over the other giving me a full view of the muddy sole of one of his Nike trainers. That sole had a thumb tack imbedded in the sole of the shoe and I believe if forensics test that shoe, they will find it matches the tread made at the crime scene this morning."

Emotions snapped inside me. Shock. Disbelief. Horror.

Rory?

I stared at Jack in disbelief while the Inspector gaped at Jack as well. Matt's head snapped sideways to look at Jack with a stunned expression on his face. None of us spoke for a few minutes while the words hung heavily in the silence.

Finally, Inspector Brooks leant forward, his forearms resting on the table. Beside him, Matt still gaped.

"You're accusing a lawyer who works in one of our Government offices of murder, Mr Curtis?" the inspector stuttered. "You had better be sure of your facts because this could go down badly for you."

My eyes were riveted on Jack's face.

"Believe me. I would never make this up."

"And you're absolutely sure of your facts?" the inspector asked, clearly in shock.

Jack turned to me. "I'll base my career on this."

The words were spoken softly and were meant to assure me of the truth but still I couldn't believe it. My mind kept screaming *Rory?*

"I'd like to know those facts before proceeding, Mr Curtis," the inspector interrupted. "These are pretty damning accusations."

I found my voice. "So would I, Jack." My voice was firm but inside my head, I was screaming. *Rory?*

Jack looked at me sadly. "That's the look I've been dreading, Sam."

The Inspector sat back in his chair, his eyes staring down at the reports on his table before looking back up at Jack. His eyes were clouded with disbelief and sadness.

"We are a small community here, Mr Curtis. A community is based on trust of our neighbours. You are telling me that one of our most respected ones is capable of such a dreadful crime?"

"Have forensics test his Nikes," Jack stated. "But do it soon before that tack is removed from the sole. It's a working day so we may get lucky. It could still be there."

He hesitated before continuing. "No one else needs to know until the findings are in. It doesn't need to leave this room."

I gazed around the room while Jack and the inspector were speaking. I was still in shock but I was trying to put the facts into a logical order in my head. I desperately wanted to believe Jack... but Rory? I heard Rory's voice last night telling us that he had given Sean an alibi for the night but later on he was told by Sean that Jessica had killed Merrell. It made sense at the time because we had forensic evidence of another woman in Merrell's bedroom. That woman had to have been Jessica. It was the reason behind Sean's confession to the crime. So why kill Jessica?

I looked across at Jack and saw his eyes watching me intently. That meant everything Rory told us last night had to have been a lie. Everything.

"Have you gone mad, Jack?" I asked in total disbelief. Even to my own ears, I could hear the shock in my voice. "Why? What's the motive?"

The inspector was nodding slowly. "I'd like to hear that as well, Mr Curtis," he said. "Before we going jumping in at the deep end, you need to fill me in on the whole story. I want motive and opportunity. And if we want this warrant processed this morning, you need to explain your reasoning very quickly and convincingly."

Jack shook his head adamantly. "Motive can wait," he urged. "With that shoe, we have evidence and that beats everything else right now. The rest we will get, I assure you, but it can come later after we verify that evidence. We need that warrant processed as soon as possible before Rory O'Donovan realises his mistake and destroys it."

The inspector opened his mouth to speak but suddenly close it.

He turned to Matt. "Have Mr O'Donovan's name placed on the warrant for the shoe immediately and take it yourself to the judge's office. And turn the sirens on, detective. Speed is the essence."

He glanced at his watch again. "It should take less than half an hour each way to and from Hobart. By then, Detective Harris will be here waiting for your warrant to take with him to the O'Donovan household."

He turned to look at Jack. "I want this done by the book. No shortcuts. We all wait for the warrant before retrieving the shoe in question. If this proceeds to court, I do not want a lawyer stating that the evidence was retrieved under false pretences without a warrant. And that means you, Mr Curtis. You stay put here. Understood?"

"Absolutely," Jack replied.

The inspector looked at me for a long time with a hard gaze before turning to Matt. "Go now, detective. And you are not to inform anyone, absolutely no one, of the circumstances as yet. Understood?"

Matt was already stumbling towards the door as the Inspector was speaking. My guess is he would follow instructions to the letter. "Yes, sir," he muttered.

The inspector turned back to Jack. "Now. I want to hear everything. You have exactly one hour to do that."

34

JACK

There are four types of murder. Accidental: where your car inadvertently slams into another resulting in a death. Justifiable: as in self-defence. Second degree: where recklessness has a big part to play. And of course, first degree: which requires premeditation, wilfulness and malice afore-thought. When it came down to it, I knew beyond a shadow of a doubt that Rory had killed Jessica in cold blood but like everyone else, I had no idea why. What I had was suspicion which mean nothing. We had evidence and opportunity but what we didn't have was motive. Every-thing went back to Merrell's murder, that I was sure of, but the big ques-tion, why, was still unknown. Until we spoke to Rory O'Donovan, everything was supposition.

Sam's eyes were glued to mine and I could see the confusion and disbelief written over her face. We'd come a long way since I'd arrived in Richmond, further than I'd ever thought possible, and it pained me to know that this could mean the end of everything before we'd even begun.

I cleared my voice before starting, trying to explain everything to the inspector logically and in order.

"Let's start with what we know for sure" I began. "The tack in the shoe and the footprints at Jessica's crime scene."

The inspector pointed an index finger at me warningly. "Let me just state that you are the only one who has seen this evidence, Mr Curtis. I have gone out on a limb here so I hope you have more than this."

Part of my routine as a detective had been to observe and calculate. I watched everyone. I looked for nuances, inflections and subtle changes in behaviour patterns. While things were fresh in my mind, I liked to jump from one interview to the next rather than lose my momentum and stop to report my findings.

Some cops run around making a lot of noise without keeping to a fixed schedule. Some, like me, note everything and never give up until the crime is solved. You hope for things like a chance remark, an ex-spouse with a grudge but you always expect dead ends. As Mel Brooks once said, '*Hope for the best. Expect the worst.*' What you know is that you've done this all before and you have the determination to pull it off. What I also know is that you have to keep going while the window of opportunity is wide open.

"This evidence is the vital part of Jessica's murder," I stated. "Once that shoe print is confirmed by forensics, we will interview..." at the dark look from the inspector, I hesitated. "*You* will interview Rory O'Donovan to gain his motives. At the moment, we have evidence and we have opportunity."

Sam's eyes were intense as she watched me and her voice sounded confused, even a little hurt. "How do we have opportunity, Jack?"

The intenseness of her gaze told me she still couldn't quite believe me. "You need to try and keep an open mind on this, Sam," I said.

I should have thought before speaking because there was a microscopic twitch. I'd wounded her.

I suddenly realised how much I'd taken for granted that her feelings for Rory were over. Of course there were residual feelings. He'd been a major part of her life before she moved to Queensland. She had imagined spending her life with him. My heart did a double flip and something inside cleaved away. A gargoyle called regret was riding my shoulders, head back, laughing and showing sharp teeth. A small taunting demon of regret whispering things that could have been but would never be. I knew the gargoyle. We weren't friends, but I knew him well.

I've always believed the future lies in the shadows of our past. It is endlessly patient, secure in the knowledge that all we have done, and all that we have failed to do, must surely return to haunt us in the end. When I was a kid, I believed nothing was to be regretted for there were more days to come. Slights and injuries would be forgotten, hurts would be forgiven, and there was radiance enough in the world to light the days that followed.

But I wasn't a kid anymore and the future didn't look too rosy for me at the moment.

As usual, Sam was reading my thoughts.

"I'm not questioning you, Jack," she stated firmly. "I'm just trying to understand. That's all."

That twitch again.

I nodded and gave her what I like to think is my knowing smile.

"Ok." I mentally shook myself trying to focus. "Let's go over what we know definitely. We know from the autopsy that Jessica died between midnight and 2 o'clock. We also know that it rained heavily between 9.30 last night and into the early hours of the morning. We have a shoe print from the crime scene with a distinctive mark on the sole and forensics have stated that it did not come from any of the known people from their list of attendants at the scene. That's 'means'."

I did speaky signs when I said means.

"I have also stated that I saw a tack on the sole of Rory O'Donovan's shoe last night and that it was around 11 pm that I noticed it."

I looked over at the inspector. He was resting his forehead on his splayed fingers with his elbow on the table, concentration deepening his frown lines. He gestured with his free hand for me to continue.

"Sam and I left the station at around 11.30 pm last night so he had time to call Jessica as soon as we left to set up the meeting. That's opportunity and those are the facts."

I looked from Sam to the inspector and back to Sam. "Right?"

Sam looked at me as if I were mad.

"Are you serious? You're saying Jessica received a phone call from Rory at 11.30 last night to meet with him and she got out of her bed, in the dead of night, put on her best blue dress, and met with him after, what, twenty years?" She snorted again. "Seriously?"

"Who said she hadn't seen him for twenty years?" I asked. "They've lived in the same small town all this time. Why wouldn't they have crossed paths? And don't forget she knew Sean was due for release very soon. Either she's been counting down to that event all this time or she was told by someone."

"But meeting with him in the middle of the night? In the rain?" she scoffed. "Why would she not simply wait until today to meet with him?"

"Unless he told her it was something that couldn't wait. Maybe regarding Sean."

Even to my own ears, it sounded iffy. But the fact remained, she *had* met with him in the middle of the night, in the rain, and in her best dress.

Sam held her hands up in the air and took a deep breath.

"And motive, Jack?" she asked softly, her eyes intense. "What could possibly be the motive for Rory to kill her?"

The ticking clock on the wall sounded like finger snaps in the silence.

Suddenly, I felt a pain between my eyes like someone had punched me. There was sweat on my face that wasn't there an instant ago. I felt it in my hair, on my forearms and behind my knees. The skin on my forearms tingled. That small intuitive part of me that always has suspected the worst had taken possession of my body. In an instant, it all became clear. The crucial piece of evidence had been there the entire time, right in front of my face. Suddenly, I knew. But the reason would have to come from Rory's mouth, not mine.

Outside I knew it was a beautiful autumn day, the kind that reminds you of the coming winter and the kind of day an old flame of mine by the name of Shannon had told me to beware of. *Bad things happen on beautiful days.* It was a beautiful day after the night of rain but there was a deep chill in that grey room.

Sam and the inspector waited in silence for me to continue.

I leaned forward and clasped my hands together on the table. I couldn't tell them what I suspected. But I had a plan.

"We don't know all the facts. Yet. Once we have proof then we can ask these questions. Only then will it be clear."

"You're talking about some pretty clear thinking in a stressful situation," the inspector noted.

"I guess I am."

The inspector sighed and shook his head. "Well, let's hope this doesn't blow up in our faces," he warned, placing his hands on top of the desk. "What I need to do is fill in Detective Harris on what is happening and have forensics here waiting for Gibson. Harris needs to be ready to leave and retrieve that shoe at Mr O'Donovan's home as soon as Gibson comes back with the warrant." He looked at his watch. "In half an hour."

He rose from his chair, a loud screech filling the silence in the room, and walked towards the door. Before opening it, he turned to face us again.

"His wife will no doubt call her husband when we leave with the shoe so Mr O'Donovan will more than likely be on his way here to ask us some questions. Hopefully forensics will have a result before he walks in our front door with all guns blazing."

He sighed sadly. "Until then, I want this kept as low key as possible, mainly due to the fact that apart from the shoe, the rest is all supposition."

35

———————

JACK

No sooner had Inspector Brooks left the room, Sam stood up as well.

After a megawatt of eye contact, she said, "I need to think, Jack. Alone."

At that, she left the room leaving me with my demons.

I had no want to sit alone waiting for the bomb to drop so I rose and made my way into the cool air outside. I needed a coffee to help me think. Across the road, the blinking lights of a small café told me the best coffee in Tasmania could be purchased there. Through the lace-covered windows, empty tables welcomed me. I looked both ways up the near empty street and crossed over.

An hour and a half later, a puff of warm air hit my face as I detective-walked through the heavy front door of the police station, reluctantly moving out of the morning sunshine and into the dusty gloom of the dark-panelled reception area, clutching my paper cup full of bitter deli coffee.

Standing to one side was Rory O'Donovan talking quietly to Sam. No doubt, Sam had already filled him in on Jessica's murder and why the police needed the shoe.

Both looked up as I hesitated at the door. Despite knowing he'd had very little sleep last night, his face was cleanly shaven, and his hair had been combed back. All this was for show.

I watched him in silence as thoughts ran across his face, a small grin appearing on his face. On a purely physical level, it was a nice grin. Charming. The kind that opens door and lowers inhibitions. It was probably the last thing Jessica saw.

Silence is one of the many tricks in my bag that tends to unsettle people. Silence affects people in different ways. My silence was making him feel awkward, or I hoped it was. He would be wondering what I knew and how much he could say without giving anything away. He turned towards me, the grin disappearing and a deep frown replacing it on his face.

"What are you trying to do to me?"

Most of my life, I've done a good job of staying away from macho histrionics. I could handle myself in a violent confrontation and that had always been enough for me because I was just as certain that there were always people meaner and tougher and faster than I was. And they were only too happy to prove it. So many guys I'd known from childhood had died or been jailed because they needed to show the world how mean they were. But lately I was tired of the pathetic depravities of the whole damn human species and tired of the sort of people who needed to prove they were smarter than everyone else.

I tried to calm myself before I spoke. "You're a son of a bitch, Rory. We'll all know that soon enough."

My voice came out deceptively calm although inside my stomach was churning with anger.

He snorted as he shook his head.

"You think you're so smart. You're like a bloody dog running around with your nose on the ground, sniffling through bushes and piles of shit until you find what you think you're looking for. Then you step back and let the hunters shoot it dead. Why couldn't you just let things stay as they were?"

It wasn't the analogy I would have chosen, but it wasn't entirely false either no matter what I wanted to think. He was right. He'd played us both for fools and I wasn't about to let it go. He was a cruel man, pitiless and vicious. He had shown that. But as I stood looking at him, I saw another side. He was stupid, too.

I saw the frown on Sam's face as she took his words in.

"It was me who stirred things up, Rory. You gave me the letter from Mum and I..." she looked across at me, "we followed up on it."

None believe they are evil, not even the evil do. I knew that he would try to deny everything and deny it with a conviction worthy of his profession. When he was trapped, I'd guessed he would turn ugly and search for someone else to blame. I'd had time to think in the café and everything had fallen into place. Once I started, everything would become apparent. If I did this right, Rory could very well be in jail today. That was the upside and that's what I was focused on.

Of course, there was a downside. If I failed, Rory's defence could look like he was trying to foist blame back on to his brother who had already confessed to Merrell's murder. But both crimes were linked, and I was going to give it all to prove it.

I was saved a reply by the appearance of Inspector Brooks, followed by Matt Gibson. The look on their faces told me all I needed to know. I saw the blood drain from Rory's face as he saw the looks as well.

The inspector walked stiffly over to Rory.

"Rory O'Donovan." His voice sounded as if he'd been gargling gravel. "I am placing you under arrest for the murder of Jessica Danvers. If you say anything, it will be held as evidence against you in a court of law. You are entitled to a lawyer, and I would strongly advise it."

I found I'd been holding my breath as I stared at the group and to get the blood flowing through my heart again, I took a deep breath. There was a whooshing sound in my ears now like the wind blowing into seashells. My palm felt clammy, opening and closing at my sides, and I could feel a balloon of heat rising from my stomach into my throat. The rush of blood to my temples pounded and a chill ran down my back.

Rory turned to the Inspector. "Oh, come on! You know me, Gavin. You've known me for over ten years. Why would I do this?" he shouted, his shoulders shaking with emotion.

He spun to face me. "You set me up," he bellowed. "You planted that evidence trying to implicate me."

There is always a moment of shock when we catch a glimpse of another's humanity. We don't want to see it but when we do, it never fails to shock us or to change us. And the shock is even greater when in our arrogance we believe that our understanding of things has reached beyond the secrets of the other person's being. Now, seeing Rory O'Donovan's soul bared, I received another shock.

"Take him away, detective," Inspector Brooks said.

Gibson stepped around him and murmured, "That's enough. This way, please," then pushed him towards the corridor I knew would lead to an interview room.

Rory spun back to face me and pointed an index finger at my face, his voice as thick as tar.

"You'll regret this, Curtis."

I shrugged but inside something was uncurling in my chest, something I haven't felt in over a year. It was like a hunter's tension, charged with a current and aching for resolution. I'd known he would try to blame someone else, but I had never imagined he'd try to turn it around to me.

Sam had stepped away from Rory when the inspector had arrived but didn't say a word. There was no reason in the world for her to say anything about his outburst at all except that we had once been partners and she knew she could trust me.

Rory was led away, shaking his head repeatedly, as Sam walked across to me. When she spoke, her face was pale and her voice came out in a murmur. She glanced over her shoulder to where Rory was disappearing into a room, then turned back to me.

"I know you want to get involved in this, Jack, but there are guidelines here that you have to abide by now. *A.* You stay right out of this because you are no longer a member of the Police Force. *B.* You don't ask to get involved in the interview. *C.* You tell me everything you know. Even what you think."

A dark thrill rippled through my chest, and I felt a burst of adrenaline. "What was *B* again?" I asked.

There was no smile in return except her raised eyebrows.

There is a gap, I suppose, between all we ever wanted and all we will ever have, and that gap can sometimes be a source of bitter regret. But sometimes, just sometimes, there is a glimpse of hope that the gap might narrow and might even be eliminated in one brilliant magical moment.

Ringing loudly in my head was one sentence. *She hadn't supported him.*

Now it was my turn.

36

SAM

The interview with Rory took barely an hour because the evidence was irrefutable. Forensics had confirmed the shoe retrieved at Rory's house was the shoe that had left the prints at Jessica's crime scene. He'd tried to accuse Jack of planting the evidence, but the tack was still embedded in the sole and his wife had confirmed that the pair of shoes in evidence were indeed her husband's. Eventually, he buckled under the weight of the evidence and confessed.

The motive given for killing Jessica had been that she was blackmailing him. She'd seen Rory and me together on the morning of the picnic at Lover's Hollow and had threatened to tell his wife about us. He didn't want to lose his children, he'd said, and in a fit of passion, he killed her.

My heart tightened at the memory of the kiss and at how close I'd been to giving in to him. *Is that what she saw?*

A burst of shame hit me but nudging me as well was the thought that I'd done the right thing and refused his advances. His children would keep him tied to his wife, no matter what he said to me, and I'd be the loser once again. His family won the first time, his wife would win this time.

Matt gave us the gist of the interview as Jack and I waited in the reception area nursing another cup of coffee. Jack's reaction was as I would have expected. First, he'd snorted, then his disbelief turned to anger.

Matt's words hung heavily in the air until Jack snarled, "Bullshit, Gibson. So what's he saying? A crime of passion?" Jack snorted. "And he just happened to have the fishing wire in the pocket of his jacket when he met with Jessica in the middle of a storm at one o'clock in the morning?"

Jack stared hard at Matt and Matt stared silently right back.

Matt's words had taken me by surprise as well. I searched his face to see if there was a 'but' to follow but he stood silently with both hands clutched in front of him, the knuckles on his hands white with tension.

"That's the gist of it," Matt mumbled. "I'm just letting you know because you were involved in this as well. But it's over now."

"Are you serious?" Jack growled. "Let me speak to the Inspector. I want to talk to him."

It was as if I'd never warned him an hour ago. There were a dozen things I wanted to say, all at the same time, and when I finally found my voice, it sounded remarkably controlled, considering the turmoil my body was feeling.

"You don't have the right to talk to him, Jack. It's over. Rory confessed."

He opened his mouth to say something, and I had a good idea what it was.

I jumped in. "Let *me* ask him." My eyes locked on to his. "If we go in together, he may allow it." I hesitated. "Rory and I have history."

Jack exhaled a little puff of air and waggled his head from side to side.

"What do you want me to do?" His voice was quiet, defeated almost.

There was another little awkward silence as we stared at each other. Then I took a deep breath before answering.

"We'll go in together. I want answers too, just like you."

37

Rory was sitting facing the door when Jack and I walked in, his hands clasped together tightly on the surface of the table.

When he saw us, he rubbed his eyes with the heels of a hands and blew a rush of air out of his mouth.

It's strange how my heart once burned for Rory and now it had suddenly turned to ice. The blinkers were finally off and I saw him for what he really was. There was indeed a primordial evil that had blown through him and caused a swath of destruction wherever he went. I had just been blinded by love.

I felt a tic at the corner of my eye that always happens when I'm feeling the most vulnerable. Beside me, Jack was silent, letting me go at my own pace. Pretty soon, I'd let him take over. That's his forte. Getting to the truth in his own way.

"What's the full story, Rory?" I asked to break the silence that had started to swell between us.

As I was speaking, Jack leaned towards the desk. His hand slid underneath the desktop and almost immediately, the red video light flickered to life in the corner of the room behind Rory. My eyes burned into his, but I said nothing.

I turned back to Rory. "What I don't understand is why you killed her."

Something rippled deep in Rory's dark eyes, like the flick of a fish tail. He rubbed his face with his hands then he smiled sadly. His gaze was fixed on the watery red sunset barely visible through the window on his left, showing itself behind the thin trunk of trees that had turned dark in the growing darkness. His head turned as he glanced down at his left hand.

I remember Jack saying once that whenever someone is about to lie to you, they glance to the left. It's a psychological thing but almost 100% accurate. I glanced over at Jack and saw he'd noticed the look to the left as well. His eyes were intense as he stared at Rory.

Here it comes, I thought.

"She wanted to expose us," Rory whispered. "And I couldn't have that. Not only would it hurt me but it would hurt your reputation around here as well. It got so that I couldn't think straight. She was always on my mind, sniggering and goading me."

I knew he was playing on my emotions, making it look like he was only doing it for me.

Be careful, a voice whispered in my head.

He swallowed noisily before continuing. In the silence, it felt cold and damp as the sun slid behind a cloud and shadows filled the room. The room suddenly felt malevolent despite the light bulb glowing steadily above us. Not a hundred feet away, cars and trucks thundered on the road outside the station and people sat huddled in the warmth of their cars heading home to their families. Not one knew that Rory was discussing how he brutally took the life of a woman.

The air pulsed around us as I stared at him, almost not breathing. I had this feeling that what he was about to say would tilt my world.

I blinked a few times. I know I did.

"I had to kill her to silence her," he finally admitted.

He straightened his back and squared his shoulders as if he was trying to smooth out a pain between his shoulder blades.

Time seemed suspended as I stared at the wall. Phones rang dimly and muffled voices called to each other outside the room but still I stared disbelievingly at the wall.

I glanced over at him and saw his eyes boring into mine. "It was 'us' I was thinking about, Sam. Us. You and me."

I heard the anguish in his voice as his eyes scanned my shocked face. As I watched him, my skin crawled and I felt my stomach turn and my head begin to swim.

Careful, came the whisper again.

"Now I'll tell you what *I* think." Jack's voice interrupted, almost in a whisper.

Rory's mouth stretched into a slow sardonic smile as he turned to face him.

"Yes, Jack. Let's hear what *you* think."

"We know you killed Jessica. That's been established. But there's another reason why you killed her, isn't there? You had to shut her up, but not for the reason you give."

Rory turned to me confused, as if Jack had been trying to explain that one and one equals three and he just didn't get it. He made a little blowing thing with his mouth and leant forward with his elbows on the table again, his hands clenched tightly as he shook his head in bewilderment.

Rory's theatrics had no effect on Jack.

"You called me," Jack grinned as he made speaky signs with his fingers, "*a bloody dog running around with your nose on the ground, sniffling through bushes and piles of shit until you find what you think you're looking for.*"

Jack dropped his hands. "And you were right. You knew I'd insist on visiting Jessica, just to set her mind at rest and you knew we'd tell her that we knew she'd killed Merrell and that we wouldn't proceed with the investigation because Sean had insisted that things stay as they are. She was safe from prosecution."

I could see the question in Rory's eyes and I knew Jack was wired into his mind somehow.

"And you also knew she'd deny killing Merrell."

Jack stared at him for a few seconds before continuing, his gaze intense.

"Did you think I wouldn't check it out, Rory?" Jack asked with a coldness in his voice as he looked hard at him.

Rory frowned and shook his head. "You've lost me. Check what out?"

Even as he said the words, I knew Jack had hit a nerve as the blood left Rory's cheeks.

"Nothing ever turns out the way you think they will, O'Donovan," Jack said.

Rory looked quizzically at Jack for a while longer before turning to me.

"What's this about, Sam?" His expression suggested he was waiting for the punchline.

Careful, came the whisper.

Just after Jack left the force, I watched him try to break a man on cross-examination. That man had once been Jack's best friend, Joseph Banner, accused of murdering his fiancé, Shannon. Shannon had been playing games with them both before Joe finally found out. But that's another story. Everything had been carefully prepared, laying out all the traps building up to a devastating blow. Jack brought out flashes of anger and emotion and showed the jury the inconsistencies of Joe's story. Joe had actually murdered his fiancé, proven later by a piece of evidence held by his wife. It taught me a valuable lesson.

Cross-examination is a way to highlight inconsistencies and expose falsehoods and painting a witness as a hapless liar. But it is not the place for crushing blows. There are too many formalities involved and too many rules to follow. But there were questions that needed to be asked and if Jack didn't ask them, then I most certainly would.

"I did some checking while I waited for the warrant to arrive and the shoe to be examined," Jack interrupted, as I was about to reply. "There was no doubt in my mind you had killed Jessica but I wanted to make sure of all the facts."

His voice was calm but there was fire in his eyes. "You see, I've never quite believed the story you fed us about Sean confessing to the murder of Merrell to protect Jessica." He shook his head. "It was just too Hollywood."

"I don't understand where this is going?" Rory said to me.

When I didn't answer, he turned his attention back to Jack.

Something was bothering me too. Something I couldn't put a finger on. Something just out of reach in my mind that teased me, flicking across my subconscious. I knew the doubt had started when I first spoke to Jessica and she'd mentioned that Rory had been arguing with Merrell at the party. But the thought kept slipping away.

Jack glanced at the window Rory had been gazing through for a few seconds before continuing.

"I rang Hobart Police Station while I was waiting and spoke to Captain Marshall," Jack stated bluntly. "I told him the whole story about Jessica's murder and how we were waiting for the shoe to be examined by forensics to prove your guilt."

His eyebrows wiggled as he smirked at Rory. "I was pretty convincing, too."

Jack paused, seemingly composing his thoughts while Rory straightened his back again, visibly trying to pull himself together as he waited for Jack to finish.

Rory knows what's coming. He's knows.

"He agreed with me that we needed to talk to Sean about the events on the night of Merrell's murder. Just to make sure we had all the facts straight."

Rory's eyes popped open and he paled visibly. "What? You didn't..."

Jack smirked and nodded his head. "I did."

"You interfering bastard! I told you not to do that," Rory snarled, his voice heavy with anger.

I simply stared at this stranger in front of me.

"The motivation in most crimes is not complex." Jack sounded like a teacher giving a lesson. "Usually people steal and cheat because they're greedy or lazy or both. People kill for reasons of money, sex, and power. Even revenge. Or, as in your case, to hide something."

He sighed before continuing, his eyes were sad as he looked over to me.

"Jessica didn't kill Merrell, Sam. Rory did."

Some people know the exact moment where their lives change. They get to look for places where pain is only skin deep. Others are nowhere near that lucky.

I felt lightheaded as the room spun and shifted around me.

Rory killed Merrell?

"What?" I muttered. "Why?"

Jack sighed heavily as he turned to face Rory. "Because he slept with Merrell and she was going to tell you."

There are sudden rips in your life, deep knife wounds that slash through your flesh. One moment you have a life and the next moment, it's shredded into another. It comes apart like it's simply unravelling. A loose thread pulled. A seam gives way. The change is slow at first, but when it starts, there is no turning back.

Believe me, I know.

I stared at Rory as he dropped his head, shoulders slumped.

"That's what Sean said?" I whispered. I still couldn't believe it. *Merrell and Rory?*

Jack nodded. "That's what the argument was about at the party," he said softly.

Why wasn't Rory denying this?

"But there's no actual evidence that Rory had ever been in Merrell's room," I stuttered, still not quite believing what Jack had just said to us. "Fingerprints were lifted but his weren't one of the ones found. Remember?"

Say something Rory!

It just wasn't adding up. I was missing something vital right in front of me. I stood up and walked to the small window overlooking the carpark, shifting my weight from foot to foot like a boxer in his corner waiting to answer the bell.

I spun around. "She was seeing your brother, Rory. What was *that* about?"

My voice began to rise as I walked towards him. "What the hell was that about?"

He'd been quiet the whole time as Jack spoke, his chin resting on his chest. I watched his chest rise and fall and felt my heart turn in my own chest painfully.

It's true? This man I'd loved so incredibly, would have given up everything for, had betrayed me and slept with my sister? Then killed her?

A voice I barely recognised spoke. A trembling, quaking voice. "She seduced me, Sam."

"Bullshit!" I spun on my heels and walked back to the window, then spun around again. "BULLSHIT!"

His mouth trembled. "She had something in her that was like no one else. I know how much you loved her but she didn't care about anyone but herself. It was as if she was practicing on all of us, perfecting her routine for when she went to Melbourne to find some rich businessman to marry. I couldn't help myself."

I snorted loudly.

"I couldn't, Sam. I loved you but I became obsessed with her." He dropped his head again. "Remember when we'd sneak out and come across her and Sean together by the river. She'd touch me when no one was looking and eventually, she seduced me. It only happened once but she was going to tell you. She laughed about it."

"An obsession?" I almost sobbed.

"She was going to tell you." He sniffled and ran his hand brusquely under his nose.

"And the alibi?" My voice came out sounding strangled. I was trying to calm myself but the hurt kept bubbling up.

"The alibi was for him, not Sean," Jack interrupted.

I frowned, spinning to face Jack. "Pardon?"

"By saying Sean was with him at the time of the murder is just the same as saying he was with Sean at the time. He couldn't have done it if he was with Sean. He gave himself an alibi."

"And the lack of fingerprints in Merrell's room? What about that?"

Maybe it was the catch in my voice that betrayed me, because Jack stared at me for a while in silence before answering.

"Do you remember when James Russell told us that Tim Logan was the head of the fingerprint lab at the time and he was barely sober in those days? Most of the time when he showed up for work, he didn't know one end of the microscope from another. That's a quote. And when James began comparing his report and the lifts from the scene, he discovered they didn't all match. They were close. But there were several minute differences in some prints. And most were only partial at the best. Rory's would have been there but there wasn't enough to accuse anyone of the crime."

I sat down heavily and my fingers curled into fists in my lap as my breath quickened. I took a deep breath and blew air out through my mouth in a loud push.

I sometimes hope I will eventually feel settled about the choices I've made but then I wonder if I'll always look back and think about all the things I could have done. I had such high hopes when I joined the force of putting this all behind me and now I look back on my life and all I feel is exhaustion and bitterness. They have lodged themselves deep in my bone marrow.

Jack let the silence linger for a few seconds before he spoke. "Do the right thing, O'Donovan. Explain to Sam what happened that night."

Rory raised his head to look at me. His haunted eyes will stay with me forever.

He sighed heavily, his mouth a perfect O as he exhaled breath noisily from his lungs. He wiped the back of his hand across his mouth and sighed again.

"She told me at the party she was going to tell you," he began. "I tried to explain that I never meant it to happen, and she just laughed. She said she was tidying up her life. She'd already told Sean and it was your turn next before she left this no-hope town."

His chin quivered. "Sean was furious. I've never seen him so angry. We left the party and he just disappeared." He gulped. "I had no idea where he was."

I watched his chest shudder as he took a few shaky breaths.

"I found him later down by the river. We sat for a while talking." He looked shamefaced, "well, fighting is more what we did. Merrell called while we were there but Sean didn't want to talk to her. He just let his phone ring out. Eventually, he said he wanted nothing more to do with either of us. He left me sitting there and drove away."

He lifted his eyes and stared at me. "I lost everything, that night, Sam. My brother. You. And it was her fault. All her fault."

Suddenly, there was sweat on my face that wasn't there an instant ago. I felt it in my hair, on my forearms and behind my knees. The skin on my forearms tingled.

This is it, I thought.

"I didn't plan on killing her," he muttered. "I just wanted to change her mind."

When most people think of a murderer they think of a glassy-eyed lunatic. Someone who looks the part and acts the part. Actually, the typical murderer is something completely different. They're the kind of person you would never imagine being a monster, sitting quietly with his chin on his chest.

Beside me, Jack was staring hard at Rory.

"When you arrived at Neil's Pub, you climbed up to her room to find that someone else had already been there. Isn't that right?" Jack asked.

Rory nodded. "I climbed up the trellis to her balcony and the French doors were already smashed."

There was a pause where he seemed to try and compose himself. He nodded again, resigned, like he was happy to get this finally out in the open.

"I went inside, and she was sitting on the bed wiping some blood off her cheek."

His tone throughout the speech was monotone but when I turned to Jack, he was staring at Rory with hostile anger in his eyes.

"She laughed and said I was the second visitor that night. Jessica had already been there. She pointed to the cut lip and told me Jessica had hit her for taking Sean away from her." He glanced up at me. "That's when I couldn't hold back. I pushed her back on the bed and put my hands around her throat."

His eyes pleaded with me. "I never meant to kill her, Sam. I didn't. I tried to get her to say she'd never tell you, but she just laughed."

His face twisted in a snarl. "I hit her head on the backboard of the bed, over and over, until she stopped laughing."

He swallowed hard and his face softened. "I didn't mean to kill her. She made me do it."

I simply stared at this stranger in front of me. I'd spent twenty years as a cop interviewing rapists, murderers and child molesters and none had looked like fiends to me. Some looked harmless. There is no 'killer look'. I couldn't see it in his face, but I knew his heart was black.

"Why did Sean confess to the murder if he wanted nothing more to do with you?" I asked shakily.

"No one knew I'd been there. When we heard that Merrell was dead, we were all in shock. That's when Jessica told us she'd been to Merrell's room and hit her. She wanted Sean back, she kept crying, and Merrell had taken him away from her. That's when she told him she was pregnant with his child and all the wind just went out of his sails."

Tears shimmered in his eyes. "I didn't know I'd killed her. She watched me walk out through the broken door. I swear."

He blew air through his lips. "Anyway, Jessica thought she'd killed her and she was in a panic, waiting for the police to walk through the door and arrest her. But no one did. Two weeks later, she miscarried the baby and Sean was distraught. It was all his fault, he kept saying."

Rory shook his head. "I couldn't tell him it was me. The police were bloody useless. They were still scratching their heads. But Sean thought they'd eventually find out it was Jessica who'd been in the room and killed her, and he didn't want that on his conscience. So, he confessed."

Jack glared at him. "And you never told him the truth. You just let your brother go to prison for twenty years for something *you* did."

Rory closed his eyes and lowered his head.

Jack's mouth twisted in repulse as he watched him. "Well, he knows now."

I'd suddenly had enough. I stood, pushing the chair away with a screeching noise on the wooden floor. Rory's head shot up quickly.

Eyes I had lost myself in twenty years ago, looked pleadingly at me. Memories ran through my mind of lying on soft, cool grass with him lying beside me, his eyes greedy for me, travelling over my body, then the sun blocked out by his head as he lowered it to kiss me tenderly. My heart clenched as I remembered his soft breath on my neck and the ache I felt in my very being, eager for his touch.

I calmly pushed the chair back in and said, "Who the hell are you?"

Then I turned and walked out the door.

38

———

The gusting wind whipped around me and flattened my woollen jumper and jeans against my body. In the distance, the ocean roared and I knew the beach would be strewn with shells and driftwood, mollusc skeletons and some dead fish half eaten by scavengers. Trash was blowing down the street as well as cans and sodden paper. Muffled country music drifted through the air.

I stood with my arms hugging my body, as much to keep myself warm as to protect my heart from the almost physical pain I was feeling.

A movement behind me told me Jack had left the interview room and had come to join me.

"They're taking his statement now. But as you saw, I had the camera on so it's just a formality."

He glanced across to the café across the road, brimming with teenagers on their way home from school, buying packets of potato crisps and cans of coke to keep them going until mealtime.

"It's over now, Sam," he said, touching my back softly.

"And you think that's somehow going to change everything I'm feeling?"

It was a curt reply and I regretted saying it immediately.

"We can only hope," he replied after a second or two's hesitation.

I shook my head. "Hope is nothing."

"Hope is everything."

He was watching my face for a reaction. When he spoke again, his voice sounded dry.

"I have to leave tomorrow."

I turned to face him. "Instead of Saturday?"

He nodded. "Frank called and I'm expected. There's a case waiting for me and I have to start straight away."

I tried to speak, to communicate, but in the face of grief, words have no power.

"This new job of yours?" I eventually asked.

He nodded. "And we'll see each other when we get back home?" he asked.

I smiled softly. "Of course."

Only a day or so ago, we'd taken tentative steps towards knowing each other a little better. Now, everything had changed, and it seemed like we were back where we started. Which wasn't too bad if friendship was what you wanted.

The silence dragged on. He breathed heavily, his eyes searching mine, but said nothing.

"I have to see Kathleen tonight, Jack, so I'll have to skip dinner with you. I had planned on catching up with her Saturday but there are things I want to talk to her about. She knows nothing about this diary, and I want to explain about Rory." I swallowed noisily. "I want to get away from Richmond as soon as I can. I have some last-minute tidying up to do, then I'll leave on Saturday morning."

In the silence, the sea sounded muffled in the distance. By now, the streets were sprinkled with rain and clouds were beginning to gather on the horizon.

For something to say, I looked up at the sky and said, "Looks like it's going to be another big one tonight."

"It'll get better, Sam. Trust me, I know."

I turned to face him.

"Someone told me once," he began, "grief is just love with nowhere to go." He smiled sadly. "You just have to find another channel for that love."

I squared my shoulders. "Well, luckily I love my work."

I looked at my watch before looking back up at Jack.

"Kathleen will have picked Rianne up from school by now. I want to get there before the storm starts. Do you mind?"

I felt like such a shit. He'd come all the way down here to support me and here I was, leaving him to his own devices on his last night in Richmond. But I couldn't help it. I had a lot to talk to Kathleen about and it couldn't wait.

"I'll be fine," he nodded slowly. I could see the uncertainty in his eyes mingled with sadness. "I have an early start myself tomorrow so it will give me time to pack and get an early night."

He hesitated. "See you when we get back?" he asked again.

"Of course," I repeated quickly.

39

———————

FRIDAY, 26TH MAY

I woke up with the knowledge it is my last full day here and I suddenly wanted to see it all one more time before I left. I had no plans to return. There were too many memories I wanted to leave behind.

The talk with Kathleen last night went better than I thought and once again, regret raised its ugly head. We'd never been close, mainly because of the age difference, but I had been a tough teenager to like.

Something last night changed as I talked to Kathleen. The pain and hurt seemed to slowly melt away.

She looked at me sadly after I told her about Rory's confession.

"Even before mammy told me about Dan O'Donovan, I didn't like that family. Always looking at us slyly. Mind you, they were easy on the eye, but beauty is only skin deep, so they say. And that Rory O'Donovan has proved the saying to be true."

Slowly, I began to see things in a different perspective. The truth always clarifies but with that clarification comes emotion and the tears came freely. I'll never forget how I felt about Rory all those years ago but I was beginning to wonder if that attraction was built because I was ordered not to see him. Again, youth and hormones.

"It's been twenty years, you silly sod," she laughed to me. "Time to move on. We can't bring Merrell back but we can remember the good times with her."

As I looked outside, the sun shone gloriously after the storm that had hit again last night.

It'll be good to go for an early morning jog, I thought, before everyone wakes to begin their day. I remembered Nana Peg telling me it's the best part of the day and looking outside, with shadows rippling across the water, the sun peeking through the trees, I believed her.

We'd had days like this when I was a child, I know we did, but there was so much going on in my young life, I never appreciated it.

Five minutes later, dressed in an ancient tracksuit I found in the back of the wardrobe, I was jogging down the familiar road towards the supermarket. I'd emptied out the fridge and there was nothing left in it and I desperately needed a coffee to help me sort out both my thoughts and packing. Jack was leaving later this morning and tomorrow I'd be gone too. My life back home in Surfers would resume.

The cool, offshore breeze fanned my face and I inhaled it deeply, lengthening my stride as I drew it into my lungs. I'm leaving tomorrow, I thought, and I can't remember when I last felt this surge of energy before. It was running through my fingers, my face and into my feet as my legs stretched into long strides.

Despite the coolness of the weather, tomorrow the visitors to Richmond would arrive carrying picnic hampers full of food and drink, wearing windbreakers and carrying umbrellas, sunscreen and towels for the kids.

When I glanced up, Jack was standing outside the supermarket, a takeaway coffee in his hand, and a surprised look on his face.

I slowed my pace to a walk and joined him.

"I never took you for an early bird," I smiled. *Why was my heart skipping like this?* "I was going to come over and say good-bye later on," I lied.

"I'm happy to see you now." He smiled as his eyes roamed over me in my tacky track pants. "And looking so glamorous, may I add."

I punched him lightly on the arm. "Walk me back to the pub," I said, taking the cup of coffee from his hands and taking a slip. I handed it back to him as we walked slowly but he waved me off.

"Keep it. It's yours. I'll get another one when I get back."

We walked in silence for a few seconds, leaving the supermarket behind us and following a dirt track through the trees that was a short cut back to the pub.

"It's beautiful here," he muttered. "Last night, I took a late walk to the beach to watch the tide come in. It's different somehow from Surfers. I walked further up the beach, close to a little cliff, and just sat, watching the incoming tide in silence. It helped me think. I'd forgotten how the quietness is intoxicating and I guess that's what's different from Surfers. I hate to admit it, but we get used to the noise and the crime. We take it for granted that this is what our life is going to be like and that everywhere we go, there are evil people lurking around the corner waiting to take advantage of us. I may not make much of a difference, but I want to try and change that." He glanced over at me. "Hence the new job."

He stopped and looked into my face and what he saw made him falter.

"You're something else, you know," I smiled, stopping beside him.

He was looking at me with soft eyes and I felt my heart twinge.

"You're not like the rest. You're not hard and uncaring. You feel things far beyond what others feel. You won't admit it but inside, you're tender. And that's what makes you special."

I have no idea why tears burned behind my eyes, and I had an awful feeling I was about to blubber. *What the hell was that for? Leaving Richmond? Couldn't be. Maybe a more unsettling thought, back to my old life with no one in it?*

I needed to change the tone of the conversation.

"You're right, as always," he grinned, although a blush was rising up from his neck. "I don't think I get enough credit for the fact that I do this unmedicated."

His voice came out a little tight, but the softness around his eyes deepened.

Instead of the expected laugh, I remained quiet.

"Oh, come on!" he laughed. "That was funny!"

I swallowed audibly and glanced down at the remains of the dark liquid in my cup.

His head tilted to the side. "Are you okay?" he asked softly.

When I looked up, his eyes were travelling over my face.

"I'll be fine," I whispered. The prettiest of lies versus the ugliest of truths.

I tilted my head to the side. "You look...different somehow," I began.

"More handsome?"

I smiled. "Yes."

"Calmer?"

I nodded.

"I know. And all my tea towels are lined up neatly in the kitchen. Can we move on now?"

I grinned and suddenly, it hit me. There are moments in your life when you know you have to make a decision that will affect your life. Everyone is scared of taking that first step, especially when you can't see the whole staircase. The decision might come after long deliberation or after no more than a second of thought. But it carries the potential to change the direction your life takes and whether conscious of the fact at the time, looking back, you are aware of the changes that decision brought. I was having just that kind of moment.

Thoughts jumbled around in my head as Jack's eyes stared into mine. What was I nervous about? Was I too scarred by the past to have a future? The thought made me catch my breath. What was I thinking? If I hung on to regrets, I'd be stuck in the past. Because of my feelings for Rory, and my divorce from Ryan, I have hovered on the edge of relationships, waiting to be close to someone but keeping my distance until another Rory came along. Over the years, *that* Rory had grown and become almost a god.

I'd learned something about myself since coming to Richmond. The euphoria of seeing Rory had been temporary. Soon the hurt reappeared and I guessed it would last a long time before I could rid myself of it. What I needed was to move on.

Did I need a man in my life?

No.

Did I want a man in my life?

Yes.

What were the words from that song? I'd rather be sorry for something I did than sorry for something I didn't.

I closed my eyes for a second, centring myself, before I continued.

Jack's eyes were still watching me, a small frown on his forehead.

"I'm wondering whether I should tell you something," I finally said.

Jack sighed heavily. "I'm not up to these games right now, Sam. What is it?" he asked tiredly, shaking his head. "I don't know if I want to know where this is going."

I stepped forward and kissed his lips, a light kiss with our lips barely touching. When I pulled back, he was smiling. He pulled me close and this time the kiss was firmer. As our mouths tightened on each other, our bodies followed, burying deeper until we are pressed full length against each other, our arms wrapped tightly around each other.

We kissed for a long time. Afterwards, we kept our heads close, foreheads touching, our ragged breath mingling.

"We certainly have some unfinished business between us when we get back home," he whispered.

9 781763 554825